*Phil,
hope you like it*

# UNDER FALSE COLORS

by

Peter A. Neissa

*Peter Neissa*

*2001*

All rights reserved.
© Copyright Peter A. Neissa
No part of this publication may be reproduced, stored in a retrieval system, or transmitted, in any form or by any means (electronic, mechanical, photocopying, recording or otherwise), without the prior written permission of both, the copyright owner and the publisher of this book.

ISBN: 1-930879-03-2
Ediciones Nuevo Espacio, 2000
http://www.editorial-ene.com
ednuevoespacio@aol.com

Ediciones Nuevo Espacio

For my sister Susan

*Wide is the gate that leadeth to destruction.*

*Mathew 7:13*


*The FBI wouldn't tell the DEA what they were doing, the DEA wouldn't tell the FBI what they were doing and nobody talked to Customs.*
*-- Max Mermelstein*
*Testifying before Senator Biden's*
*Senate Judiciary Committee*

## Author's Note

The term 'under false colors' is an ancient expression meaning deception. It was used quite often by sea-captains and harbormasters when referring to the duplicitous way in which pirate ships would stalk their prey or gain admittance into a harbor by flying a friendly flag. Unfortunately, by the time the deception was uncovered it was already too late to save the day.

Today's drug lords are just as devious. Their aircraft use fictitious registration numbers, so that, in effect, they use the same deceptive measures as did fourteenth and fifteenth century pirates, because an aircraft's registration number has the same significance as a national flag. Every country in the world is assigned one or two letters, followed by a series of three to five numbers for registering their aircraft. The first two letters used by a United States aircraft are NC and for a Colombian aircraft would be HK.

## Acknowledgments

The research on this book would not have been possible had I not received the help of many people, especially:

In Bogotá: Many thanks to the law enforcement agencies F-2 and DAS.

In Washington: Guy Gugliotta whose advice and knowledge on the drug trade served me well in the preparation of this manuscript as it did in my previous novel, THE DRUG LORD. His non-fiction book, KINGS OF COCAINE, co-written with Jeff Leen is the best non-fiction book on the history of the drug trade.

I would also like to thank the United States Department of State for their assistance in obtaining documents.

In Boston: The Office of Senator Edward M. Kennedy for helping me obtain the relevant documents on the Medellín Cartel. I also thank the Drug Enforcement Administration in Boston for advising me on the history of the DEA.

In New York: James M. Neissa for instructing me on the nuances and regulations of international banking and on the United States Tax Code. Any errors in respect to banking or taxes are mine and not his, because I had to alter some facts to suit the plot of the novel.

Finally, I would like to thank all those pilots who shared their knowledge and know-how on flying the single, twin and jet aircraft.

The late afternoon of October 24, 1999, had, as it did during that time of the year, turned nasty. A cold mountain hailstorm fell and clattered over the Spanish tile around the entrance to the American Embassy in Bogotá, Colombia. The white marble-size pellets hammered the US Marine gatehouse's corrugated tin roof, drowning it in noise and blinding it from the outside world for six minutes, then ceased abruptly, leaving behind only the cold and the melting hail.

The embassy, known to bogotanos as The Compound, is an appropriate description. It is an imposing structure on Avenida Séptima. The huge concrete multi-storied building rested on an entire metropolitan square block, in what is regarded as the most expensive real estate property in the city. It is also quite windowless and everyone's first impression of it was that it looked like an updated American prison.

To enter one had to walk past the US Marine gatehouse and into Fortress America. The fluorescent bulbs inside the building managed to splash a harsh light into the most remote corners and even seemed to brighten the faded colors of the American flag that hung over the lobby's entrance, which hadn't been replaced since the early seventies. In the lobby of the architectural monstrosity that was the embassy, framed pictures of the American President and Vice-President hung on the lily-white walls as well as some other forgettable bureaucratic leaders of the present age. The attendant secretaries, sitting behind the protective bullet-proof glass window, lent an air of respectful industry and conveyed a message made clear by its artifice: Here serious business is conducted.

At any rate, people walked in and out of the place with metronomic regularity. Americans, Colombians, rich people and poor people alike -- gaining access only after demonstrating proper identification to the Marine guards standing at the front gate -- entered the building to obtain the much valued entry visa into the United States of America, or, in the odd case, to ask for political asylum. Yet, once people were inside they were not really inside. They were in a front lobby that was really a huge white room whose far wall was really bullet-proof glass where two administrative assistants sat in cinema-looking booths and took enquiries and visa applications through small portholes.

It was at this moment that a woman entered the lobby. There was something about the woman that suggested danger, many would think later on when they viewed the embassy's video security film. Nevertheless, at that moment no one had taken a full measure of the woman.

There was no doubt the woman was a Colombian, an educated Colombian, at that. Only a Colombian woman would have been able to walk in out of a hailstorm looking like a million bucks and not miss a beat. The woman wore a black oversized raincoat with high-heeled shoes. She seemed to study the area as if to make up her mind how to walk across it. "She was class," they would say about her later on. "Come the angels with doom on their lips, that woman was never going to lose sight of that fact."

In any event, the woman walked up to the furthest right handed booth, one of six and watched as the administrative assistant leaned closer to the video screen as a last measure of avoidance. But the Colombian woman was not deterred.

"Good afternoon, ma'am?" the Colombian woman greeted.

"Yes?" the administrative assistant replied rudely and without even looking up or breaking the rhythm on her keyboard. She had planned on avoiding the woman altogether, but the woman had spoken English and that had peaked a measure of interest. "How can I help you, ma'am?"

"I am looking for Mister John Whitney," the woman said. "I have a letter for him."

"I'm sorry, but Mister Whitney has been called away from his desk. I could make sure he gets the letter, if that's what you're worried about."

"You are very kind, thank you." The woman opened her pocketbook and retrieved the envelope, which had the words, For Mr. Whitney's eyes only written on it. Then she passed the letter through the porthole in the glass booth and smiled.

"Who may I say it's from?"

The woman hesitated. "Liliana. Liliana Santander."

"You're going to have to sign for it, Ms. Santander."

The woman was stunned and the assistant began to get a strange feeling in the pit of her stomach, even though as the moment unfolded she could not say why.

The woman was stunned and Miles knew by her reaction that she had done the right thing, even though as the moment unfolded she didn't know why.

"Why?" the woman asked.

"Embassy rules, Ms. Santander."

The woman nodded and the assistant handed her a paper and a pen, which the woman used to sign her name, address and telephone number. It was during this time that the assistant took a good measure of the woman.

She was not only beautiful, but intelligent. It was obvious, the assistant told herself. There was something about how her eyes sparkled, like an old Bette Davis movie she'd seen long ago. It was at that moment that she wondered if John Whitney was having an affair with her, but the idea faded when she noticed the wedding ring on the woman's finger.

Then the woman handed back the paper where she had signed for the letter she was dropping off and said, "Thank you. It is very urgent that he read it soon, please." The assistant nodded but didn't believe it, because in Colombia everything had to be done the day before yesterday and was rarely done the day after tomorrow. The woman then took one last look at the letter in the assistant's hands and left.

John Whitney, the DEA Section Chief in Bogotá, received the letter a few hours later and had been intrigued by assistant's story. He scratched his right temple with his right hand, a bad habit he had when trying to concentrate.

"What did she look like?" he asked.

"Gorgeous," the assistant said with some envy.

John was surprised. "Really?"

"Supermodel material," the assistant said and handed him the envelope. "I also had her sign this."

John weighed the letter in his hand. It was light. He had been with the DEA for twelve years and the last two as Bogotá Section Chief. He was a man of average height, of olive skin and jet-black hair. He also sported a mustache which he was very fond of. He had thrown himself into the job as deeply as any man could possibly go, but the deeper he delved into the job the more doubts about what he was doing surfaced in his mind. He had doubts whether America was really committed to ending the drug trade because, whenever he asked for manpower or monetary assistance, he was met with a barrage of bureaucratic red-tape. In his two years as Section Chief he had seen the level of drug traffic and the level of rhetoric from the States increase twenty-fold.

Months later, the assistant would testify in front of a Congressional sub-committee on how the color had drained from John Whitney's face when he read the letter. John, by the time he had finished reading the letter, had forgotten about the assistant standing in front of him. He simply kept reading and re-reading the letter to make himself sure that he was really reading it and not dreaming it up. But it was real, because the author had affixed his inked fingerprint to it for proof. The letter was so simple it nearly looked like the memos he sent to DEAHQ in Washington, he would later explain to the committee.

John read it again:

To the American DEA,

My name is Ernesto Camacho. You may know me as the bank launderer for Juan Calderón. I am writing because I have a deal to propose. My son has been diagnosed with cancer. If he is to survive he must receive treatment in the United States. I, therefore, propose an arrangement. I provide you with all my knowledge on the cartel in exchange for medical treatment for my son and immunity from prosecution for myself and my family, plus relocation under your WITSEC program. I can be reached through, and only through, my sister Liliana Santander. She's in the

telephone book.
Ernesto Camacho

John finally looked up at the assistant, smiled warmly and told her not to worry about any of it and sent her home for the weekend. It was, perhaps, the only happy ending in the heartbreaking and dirty affair. So, when people would think about the operation, they would try to imagine the assistant walking out of DEA section chief's office with the steadfast belief that she had done something good for her country.

Everyone else, on the other hand, held no such illusions about their part in it, or anyone else's. However, for the purposes of this fact-finding Congressional Report -- whose sole objective is to report the truth about what happened, which no government agency will ever care to own up to. Therefore, this report will probably be buried or mislaid in some dark and secret warehouse, where all reports of such kind eventually come to rest once the roar of the public outcry has blown away like the topsoil on a freshly dug grave.

# CHAPTER 1

It would be nearly five full days after Liliana Santander had passed the envelope to Miles Cooper, when the DEA reluctantly met to discuss the contents of the letter. And after every department had read and analyzed it, they called in yet another hallowed Washington institution, the White House Chief of Staff, to see if he could shed some insight as to what the President might think on what had become the biggest thing since the Gulf War.

Yet the case began quite simply and without fanfare, but with a few words from Donald Harkin, the Director of Operations for the DEA.

"Something just came in, sir. It's encrypted. Administrator's Eyes Only. It's from Bogotá. John Whitney, sir." Doctor Alfred Stevens, the director for the Drug Enforcement Administration, also known as the 'Administrator', looked up from his desk with a puzzled look. "He's the Bogotá Special Agent-In-Charge, isn't he?" Stevens asked.

"Yes, sir."

"Is he running something I should be familiar with?"

"No, sir; at least nothing we know about except for routine surveillance."

Stevens was a six-foot gray-eyed New Englander with the blue-blood to prove it. He was in good physical shape, which made him look younger than his fifty-five years, but the bags under his eyes betrayed his age, if one looked closely. He wore austere blue-thin pinstripe suits from Brooks Brothers and Burberry coats. He was Yankee blue-blood all the way back to the Mayflower and with all the right labels given to him along the way: St. Paul's Prep, Yale, Skull and Bones, but, despite his education, he was not unfortunately, a man of great intelligence. The prestigious education only had been a right of passage rather than the augmentation and training of an exceptional mind. He was a man who never gave himself time for introspection because, in his opinion, he could use that time to think about how to advance his political career. Everything he thought and did had been carefully weighed and measured against his political future. To understand his mind one simply had to gauge from where the prevailing political wind was blowing. It was, therefore, no secret to anyone that he was seeking a higher post than the DEA administratorship. Alfred Stevens was aiming for White House Chief of Staff, but dreaming of the Vice-Presidency.

Stevens had married twice. His first wife had died early on in their marriage and he had remained a bachelor until two years before, when he met his current wife, who was twenty-seven years old and younger than his only daughter.

But on this day when Don Harkin handed him a computer disk, as he sat behind a wall of bureaucratic paper, he sighed and inserted the disk into his own computer terminal.

"Well then, let's have a look," Stevens said as he gained access into the mainframe computer by typing in his own personal codeword.

Once the mainframe identified his access code it would scroll the message across his video screen. Stevens then put on his thick reading spectacles and began to read the message.

"Dear God!" Stevens said with an accent that sounded a lot like John F. Kennedy's, so that 'Dear God' sounded more as, "Dea' Gawd!" Then he pushed himself away from his desk and looked up at Don Harkin. "It's a joke, right?"

Don looked at Stevens with a curious look. Don had been with the DEA for twelve years and fifteen years with the US Marines before that. He was of average height, sandy hair (receding), and, to his detriment, he was overweight by at least forty pounds. In September, he had celebrated his forty-fifth birthday and his twenty-two year marriage to his Marine Corp flame, Jennifer.

He was a family man, burdened by the demands on a civil service salary made by his five daughters and two sons, pressures exacerbated by the fact that four of his offspring were in college and two more who were eight months away from joining them.

Lately, Don had begun to change his style because, as his wife Jennifer informed him, if he was to earn more income he would have to rise further in the present administration. They already had discussed the fact that a civil-service job would not be enough for them in the long run, but if Don were to play his cards right he might become a power player in the nation's capital. If he did, he might be able to parlay that position into a directorship of some private corporation. So, Don traded in his old Chevy Impala for a Saab Turbo and his old leisure suits for new tailored ones.

All this, of course, was far from his mind as he watched the Administrator's face pale. Instead, he ran his hand over his thinning hair -- a nervous gesture, as if he were checking to see if it was still there.

"Perhaps I might be able to help, sir, if I were permitted to read the text."

Stevens punched a few keys on his keyboard and his laser printer printed out the text in hard-white, bonded paper.

Harkin picked the paper off the printer tray and read the message quickly. "Jeez," he said, momentarily at a loss for words. Then he shook his head and added, "It's no joke, sir. If John Whitney sent this, then we better take it for what it is, a miracle."

Stevens stood up and began to pace the office. As an old New Englander, his office tastes ran to the colonial, with deep, dark and heavy woods, and oil paintings that depicted whaling vessels sailing off the coast of Nantucket.

"Where is John now?" Stevens asked.

"Standing by, sir."

"Good, good." Stevens stopped pacing. "Okay, this is what we're going to do. I will go and talk to Lewis, because I'm sure he'll want to inform the President. Once Lewis gives us an inkling of what the President thinks, we should set a meeting: Intelligence, Operations, the works. For the moment, send Whitney to set up a surveillance of what's her name...Liliana Santander. And let him know that this is to be kept in-house and strictly on a need-to-know basis. By the way, where's Dusty?"

"In the cellar, I suppose."

"Get him in on this, just in case it blows up in our faces.

He was not much to look at and he had never been any good at sports. He had never been overweight, but neither was he ever the embodiment of physical fitness. He was a tall and awkward kind of fellow, who stooped slightly because he usually hit things with my head if I don't. I'm tall, very tall, six feet eight inches, and usually the first question anyone ever asked him was if he played basketball professionally. His limbs, especially his arms, were quite long and he seemed to be totally at odds with them. Usually they were flapping around in some disconcerted fashion many people called uncoordinated. His eyes were very blue and his hair was black. He also looked better in jeans and sweaters than in shirts and ties.

Dusty had never been his real name, it was Joseph Malone. From grammar school to Jesuit School -- Boston College -- he had always been known as Joe, until he joined the Narcotics and Dangerous Drugs Bureau, which was the old agency that merged with a branch of the Customs Service to form yet another agency, which became the Drug Enforcement Administration or DEA. But it was there at DEA where he became Dusty, short for Dustman. He had spent a quarter of a century doing what he did, which was, in effect, to clear other people's screw-ups by burying them in a morass of unsubstantiated facts intended to confuse even the most competent and able reader. He was a trained Political Scientist from Boston College, a criminal expert with a Ph.D. in Criminal Justice from Northeastern University, and, in rather vague terms, an officer of the law sworn to uphold the honesty of the profession, but he had, without pity or second thought, ignored some of its more ethical tenets in the name of need-to-know-basis or whatever happened to be the catchall phrase of the day.

He married when he was young, but his wife Elizabeth, like his profession had soured like a bad wine. He blamed himself because when he started out in the business he had done his best to ignore her and when he finally turned to her in need, she had found someone else. "If you play dirty, expect to get dirty," she had told him in one of their more bitter fights.

Her punishment though, had not been to sleep with other men, but to remain married to him.

It was also the reason why he sat in that office, never making waves, working behind a desk that only saw even bigger lies come across it. So it was there where he learned about all the operational foul-ups, because it was his job to bury them in obscure administration doublespeak for any Congressional Sub-Committee to pour over and make sense of whatever it could. The Santander Case was, perhaps, the prototypical case of how things had been going on at the DEA for nearly two decades in what had become known as 'the war against drugs'. But some days, while he sat there behind his desk thinking about his job, he told himself, while he buried the junk, that things would change.

So when he watched the Administrator enter into his office at DEA Headquarters, across the Potomac River in Pentagon City, he told himself, here we go again.

The Administrator was brief. "Dusty, get your wares together and come upstairs. We're having a pow-wow."

Dusty nodded and turned off his computer terminal. "I'll need a few minutes to secure some of the material on my desk," he said, but Alfred had already lefty his room.

For years Stevens had come to believe that the DEA was considered second banana to the bigger law enforcement agencies in town, but with this meeting he had seen it as a 'I have arrived' sort of thing. He was attentive and respectful to those invited to his sancto sanctorum.

Dusty turned up on the top floor of DEAHQ, otherwise known as Lincoln Place -- for the library collection Abraham Lincoln, which Alfred Stevens bought at considerable taxpayer expense. The DEA's lair of power was for Dusty rarefied air. There was a special conference room where Stevens and Harkin usually held their meetings, and it was decorated in the style known as government drab: white walls with cheap framed prints, a large Scandinavian table surrounded by a dozen awkward and synthetic chairs which neither improved the aesthetics nor the comfort of the room. At the center of the table rested a clear crystal pitcher of water surrounded by a dozen upturned glasses. The pitcher was depressing to Dusty, because he had come to equate them with long boring meetings.

It was Don Harkin who greeted him first.

"Hello, hello," he said with his new welcoming voice and newly polished style. "Good of you to come, Dusty. How long has it been, three or four months? Gees, I'll have to remind Jennifer to have you and Liz over soon. How are you?"

Don had been overweight for most of his life, but at a glance one could see he had dropped some of those extra pounds. He still had to drop another forty before one considered him fit, but those were going to be the hardest pounds to shed. It would be akin to a polar bear shedding its Winter pelt in January.

Dusty replied to Don's question timidly by saying something like how time flies, but before he could finish Don was moving away to greet someone else. So, Dusty took a seat, afraid that if he didn't, he'd probably have to stand up throughout the meeting and that wouldn't do at all.

Dusty had been suffering for quite some time with feet problems, so much so that regular shoes felt like bear traps. The doctors had some long complicated name for it, which was to say his feet suffered from chronic swelling. The doctor's remedy was to get himself a pair of German sandals, which he wore religiously with his suits. When he first began wearing them, people laughed at them or at him -- a person standing beside him could never tell -- but lately Dusty had seen them spy at his sandals with a little envy, especially at the end of a long working day.

Dusty sat himself down and managed to massage his feet and eyeball the room. The Administrator sat at the head of the rectangular table. To his left, which surprised him and should have triggered an immediate danger signal, was Norman Lewis the White House Chief of Staff; James MaClean, Head of the Intelligence for the DEA, and Lisa Mejía, who was Don's immediate subordinate.

Sitting to the Administrator's right, which was Dusty's side, was María Jacobs, DEA Liaison Director who kept things running smoothly between DEA and F-2 Police in Colombia. The F-2 was Colombian Intelligence. María gave Dusty a friendly smile and he promptly returned it.

The meeting officially began when the Administrator looked up from his desk and said, "I call this meeting to order."

Dusty thought, at the time, that he might as well have said, "Send in the clowns."

"I assume everyone here has read the letter," Alfred continued. "Does anyone have any suggestions?"

No one replied, so Dusty raised his hand as a schoolboy at his first day at school.

"Excuse me," he said timidly, his voice barely above a whisper. "What letter are you referring to?"

Lisa Mejía handed Dusty the letter. He then removed it from the envelope and read it. It didn't take long. His first impression was that the letter was somehow a fraud, but then belief slowly superseded that first impression. Then he thought, 'poor pitiful bastard.'

"Well," Stevens said, realizing the meeting was going to be more difficult than he had anticipated. "I think everyone will agree that we're going to have to get a man close enough to Camacho in order to establish communication. Camacho himself tells us that his sister Liliana Santander will act as a liaison of sorts, so all we need to do is set up a link with her."

There was some general mumbling in agreement, except for Lisa Mejia who was frowning. She had been with the DEA for nine years. She also was the Deputy Director for Latin American Operations, which in effect made her Don Harkin's second in command.

Lisa had been born and raised in Miami's little Colombia. She stood at five feet five inches with dark hair, brown eyes and olive skin and was as thin as a rail. She was also a Harvard Law School Graduate who in the past six years had made more cocaine-related arrests than anyone in the Miami area.

Lisa Mejía was the DEA's golden girl, a bright woman of thirty-four whose self-possession and professional competence would take her far in the administration. There was little doubt in anyone's mind that she was on the track for the high post, despite the rumors from the Miami law enforcement officers who stated that her arrests had been too easy. It didn't matter, because professional jealousies at her level went along with the job and especially if the professional was a woman.

Everyone liked her. She was attractive, except on days she had stayed up all night and her eyes were blood-shot and puffy. She told people that she was an insomniac and usually didn't get to sleep before three in the morning, but she had an excellent sense of humor and everyone was aware of that. However, she disliked her nickname, Ostrich, like the bird, because her legs were thin and she devoured all types of food and never seemed to put on weight. The female secretaries envied her thinness, because they had seen her sit down and devour a meal and then go for seconds.

Alfred, however, had taken notice of her frown and asked her, "You don't like the idea Miss Mejía?"

"It's fine, sir," Lisa replied. "I agree that contact must be established with the Santander girl, but I also think we have to set up a direct link with Camacho. I'm sure this will become evident if we agree to his proposition."

Norman Lewis cleared his throat. "The President has agreed to the idea, but he wants to see the terms on paper once we establish contact with Camacho or the girl," he said.

Norman Lewis was of the same mold as Alfred Stevens. He was tall with angular features, dark brown hair, brown eyes, and the quintessential politician's bearing: Polished, refined, cultured. The only difference between Norman and Alfred was that Norman was a survivor. He had been in the political arena long enough to know how to protect himself. He also knew a losing proposition when he saw one.

"Do you have an idea, Miss Mejía?" Alfred asked.

"Maybe, sir. Do you remember Operation Fly-School? It was the investigation which targeted drug-pilots during the late seventies? I think we might be able to use some of those ideas now. We know the cartel has lost its best pilot, so we should assume that they are in the market for a new pilot."

"And you think we should provide them with one?"

"Yes, sir. That's it exactly."

"Where are we going to get this pilot, exactly?" María Jacobs pressed Lisa. She was a small black woman with remarkable green eyes, who had come up through the ranks in the DEA.

James MaClean, Head of Intelligence, answered, "That shouldn't be a problem. After all, we have a whole slew of pilots flying for us, don't we?"

María shook her head. "That won't work, because the cartel has a positive identification on every pilot that flies with us. If we are going to get someone to fly for the cartel on our behalf, we'll have to go outside. In my opinion, I think trying to get Camacho is a bad idea."

"Oh?" Alfred said in genuine surprise.

"Sir, we should blackmail Camacho, in my opinion. What happens if nothing comes from this deal but another immunity from prosecution deal? There will be hell to pay. The people in this country are sick of letting people off the hook because they rat on their friends, which in the end rarely seems to work."

It was quite a statement and a dead silence followed it. María had always thought of repercussions if things didn't go as planned; it was her nature, but there was something more. In her statement, only later did people seem to recall that it was filled with disillusionment; perhaps even María hadn't either, but it was there nevertheless, hiding under the surface.

Alfred in his usual affable way ignored the advice, because he didn't understand it. He had pursed his lips, which everyone knew was his way of superficially showing he had given it his utmost consideration. "I'll make note of that suggestion María," he said and then moved on.

"Where would we find this pilot, Miss Mejía?"

It was Don who answered: "He will have to be someone with jet-fighter experience in combat, which would make him a pilot who has flown during the Gulf War."

"You sound like you have someone in mind, Don?" Norman asked with a pleasant smile.

"I haven't asked him, of course, but I think he might be persuaded. His name is Martin Black. He works...used to work for us, but before that he was a pilot for the Marines. He flew a Harrier in the Gulf. He's been awarded several medals for bravery and for flying. He lost two fingers when he was shot down over Iraq, which was his reason for his discharge from the Corp. The guy's a patriot."

Alfred lowered his eyes in suspicion. "You said he worked for the us, what happened?"

"I think he might have been one of the people who was let go after the famous budget axe. If you're worried about his integrity, sir, I am sure his job evaluations will recommend him highly."

"You know him?" Lisa asked Don.

"Marines. I had lost touch with him, but last month I discovered he was making a mint off rich tourists in Florida. He owns a yacht of some sort, which he charters out to the rich and famous."

James let out a chuckle of disbelief. Then he asked, "What makes you think Martin Black is going to leave such a comfy life just to help us bring in some shady character from Medellín?"

"I thought someone might ask that, but there are two things that tell me he'll do it. First, he's been reporting drug flights to Miami DEA every time he spots one when sailing from Key West to the Bahamas. The second reason is because he's a man who will do anything for his country and I don't mean to sound corny, but the guy has won a CMH."

Alfred smiled pensively. "I've been in this town thirty-three years and I've never met someone who's been awarded the Congressional Medal of Honor. Get in touch with him, Don. ASAP."

Then, unexpectedly, Norman handed Alfred the reigns of responsibility in an off-handed manner. "This seems to be your area of expertise, Alfred. Why don't you run with it, eh?"

Alfred nodded somberly, but inside himself he was smiling wide. He had always wanted to play in the big leagues and his big chance had finally arrived. Norman Lewis, in effect, had just tossed him the ball and he was running with it. For better or for worse, Alfred also realized he had just been maneuvered with kid gloves into taking charge of an operation whose ultimate goal was yet unknown. It was a disaster in the making. Alfred was taking the helm of the Titanic and Lewis and Harkin knew it.

But from that moment on, Alfred Stevens, the 'Administrator', decided to go by the DEA book. Everything was to be recorded, audio-taped, video-taped and generally catalogued for easy access. However, before all that could be done, Alfred would have to institute chapter one of his book into action, which called for signing Martin Black onto the good-ship Titanic so that they could all begin the voyage of the dammed!

# CHAPTER 2

Martin Black slept in the aft cabin of his steel-hulled sloop which he had christened Windraider. It was a dream-filled sleep and in the dream he was in a snowstorm, which fell from a clear blue sky. Then he slipped out of the dream and into nothing.

Suddenly he awoke with a start. He tensed and listened to the tiny waves that were lapping the hull. He concentrated harder and heard what had awakened him. Someone was on Windraider, because he could hear the light footsteps moving across the deck. He reached for the gun he kept in his nightstand, a .38 Smith & Wesson from his old DEA days, the one he did not turn in to the DEA after being canned.

Martin quickly checked its status; it was loaded. He slipped the safety off and slowly got out of bed. Cinnamon, his only pet and angry cat was listening at the intruders' footsteps and not liking it one bit. Her hackles stood on end and her back arched like a bow.

Martin ignored the cat and began moving quietly through the galley. The lower deck was littered with supplies and groceries he had purchased the night before and was too tired to put away, forcing him to move in a zig-zag motion. Then he found a man standing in the navigation room, looking at his instruments. The man seemed not at all concerned to be trespassing, because he actually appeared to be enjoying himself.

"I could shoot you right now and ask questions later," Martin said, his voice breaking as he spoke the first words of the day. He cleared his throat and added, "Put your hands up and turn around...slowly."

The man did nothing of the sort; instead, he began to laugh.

Martin fired a warning shot through the open porthole and the man turned on him angrily.

"Are you fucking crazy?" Don Harkin asked as he reached for a handkerchief to wipe his damp brow. The Florida heat was wreaking havoc with his sweat glands.

Martin's smile spread slowly across his face when recognition of his old friend came back to him. "Don?" he asked tentatively. "Don Harkin?"

Harkin was still quite angry. "You bet your ass it's Harkin, but I have a mind to go over there and kick your ass!"

Martin let out a roar of laughter. "Jesus! What in the world brings you this far south?"

"I'm afraid it's business," Harkin said, his anger dissipating rapidly as thoughts from long ago filled his mind with bits and pieces of a war fought years before and far away.

"Its been a while, Martin. How long, seven or eight years?"

"Thirteen. What happened to you, Don? You're fat."

Harkin looked indignantly at Martin. "I'm not fat, I'm well-made, so I am."

"I'd say, too well-made," Martin rejoined, letting anyone who might be listening know that they were old and good friends.

"Is it a man's fault if his wife keeps him in proper health?"

They laughed.

"Come," Martin said, securing the gun, "I'll give you a quick tour of the boat and we'll talk over some orange juice. By the way, how is Jenny doing these days and what about the kids?"

"She's got her hands full with the kids, but she sends her love...Jesus, Mary and Joseph! I almost forgot. I came down here with someone else. Dusty!"

And with that shout Dusty entered into the life of Martin Black.

His footsteps clattered on the deck as if he were a tap-dancer. He had to stoop to get inside the sloop, but he managed quite nicely. The opulence inside hit him at once and overwhelmed him. There was no doubt, he thought, that Martin Black was doing okay for himself.

Don made the introductions and Dusty shook hands with Martin Black. Dusty felt Martin's firm grip, as opposed to his own, which was stiff and awkward. They stood quietly for a moment and appraised each other, and Dusty wondered what he saw in him. What he saw was not unlike what he thought, a middle-aged bureaucrat who had had the life wrung out of him a couple of decades before. But Dusty had also appraised Martin as well in those few seconds, but he knew quite a lot more than what he saw. On his flight to Florida he had read everything there was to know about Martin Black in the file Don had given him.

Dusty instantly recalled the facts of the man who would change the course of his life, as he did Martin's. The first thing Dusty remembered reading about Martin Black was that he was a hero from daybreak. Physically, he was six feet two inches and weighed two hundred pounds. The face was a handsome one with a knife-blade nose and deep-set blue-eyes. His hair was jet-black and longish, but fashionably cut. He wore a pair of paisley boxer shorts and didn't seem embarrassed about it, but Dusty thought with a body like his who would. The body was a cluster of ripples, troughs and swells that said he was ten years younger than his forty years. He was a man to be reckoned with, whose size announced him before words.

Martin had been a young pilot in the Gulf War, Dusty had read in the dossier. He had been shot down over Iraq and captured by the Saddam Hussein's Elite Guard. After three weeks in captivity he escaped and at the risk of his own life took two injured prisoners with him. It had earned him the CMH. He had served with the DEA as an analyst when he was laid off. After that he took whatever money had saved and headed south to start up his present business of chartering his steel-hulled sloop. His current tax returns and bank statements, which he had no idea Dusty was in possession of, showed him to be doing quite well on the financial end of things. His earnings without expenses and overhead were nearly two million dollars, which put him easily in the American upper class.

Martin, unlike Dusty, had never been married. The quick surveillance they had imposed on him in the past few days showed that he lived relatively alone. Other than his temperamental cat, Cinnamon, there had been nothing else to show what his emotional make-up might be -- he was a blank page. The Administration didn't like that, because the saying was: 'It's better to know the devil you deal with than the devil you don't.'

"Why don't we go up on deck," Martin said, motioning for Dusty to lead the way. He then turned to Don and asked, "How many kids do you have now?"

"Five," Don replied. "Three daughters and two sons."

Martin drew in a breath before he said, "My God! You're trying to kill her!"

Don laughed. "That's what she tells me every morning."

Don and Dusty settled at the stern of the sloop, around a small table as Martin went below to fetch some orange juice. He returned with a cooler and set it under a small table. The cooler contained some cartons of orange juice, which he handed to them.

"She's a beautiful boat, Martin," Dusty said, looking at Windraider from bow to stern and deck to top mast. "There aren't many like these around anymore. You know the old cliché, they don't build them like they used to."

Martin looked at Dusty. He seemed pleased with the compliment. "Do you sail, Dusty?"

"Whenever I can, which is not often. Once a year I sail out of the Chesapeake Bay to Nantucket on a thirty-eight foot sloop."

"I didn't know that," Don said with genuine surprise. "How long have you been doing it?"

"Fifteen years."

Martin didn't say anything. He just looked at Dusty and cocked his head to one side, then raised his carton of orange juice in a toast. It was a fleeting momentary gesture from one sailor to another, but in that single gesture he had won Dusty's loyalty. He would follow Martin to the crack of doom if he'd said it was the right thing to do.

Finally, Martin pressed the issue of their visit. "Let's be havin' it, Don. What's the business all about?"

"Dangerous, Martin," Dusty said, jumping the gun, as if warning him that no good could come of it.

Don gave him a grave look and then turned to Martin and told him all about the Camacho business from the beginning to the very end. It took him forty minutes, but when he finished he became quiet as if the telling of the story were a draining experience.

Martin sat quietly for a few minutes, digesting the facts which Don put to him. Then he spoke easily, without stress of any kind. "I suppose you want me to pose as the wild pilot who will fly for the cartel in exchange for money, all the while trying to get this Camacho character and his family out of Colombia. That's it in a nutshell, isn't it?"

Don nodded. "You would be the direct link with Camacho or the girl, but how you establish the link is up to you. We believe you will be able to get close enough and talk to Camacho directly."

"Why me, Don?"

"You fit the profile the cartel is looking for, a pilot with combat experience. The pilots who fly for us are known to the cartel, so we can't use them."

"What about Liliana Santander?"

"We'll send another operative to deal with her if that concerns you."

Martin stood up and looked out towards the Gulf of Mexico. It was early in the morning, before ten, the sky was still crisp and blue, and the visibility was perfect. Don and Dusty could see that Martin's thoughts were taking him away, somewhere beyond their reach. It was almost a physical thing when Martin let his mind drift in thought, everyone would remember later. He could be standing or he could be sitting, it didn't matter because when he drifted in thought he never moved a muscle; he was as a cataleptic.

Don became nervous when Martin assumed this state; he felt that he might turn down the proposition and Alfred and Norman might look at his suggestion for what it had been, a critical waste of time. The fact that Don had dressed badly for Florida -- wool pants, coat and tie -- heightened his anxiety while he tried to stem the sweat pouring out of him.

Dusty, on the other hand, had dressed in the local garb and gone native. He wore cotton pants and a white, loose-fitting short-sleeve shirt. On his feet he wore his German sandals, but despite them his feet were still swollen from the flight.

Dusty began to think about the words he'd used earlier in the morning to tell Elizabeth that he would be out of town for a few days. "I have to do some mumbo-jumbo stuff out of town, honey. I'll be back in a day or two."

Elizabeth didn't take it well and threw the words right back at him with a vindictiveness he had been unprepared to receive. "Good," she said. "I'll be mumbo-jumboing with my friend, so don't hurry back too soon." Dusty couldn't help wondering who the friend was, but he didn't wonder too long because he didn't know any of Elizabeth's friends.

Don and Dusty didn't know how long they had sat there as Martin looked out towards the horizon, but an hour would not have been a bad guess. Finally when Martin spoke up, he startled both of them. They too had become hypnotized by the sounds of the sea. "Beautiful," Martin declared. "It's what drew me down here. The ocean looks like glass, not even a ripple on it some days. It's smooth as silk. I came down here one weekend while I was working for the DEA. It was a conference on something I can't even remember. I knew that first day I would come back here and live out the rest of my life. I sold my house, closed my bank accounts, cashed in my retirement pension and headed south."

Then, suddenly, Martin changed the subject. "Why would Liliana Santander risk her life for Camacho?"

"She's Camacho's sister," Don replied. "She was married once, but her husband died in a car bomb explosion. As far as we can tell she's clean. She's also the godmother to the kid who's got the cancer."

"Will you help us?" Dusty asked. He was a bit early, but he felt his warnings were going unheeded and he was trying his level best to get Martin to refuse. He puzzled over that thought, but all he could come up with was that he had a bad feeling on the case.

"I'll have to know more, of course, but for now I'll give you a tentative yes. However, I reserve the right to pull out when everything is on the table."

"Excellent!" Don exclaimed, standing up. "You mind if I go to the marina office and make a telephone call?"

"I have a telephone inside," Martin said, but Don was already getting off the sloop. "Its okay, I'll only be gone for a few minutes."

Martin shrugged his shoulders and turned his attention to Dusty. He smiled and offered Dusty another carton of orange juice, which he accepted gladly. Dusty had the impression that he liked him and he couldn't figure out why.

Dusty smiled back at him, but his heart wasn't in it. "I suppose I should be telling you things like good man, you've done the right thing, but I think you deserve better. Martin, the odds of you making it out alive are so long, even Las Vegas wouldn't make book on you. We could very well be sending you to your death."

Martin nodded appreciatively, but remained silent. He was going, his mind was made up.

Dusty felt uncomfortable sitting there knowing that disaster was waiting for him. So, he decided to scare him with some details. "We'll give you a Citation. It's the cartel's favorite smuggling plane. She'll be under your name so that if anyone inquires about her, they'll know you're having difficulties maintaining payments on her. You will fly into Ft. Lauderdale and leave it there, while you hang out in some Miami nightspots. One of our men will then come around when the place is full of people and threaten you with repossession. We'll try it for three nights and hopefully someone will approach you. If nothing happens we move to Ft. Lauderdale itself. Once we believe the cartel has made contact, we will repossess the aircraft. Okay?"

Martin nodded again, this time without emotion.

"During the next few days we'll bring you up to speed on other cartel matters and DEA procedures. Then you will be on your own. Solo. You'll be on your way to the frontier."

"The frontier?" Martin asked with amusement.

"The cocaine frontier, where the law, morality and scruples are some vague and foggy notion."

"It sounds a lot like capitalism."

# CHAPTER 3

"Mister Camacho is Juan Calderón's right hand man," Alfred Stevens said, as Martin, Don, Lisa and Dusty sat and listened in the Miami DEA office. "He's the main money launderer for the band of hooligans who call themselves the Medellín Cartel. We estimate Camacho has laundered about twenty-seven billion dollars for the cartel since 1977. He's also, and I'm being honest, as close as we've ever got to Juan Calderón, also known as Drug King Number One."

Martin began shaking his head. "No! You've gotten the wrong man for the job. I don't know a thing about them and I feel I could mess it all up. You should get someone else for the job, someone who knows the score. I'm not the person you need."

"You're the perfect man for the job, for Christ sakes!"

"I haven't spoken Spanish in twenty years."

"Come on, who are you trying to kid? You've been living down here in Florida, for God knows how long. Hell, you can't go to the corner grocery store without speaking Spanish."

Martin smiled. "That's true, but so what? And why can't you guys get him out yourselves? If he wants to leave, why don't you help him onto a plane?"

Alfred stood up and turned up his broadcaster's voice to full volume. He also had that look and that poise that said I'm the man-in-charge. "Because we need to know if he's on the up-and-up. Once we are able to determine that, we can get the ball rolling. Our agents in place will be in greater risk if we don't find out if he's for real, since they are the ones who have to verify the information. You see, it could all be a ruse to expose them. The cartel has done that to us before. We need you to go down and see if Camacho's telling us the truth, and if he is, what does he want us to do about it."

"Why don't you just put him on a plane?"

Everyone laughed.

"We've tried it before with others," Don Harkin said, "but the cartel blew up the plane with a hundred or so passengers just to stop the witnesses from testifying."

"So what is it that you would like exactly?" Martin asked.

"We want it all," Dusty said; it was the Ph.D. in him talking. "Names, places, bank account numbers, the lot. He has to come through with it first before we get him out. We've lost too many times before agreeing to their conditions. You'll be our go-between."

Martin stood up from the couch and walked around the room. "The more things change, the more they stay the same. First Germany, then the Soviet Union, and now Colombia. The names of the players have changed, the trophy is a new one, but the game is still the same. Cold War, Hot War, Gulf War or Drug War."

"Don't fool yourself!" Alfred shot back in genuine anger. "The war we're in now is not a cold or a hot war, it's...nothing you've ever seen. The KGB boys in the Lubyanka prison would squirm like babies if they saw what the cartel did to informers."

Martin was unaffected by the outburst and took another sip from his coke can. "Why me?" he asked.

"If I had a choice I wouldn't have come down from Washington to see you, but circumstances have forced me to. We need a pilot; it's the fastest way for us to establish contact with Camacho. It might even be too late, but we've got to try. We have people dying every day by the dozens in almost every city in America because of drugs..."

"Stop, Alfie boy! Save me the speeches."

Alfred was deflated. Martin had effectively let the wind out of his sails, because when Alfred got going on the cartel he was like a television evangelist preaching about the perils of hell. It was also what got him the top DEA job. The President had seen him speak at a rally for his political re-election and figured he'd make a good mouthpiece for the fight against drugs. Alfred began rubbing the area between his eyebrows with his right index finger and thumb, as if trying to rub out some secret pain that had lodged itself there. Then he pulled his fingers away and looked straight at Martin.

"It's been a long day, why don't we call it a night and talk about it some more tomorrow after breakfast." Then Alfred turned to Don. "Can you get us some pictures ready for tomorrow? Slides, nothing fancy, just a general overview of the whole business."

"I'll set it up," Don replied.

"Mister Black, we've registered you in a room in a Miami hotel. Shall we say, ten tomorrow morning, right here in this office? You think you could manage?" Martin shrugged his shoulders as if to say, why not.

"Excellent," Alfred said. "Dusty, why don't you take Mister Black to his hotel and make sure he's all set up."

Dusty nodded.

\*   \*   \*

Dusty drove Martin to the Fontainebleau Hotel on Miami Beach, and both of them remained quiet during the ride. In the hotel, Martin's room was just down the hall from Dusty's, and although the impression was that Martin was free to leave at any time, he was not. He was already a prisoner of the DEA's constant surveillance. Two guards had been posted at each exit of the hotel and a man in a radio-car was outside just in case Martin decided to take a vacation from them.

"How about a nightcap, Dusty?" Martin asked as they stopped at his door.

"Are you sure?" Dusty asked, because no one had invited him for a drink in the past ten years. Don, who always said he'd have to have him over soon, had never come through. The unexpected invitation by Martin took him by surprise. It was a gesture he thought he should have made, but in the past ten years he had sealed himself away from human emotion in the hopes of avoiding pain and misery. It was not that he was antisocial, but it was a way of avoiding pain when someone you cared about was sold out, washed out or left to die.

"Hell, no!" Martin replied happily, "but, after what I've just heard, I deserve one, don't you think?"

Dusty laughed and they took an elevator down to the hotel's bar. It was a bit too loud for Dusty's tastes, but Martin seemed to be right at home. There were young women dancing with equally young men, but they all looked too plastic to him. Their fine, taut bodies only reminded him that he hadn't been with a woman in nearly five years. Elizabeth had denied me her sex the day he had discovered she was having an affair. Dusty shook the memory and focused on the dancers. The young crowd wore different color outfits, but their designs were remarkably similar. It was shorts and t-shirts for all. Dusty didn't think he had ever worn a t-shirt in his life, because Elizabeth had said he had no sense of fashion.

"Come on, Dusty," Martin said, slapping him good naturedly on the back, "take it easy, have a little fun."

They had two scotches while they chatted. They talked about boats, Washington and about Florida. They kept the conversation impersonal, or at least Dusty thought they were, because all the while he tried to guess what Martin might be thinking. But Martin seemed like a blank page to him, his face nearly unreadable, except for the sly winks he gave the pretty young women as they glided across the dance floor.

"How come you never married?" Dusty asked him.

"My God, you make it sound like I never will."

"Sorry."

"I've always been on the job, frankly. The DEA didn't let us play around, so to speak. I was on the job constantly and the women who had stayed around for a while got tired of waiting, I suppose. I could sleep with them, but I couldn't commit. You know the old tired cliché, I never found the right girl, well, that's me." Martin became silent for a moment. Then he asked, "What do you think I should do, Dusty?"

"I don't know. My marriage is far from being a model marriage."

Martin looked at Dusty with kindness and Dusty knew at that moment he had misunderstood the question. Martin, he realized, was turning out to be an unexpectedly sensitive man.

"I mean about the Camacho business," Martin clarified.

"If you don't do it, they'll probably use a twenty-four year old girl. She's a nice girl and she'll do it, too, but she'll die doing it. She's an amateur who still thinks being a secretary at an American Embassy is an adventure. She'll do it just to get ahead in the State Department. She's a looker too, which can help, but she's way out of her depth in a case like this."

"They're a ruthless bunch, eh?"

"Don's not a bad sort, but he's just like every other politician. Alfred, on the other hand, is a bastard. Lisa seems to be a nice woman."

"No, I mean the Medellín people."

"Oh, Jesus! I thought you meant...well, Alfred wasn't kidding. They're killers, psychopaths, with more money than the Federal Government."

"Don's changed," Martin said, looking into his glass of scotch. "He's almost..."

"Like Alfred."

Martin nodded.

"You think I've got a shot at pulling this off, Dusty?"

Dusty looked away without answering, because he liked Martin and he felt the answer might hurt him. Dusty thought he sensed that in him, because he put his hand on his shoulder and said, "I think I'll get some shut-eye." But, as Dusty watched him walk away to the bank of elevators, he was sure Martin wasn't going to catch a wink of sleep.

The following morning, Martin walked into the DEA office unshaven, but standing straighter, more confident, and with his eyes alive and soaking in everything around him. He noticed at once the new man in the suite and lifted an eyebrow in his direction.

"Leon, come on over and meet Martin," said Alfred. Leon walked over happily and shook Martin's hand. He was a small innocuous-looking individual, who wore a dark pin-stripe suit and gold-framed glasses. It was quite absurd to dress like that, because the humidity outside the hotel was really awful. One had to pity anyone who wore a suit in Miami.

"Martin, this is Leon Weinstein, our in-house psychiatric expert. He's going to try and dissect Mister Camacho and, perhaps, you'll be able to get a better read on him. If you have any questions just ask him. We've changed the slide-show schedule because Don needs a little more time to set it up."

Martin shrugged. Everyone could see that he didn't like Leon.

Alfred then motioned for everyone to take a seat and then turned to León and nodded at him to begin. It was show time for León.

Leon grabbed his briefcase, opened it and removed a legal yellow pad and prepared to take notes. No one said a word, except for Leon, who spoke at length and generally bored everyone with his silly little insights like, how Ernesto Camacho had lacked a father figure and Juan Calderón had stepped in to fill that void and all that junk. It had been Alfred's idea to bring in Leon and, although he had said it was to dissect Camacho, no one had really believed him. Leon was there to see if Martin Black was of sound mind.

Finally Leon put his pen down and said, "Thank you, Mister Black for your patience."

"Super!" declared Alfred. "Why don't we break for lunch. Then we can start on the pictures. I'm sure you'll find them quite interesting, Martin."

Showtime began a little after two-thirty. It was understood by all that it was Don Harkin's show all the way. Don had set up the slide projector so that the image would fall on the biggest wall in the office. He already had taken off the big framed print that had been on the wall and tested the projector's light on it.

Lisa Mejía then pulled on the window drapes and the office fell into darkness. Don turned on the projector light and the first picture-slide was cast on the wall. It was a gray and green blur at first, but the projector's automatic focus cleared it quickly and the city of Bogotá came into sharp relief.

"This is Bogotá, Martin," Don said. "It was taken two days ago."

Martin let out a soft whistle and said, "It looks like New York! I thought Colombia was a Third World country."

"It's biggest and fastest expansion took place between years seventy-nine and eighty-eight. It's a city of four million people." Don advanced to the next slide and the slide-projector made a click-click sound. "This is Medellín. It's almost as big as Bogotá and its construction boom took place in the last ten years."

Click-click.

"This is Miguel Contreras; he's the middle one of three brothers. He's also known as El Gordo, the Fat One. He makes the big deals. The Contreras family is known in South America for breeding the Cebú cattle. Their home turf is Rancho Contreras. It's located between the cities of Barranquilla and Cartagena. They're part of the Colombian Cartel; in fact, they're one of the pioneers of the coke trade. Their kilos of coke are marked CONTRAS."

Click-click.

"His name is Junior, the son of Fabián Pacha, also known as 'The Little Mexican.' He is the man or the boy responsible for transportation."

Click-click.

"These next few slides are people, kids mainly, who are known as sicarios or pistolocos. They are cartel shooters and hit-men. In order to become a sicario, they must prove themselves that they can handle it. They have a test called la muerte de prueba. The killing test. They must shoot someone point blank in a public place and with a lot witnesses around them. The saying is, ojo a ojo. Eye to eye."

Click-click, click-click, click-click. The slide projector went through thirty different slides before it finally came to a little girl.

"Pilar Camacho, age ten. She's Ernesto's oldest child." The girl was a cute little kid wearing a school uniform and with her hair done-up in pony tails. The picture had probably been taken while the girl was at school, because she held an open lunch-box in her lap.

Click-click.

"Efraín Camacho, age seven." He was a small child, looked more like a five year old kid. Brown hair, brown eyes, fair skin. He was in a pair of shorts, the kind that mother's buy at department stores because they think their sons will look good in them.

Click-click.

"Elena. Age twenty-eight. We don't have much on her; women are usually kept out of the business side of things...most of the time. The one thing you should know is that she's Juan Calderón's cousin."

Click-click.

"Five feet five inches. Dark Hair, forty-four inch chest, forty-two waist, size seven shoe. He prefers silk shirts over cotton, likes Rolex watches and drives a Mercedes Benz. He's Colombia's top money launderer or among the top money launderers. This is our man in Colombia, Ernesto Camacho."

Click-click.

"Do you recognize this face, Martin?" Don asked.

It was the face of a man in his late thirties, big mustache, tall with thin limbs but big in the stomach. He had dark, wavy hair and paid careful attention to his clothes -- that was obvious. The man looked harmless, because his face had that baby-fat quality one associated with children.

"His mother was a nurse. He started his criminal life stealing cars and then stripping them for their parts. He's very cool under pressure and he speaks with a very low voice that sounds cultured. He's very well-mannered, to the point that one could say he's refined. He lives in Hacienda Caracoles, his estate forty miles east of Medellín, most of the time. The farm has sixty thousand acres and he paid fifty million dollars for it. He had twenty man-made lakes put in it the year before last, so that he could sail his twelve power boats. He has also stocked the land with giraffes, camels, rhinos, hippos, lions and other exotic animals. In essence the hacienda has become the biggest zoo in Colombia, attracting nearly 60,000 visitors a year."

"Who is he?" Martin asked.

"Juan Calderón. This is who we're after in the end, Martin. Nobody has ever come close to him and that includes the Colombian guerrillas who have put a price on his head. Make no mistake about him, Martin, he's an extremely dangerous man. That is why he's the most wanted man in the world. Last November he blew up a jet-airline, killing one-hundred and seven people aboard. He did it because two of the passengers aboard were going to testify against him here in Miami. They never did."

Click-click.

The image of a young woman, impeccably dressed, flashed on the wall. She wore a short black skirt that showed off her slim but long legs, and a white blouse that was buttoned all the way up to the neck. Her hair was light brown, long and flowing past her shoulders. The face was angular, with high cheekbones and wide-set green eyes. The mouth was regular with small but full lips. The woman was a stunner and even later on when everyone looked at the picture again, she still held everyone in awe. 'Gorgeous', 'knock-out', some said in trying to describe her on that late afternoon.

It was Martin who broke the spell, "Who is she?"

"Liliana Santander."

Martin moved upright in his seat to catch an even better look at the picture, if that were possible, considering the image splayed across the wall was nearly five feet long by four feet wide, but it was at this moment while Lili's picture was on the wall that the Santander Case became an operation. Although everyone had been watching the picture-slide, Dusty had glanced over at Martin and saw something stir in him: Purpose.

"Will you help us, Martin?" Alfred asked him.

"Christ, do I have any choice?"

Nobody replied because it was a rhetorical question.

Then Martin, at whisper level, said, "Yes."

"Yes, what?" Alfred pressed.

"Yes. I'll do your bidding. I'll go down to Colombia and try to sign Camacho on board, is that what you want me to say?"

"Precisely."

It was time to scare the bejesus out of Martin. It was Dusty's version of the Spanish inquisition, and he didn't know why the task fell on him, but he supposed it had something to do with his size. He was tall, and people were disarmed by that fact. So Dusty laid it all out for him. He was now a D.E.A. Special Agent and he was liable to all the rigamarole that went along with that privilege. "You fuck up," Dusty told him, "and you'll be swinging from the highest tree limb by the neck until you're dead. We're giving you a pension and retiring you at the end of the operation. They'll be coming after you, hired gun-men. Maybe not, but you'll have to keep a good eye on the lookout."

"Is that it?" Martin asked Dusty when he stopped talking.

Dusty was frightened by the question. He wondered if Martin had heard the import of his words, so he tried to shake him up, for real.

"The cartel will never forget and you will not be Martin Black again, because when you get back stateside, we'll have to give you a new name and a new life."

"What about my boat?"

"You will have to change its name, of course, but you would get to keep it. You might even have to undergo plastic surgery, but we can talk about that later. Tomorrow we'll put you through an intensive weapons course and then some electronic spy stuff. Then will put you out there to make contact with the cartel and you'll be up and running. How do you feel?"

"As ready as I'll ever be."

# CHAPTER 4

The nightclub was in Miami Beach, on Collins Avenue, in the section known as South Beach. It was a place where usually wealthy people met to have a good time and that meant an occasional drug runner or two. Generally, South Beach was free from drug-traffickers, but a few had been spotted a couple of times and the DEA thought Martin should start there. He sat up by the bar and sipped at his scotch and soda as he looked out at the young crowd. He felt comfortable, because he had become used to young tourists in Key West.

It was nearly midnight and Martin had been there for three hours. He had lost track of how many scotches and sodas he'd put away and was about to leave when a man in a business suit walked up to him and tapped him on the shoulder.

Martin turned to face a small man with thick reading glasses and carrying a briefcase. He was the very essence of a modern-day pencil pusher and he even had the banker's pallor. Martin had seen the man before, it was a familiar face, but one could not tell by the look on his face. Alfred had introduced Martin to him the night before and told them how tonight would proceed. They had rehearsed their lines, too, for effect and as the scene unfolded, it was obvious the rehearsal had paid off.

"I've been looking for you, Mister Black!" the man declared angrily as he put his briefcase on the bar counter. The bartender flashed him a disapproving look, but the banker ignored him.

"Fuck off!" Martin replied.

"Listen, Mister Black..." The accountant began opening his briefcase. His real name was Mike Fitzroy and he worked for the payroll department at the DEA. He had been asked by Alfred to play the part and he had been eager to do it. He was middle-aged, heavy through the middle and with a bitter looking face that qualified him for the job. "By our accounts you owe us nearly thirty-seven thousand dollars. That little plane you're so fond of is, by the letter of the law, now ours."

Martin extended his hand and sent Mike reeling across the floor, knocking tables and spilling liquor everywhere as he stumbled backwards. The crowd moved aside and conversations hushed as they witnessed the commotion. They were setting the scene as, Don and Dusty witnessed it through their surveillance cameras. They had had two of their special agents smuggle in small cameras so they would be able to watch it and tape it for later viewing.

Mike stood up with an air of quiet dignity. He was the banker through and through, and said, "That's it, Mister Black! You can kiss that plane of yours good-bye."

"Fuck off!" Martin said and turned back to his drink and noticed that it was empty. "Hell! what does one need to do to get a drink 'round here?"

Mike stood there pretending anger and then lifted his chin in defiance. "We'll see, Mister Black, who gets fucked over in the end." Then Mike walked out and the scene ended. The tourists and the regulars shrugged and began to talk to each other again. The show had gone exactly the way it should have, just a small scene that would bait a big fish, or so everyone hoped.

The night before, when Martin had run through the scene, he had pushed Mike across the room so hard he had injured him. He felt embarrassed about it, as if he were some big bully putting on a show. Martin was like that; he wasn't a vicious or a violent person but a man unaware of his physical potential. Like most big and strong men he was gentle rather than brusque, which attracted people to him. To make it up to Mike he made sure to spend some time thanking Mike for putting up with him, but it was doubtful Mike even listened to him. At the end of the night's session they had a going away party for Martin; a bon voyage of sorts and Mike had been the most intoxicated of the bunch.

Dusty had spent most of the night watching Martin. He could not see any nervousness in him, which was to him quite surprising. He should have been quaking in his boots, Dusty thought, but he was cool as a cucumber. It worried him, after all, a man didn't go into a lion's den without being a little worried. Then, later in the night when everyone had departed from the office and he had driven Martin back to the hotel, Martin told him he wanted to give him something and whether he would come to his room and get it.

Martin gave him a big manila envelope and said it was his life-insurance policy, the ownership papers to Windraider and his last will and testament.

"There is a letter with instructions inside the manila envelope. If anything...happens to me, Dusty, I want you to get in touch with my attorney. He will be the executor of my estate. I don't want Alfred or Don poking into this..."

"It's against the rules," Dusty said. "I have to bring this up with Alfred, you know that!"

"I know, but I'm hoping you won't. My mother is my only living relative I have, so please see that she gets what is in here. Will you do it?"

Dusty looked at Martin with a level gaze. "Why did you ask me, and not Don?"

"I trust you," he said and Dusty groaned.

"Oh! You shouldn't have said that, Martin. I'm the last person anyone should trust. Hell, I don't even trust myself, because I don't know what way I'll bend. You'd be better off giving this envelope to Don. I let people down all the time, even my wife thinks so."

Martin laughed. "That's why I picked you, because you have no ambition in the administration. Will you do it, Dusty or shall I look for another friend?"

The word 'friend' stunned Dusty. "You hardly know me, how can you call me friend?"

"Okay, we're enemies. Do I need official papers for that?"

Dusty had let out a laugh, realizing how stupid he'd made himself out to sound.

Now as the bartender refilled Martin's glass with the scene just played out, he asked, "You have a plane?"

"Had," Martin said gloomily. "That bastard was with the bank and he's going to take her away from me."

"Time's are tough."

"They are."

"How long have you been a pilot?"

"Forever."

Martin didn't say anything else. He left one hour later. He walked back to the hotel room he had rented with the money he had been provided with by the DEA. It was a small room in the Century Hotel. He liked it, but he was too nervous to enjoy it. He was on guard every minute of every second of the day, waiting and listening to other people in the hallway as they passed his room, all the while wondering if it was the cartel coming for him. He didn't sleep much that night; Don and Dusty knew, because they had bugged his room, in case someone approached him there.

During the second night in the same bar as the night before, Martin met with success. Twenty minutes after he sat on the barstool the same bartender greeted him as if he was a regular and brought him a scotch and soda.

"I didn't order a scotch," Martin said.

"It's from Señor Bonilla," the bartender said and nodded at the corner of the nightclub. "He asks whether you might join him."

Martin glanced at the man the bartender had nodded his head at. The man was dressed in an expensive silk shirt and blue-jeans, the unofficial uniform of South Beach. He also wore a gold Rolex watch that dangled from his small wrist and his hair was combed back with a greasy gel. He had the cool detached confidence, Martin noted later on in his report, of someone used to getting his way.

"Hey, pal!" Martin said, reaching out for the bartender's neck. "Tell the fucker I'm not that sort of guy."

The bartender recoiled in shock. "Please, Señor Bonilla is not..."

"It's all right, Mike," Señor Bonilla said with a Spanish accent as he took the barstool next to Martin. "My name is Señor Bonilla. My friends call me Lucio. I'm told by Mike that you are a pilot and you're having some difficulty with its financing."

Martin gave the bartender a dark look. He genuinely felt sorry for him, because he knew that, from that moment onward, the bartender would forever be classified as a cartel contact. Martin gathered his wits and said, "Yeah, so what's it to you?"

"Maybe we could be of assistance. My corporation is in need of a pilot and you are in need of some money, no?"

Martin turned around in his chair so that he might look at the crowd on the dance floor. He was acting the part of the disinterested potential employee. He could take the job or leave it, but he managed to say, "Go on."

"My people would pay handsomely for the right pilot and I believe you might be it. That is, of course, if you can fly all types of aircraft."

Martin let out a chuckle, as if the man were trying to get on his nerve. "I don't know what rock you climbed out from under, but I was flying F-15's in the Gulf when you were still sucking on your mother's tits."

Lucio swallowed the insult and managed a smile, perhaps, remembering what his boss had told him. That American pilots were an arrogant breed of men, for reasons not quite clear to him, but he supposed it had to do with an unwritten code among flyers. "Please, excuse me. I did not mean to insult you. I merely needed to ascertain your experience."

"No harm done."

"Excellent. As I was saying, the industrialists I work for need a pilot to transport some sensitive cargo from Miami to Colombia and vice-versa, and because of certain import and export regulations from both countries our pilot would have to...shall we say, be creative with his flying."

"You mean fly under the radar net?" Martin asked as he motioned the bartender for a beer.

Lucio became cautious and looked around. "I don't know about such technical matters, but if you were spotted by radar, shall we say your life...."

"I see."

"We would pay the standard rate, of course."

"Which is?"

"One million per flight. If your flying was determined to be good and everything went according to plan, then, perhaps, we could talk about a raise."

Martin gulped. "One million? Is that in pesos or good old American greenbacks?"

"Dollars. There would be incentives, too. We would also provide the plane, by the way. Here's my number." Lucio handed Martin a card he had retrieved from his shirt pocket. "Think about it and call me if you're interested. If I'm not at that number just leave a message." Lucio then stood up. "You have a good-night, Mister Black."

The following morning, the DEA repossessed Martin's supposed Cessna 182RG with many shouts and threats from both sides as witnesses looked on. Then, in between the shouts, Don told him to wait for two days before calling Lucio Bonilla, and when he did, Martin told them later on, that Lucio was blasé about the call, but he told Martin to be at a small clearing north of the Tamiani Canal, and that he was to bring nothing but himself. If he was not there by two thirty in the morning he wouldn't be hired. And at that very moment the Santander Case became operational.

# CHAPTER 5

It was nearly twenty past two when Martin found the meeting ground. The only lights he used to find his way with, were the headlights on the Chevy he had rented from Rent-a-Wreck. The night was humid and, with no moon, a filthy night. The field, he noticed, was a clearing at the edge of the Florida Everglades. At first Martin thought he might have gotten the wrong field because he couldn't spot another soul, and, as he was about to turn back he saw a small light flicker on and off and he knew he'd arrived at the spot.

The plane and the men had been well-concealed behind a military camouflage netting. The plane, a 182RG, looked so much like the one the DEA had given him for his cover he had to squint and check the registration number to make sure.

The moment Martin stepped out of the car four men approached him, each brandishing a new shotgun. They turned him around and quickly searched him, and, having determined that he was neither carrying a gun nor a microphone they moved away.

"Are you Black?" A short mustached man asked.

Martin straightened out and asked, "Who are you?"

The man smiled. "Rafael Sanchez. People call me Rafa. I am Lucio's boss. Now, will you tell me who you are?" The man raised his eyebrows and waited for Martin to reply.

Martin heard a gun being cocked behind him and said, "Martin Black," and stuck out his hand. Rafa shook it.

"We'll be taking a little trip, my friend," Rafa said, now turning towards the airplane.

"Where to?"

Rafa grinned. "Colombia, where else?"

"In that?" Martin asked. "That plane doesn't have the range!"

"Oh, don't worry. It's been modified. Look, you can see for yourself."

Martin saw and was immediately ill. Inside the Cessna a water-bed had been filled with fuel and was connected through bladder lines to the main tanks. The waterbed was a Mickey-Mouse fuel tank and it scared the living daylights out of him.

"My workers were about to load her when you showed up."

"Load her?" Martin asked bewildered. "You've got to be joking! It's probably past her cargo weight as it is with all that fuel in the back seat."

Rafa dismissed his complaint with a wave of his hand. "Oh, that's nothing." Then he turned to the others and barked a command in Spanish.

The men began to load the Cessna with weapons: M-16's, Mac-10's, Uzi's and Magnums, while Rafa spread out a map and showed Martin their flight path and destination. He told him how he would fly north of Cuba and then south over Haiti. Martin said nothing as Rafa explained, because the flight was so preposterous it could only end in disaster.

Rafael Sanchez, Martin noticed, was a short wiry Colombian who projected an air of confidence. His dark brown eyes had a slight slant to them, which Martin figured to be a trait from a South American Indian tribe. His mustache, however, was his most distinguishing characteristic. It was waxed and well-kept.

Twenty minutes after the four men loaded the Cessna a man declared to Rafa, "Doscientos kilos."

Rafa then turned to Martin and said, "That's it, Mister Black. Two hundred kilos in weapons. Now we see how good a pilot you really are. Get in and let's get going."

"We?"

Rafa grinned. "Yes, you and me."

"Christ, we're too heavy! The field isn't long enough."

Rafa shook his head slowly and removed a gun from his shoulder holster. He checked the slip action and then pointed the muzzle directly at Martin's heart.

"It's going to be like this, Mister Black. You fly or I kill you. What's it going to be?"

Martin stared. Rafa's voice hadn't a trace of bluff in it. He would kill him without a second thought. "Yeah?" Martin said trying to sound equally tough. "Well, where is my money?"

Rafa nodded and one of the men brought up a briefcase and set it flat on the ground. He opened it and allowed Martin to inspect its contents: Five hundred thousand dollars in thousand dollar bills neatly stacked in ten piles of fifty.

"You'll get the first half now and the other half on arrival."

Martin smiled and said, "My mother said I should've been a lawyer, but I don't know any lawyer who makes this much in a few hours."

Rafa laughed heartily. "I think, Compadre, that you and I are going to get on famously."

It was three in the morning when Martin and Rafa climbed aboard the Cessna. The hot and humid air of the Everglades enveloped them, so that their shirts stuck to their skin and their movements seemed more restricted. Rafa sat in the right seat. He had his gun on his lap. Martin sat in the left seat and ran through his pre-flight check-list. He used the light of the instrument panel to make notations. The weather forecast was good with a five-knot wind out of the West.

"Okay, let's get to it," Martin announced. Then he shouted through the tiny window, "Clear!"

He made contact and the engine sputtered to life. He switched on the taxi and landing lights and got his first real view of the field. "Jeeesus!" Martin declared when he realized the field was just that, a field. There was no runway, just good old reedy Florida grass. Then he drew in a big breath, put in flaps, trimmed for take-off and let the engine gather rpm's as he kept his feet on the brakes. The plane, reeking of fuel, vibrated wildly as the rpm's climbed to full power.

"Here we go," Martin said, releasing the brakes and shoving the throttle forward, but not before he caught Rafa crossing himself religiously.

The Cessna seemed to crawl forward at first, but then gathered speed and began to chew-up the remaining field under its wheels. Martin watched the airspeed gauge climb;

forty, fifty and finally at sixty knots he pulled back on the control column with the trees looking like a wall in front of him. The Cessna lurched into the air and then seemed to sink for a moment, but then found its lift and climbed up and over the trees. Martin brought the gear up and the speed rose to one-hundred knots as he leveled out.

Rafa chuckled. "I guess you are a real pilot," he said; "you had half a field left." Both of them laughed.

Martin leveled out at three hundred feet and his speed rose to one-hundred and fifteen knots. His concern now was not speed, but the electrical power lines Rafa had warned him about before take-off. Nevertheless, he was still amazed that his next stop would be Ríohacha on Colombia's Guajira Peninsula.

"How many times have you done this little trip?" Martin asked.

"Like this or by jet?" Rafa countered.

"Like this."

"Hundred, maybe one-hundred and fifty. By jet, three times a week."

Martin glanced at Rafa and watched him settle into his seat and relax.

Thirty minutes later Martin banked to the southeast and dropped to forty feet above the dark and ominous sea.

"Look at that!" Rafa declared. "We're about to wake up some people."

Martin's eyes opened wide. He pulled back on the control column to avoid clipping a radio mast on a cruise ship with his right wing. He braced for impact, but the Cessna cleared the mast by a matter of twenty-feet.

Rafa laughed as he retrieved a cigar from his coat pocket. "It's not an easy way to fly, Compadre."

Martin looked at Rafa, horrified. "You're not going to light that in here!"

"Relax, I just like the feel of it. The only thing you have to worry about is the Cuban radar, so fly low and keep out of sight. By the way, there is a thermos of Colombian coffee under your seat."

Martin nodded. "For who is the stuffed teddy-bear?" He had seen one of the workers store one along with the weapons.

"My daughter Marisol. She's nine years old."

"Are you married?"

"Ten years." Rafa grinned. Then he pulled out a wallet from his back pocket and handed Martin a picture which he saw by the light of the moon. "My wife Paula."

Martin saw that she was a homely looking woman with big eyes, a big mouth and big hips.

"She's two years younger than I am, so that makes her twenty eight. She's from my hometown, Medellín. Her father and my father worked for the same coffee plantations in Antioquia Province. My parents like hers were peasants, but in Colombia we call them campesinos. Good, hard working people who were taken advantage of by the feudal lords who owned the plantations. They had a hard life, Martin." Rafa shook his head. "Today, I can make more money in five minutes than they could in a lifetime of hard labor. My father was paid fifteen cents a day, you know? But I've changed all that. Nobody in my family will ever have to worry about money again. If I die tomorrow I will be remembered as the son who did well by his family. What more can a man ask for?"

"What does your wife think of what you do?"

Rafa gave Martin a hard look, but then he softened it and shrugged his shoulders. "The day of her graduation her father took her to the ceremony in a zorra. Do you know what that is?"

Martin shook his head.

"It's a cart made of wooden planks and four used car tires, like the wooden trailers you see horses being transported in the States. Except what transports this cart is a burro. Can you imagine yourself driving through Miami streets in one of them while wearing your best clothes? No you couldn't. Well, my wife now drives a Mercedes and her father drives a BMW."

"Is that why you married her?"

"Of course! I saved her! Why else would I marry her?"

Martin thought about love, but he wasn't about to bring the subject up. He could already see that Rafa thought of himself as the heroic and noble type.

Rafa remained quiet and, soon after, he cocked his head over his right shoulder and fell asleep.

Martin flew past Cuba and turned South over Haiti, because Rafa had explained that it was preferable to fly over Haiti than through the Mona Passage, because it meant risking interception by American aircraft out of Puerto Rico. When Martin had asked about Haiti defensive aircraft, Rafa had replied with another of his patented laughs. "Compadre, Haiti knows we're coming through," he said, then added a warning, "but you have to be careful, because the Massif de la Hotte is nearly three thousand meters high."

An hour later, the Massif was a dark mountain that seemed to block Martin's path, but the Cessna climbed over it and then again faced the wide blue sea. Then like spilled milk he saw the dawn's early light splash on the eastern horizon as night receded into the West.

It was a straight run now, Martin thought, six and one half hours straight to the Colombian Peninsula. The Cessna was holding up well and was cruising at 150 knots despite the slight headwind.

As the engines began to drain the fuel tanks dry, the plane became lighter and faster. Martin then set the Loran and the auto-pilot to fly the aircraft and he felt the tension lift from his shoulders.

Martin watched the sun rise as the Cessna flew two hundred feet above the sea. He remembered the thermos of coffee under his seat and poured himself a cup of dark brew. It tasted bitter, so he brought it close to his nostrils and smelled brandy in the mixture. He put the cover back on and placed it back under his seat. He was feeling too good to be mad, because it had been a long time since he had flown a plane. The engine whirred on noisily while the gauges showed that all was well. Every now and then he glanced at Rafa and realized that there was something really likable about the man. He was a man with an almost magnetic personality. He was cheerful in all matters and he never seemed bothered in the least about anything, but Martin didn't try to fool himself; he knew Rafa would kill him at the drop of a hat if he had cause. Then his thoughts wandered to Ernesto Camacho and what would it be like when he was in the thick of the cartel. Had he been too hasty in accepting the DEA offer, he asked himself, but he couldn't answer his own question.

One hour out of Ríohacha, Martin checked the instrument panel and discovered that fuel was beginning to run low. He looked behind his seat and saw that the bladder tank had already emptied out into the main tanks. Everything was now down to a question of fuel and distance. Quickly he worked out the calculations in his head. They were flying at one hundred and fifty knots, but they're ground speed was one hundred and forty, which meant they were flying into a headwind of at least fifteen knots and their fuel consumption was thirteen point seven gallons an hour. Instinctively, he knew it was bad. Then he checked his own calculations against the Loran, which told him the remaining time on the fuel-flow meter.

"Damn!" Martin cussed sharply.

"What's the matter?" Rafa asked, coming instantly awake.

"We have a headwind and fuel's running low. It's going to be a close call."

"How far are we?"

"Forty-seven minutes, but we only have thirty-nine minutes of fuel left."

"Well, there's not much we can do about it now. We either make it or we don't. Relax, Black. En la vida todo tiene solución menos la muerte."

Martin looked at Rafa. "What does that mean?"

"In life there is a solution to everything, except for death."

"Wow, I'm flying with Socrates."

Rafa laughed. He liked Martin Black. Rafa was always envious of men Martin's size. Men who were big, strong and worried too much, but when push came to shove they loved danger as much as he did. Rafa, perhaps, could guess that even though Martin complained a lot he was enjoying himself immensely. Martin, Rafa thought, was a born drug runner.

But now Martin was doing something he thought he would never do. He was hunting the wind, looking for the soft spot in the headwind, trying to find the path of least resistance. He reduced power to seventy percent, dropping his airspeed down to 135 knots. The ride became a bumpy one, as the day's heat thermals rose into the atmosphere and buffeted the plane.

When the Guajira Peninsula rose from the horizon, the fuel needles were on empty and Martin with his peripheral vision could see Rafa looking at the gauges, then at the coast, and then finally at him. Rafa didn't have to ask if they were going to make it, because his guess was as good as Martin's.

Then Martin thought of dumping the cargo, but the thought soon faded when they spotted the Colombian Coastline.

Then Rafa picked up the radio and tuned into a predetermined frequency and began to radio for instructions. "Alpha one, this is Alpha two. Requesting landing instructions."

Suddenly the radio became alive with a heavily accented English voice. "Alpha two, this is Alpha one. Change heading to new course two-six-zero. You're cleared for landing."

Rafa put the microphone back on the instrument panel as Martin executed the maneuver. Precious minutes seemed to pass, until the runway appeared in front of them like an open wound on the landscape.

"That's Juan Calderón's private runway. You could land a 747 on it, I am told. Ríohacha airport is down the road."

Martin lined up with the runway and began his final approach. He lowered his flaps, then his gear and the Cessna quickly lost airspeed. Holding the control column steady the gear touched down softly as a goose feather. The plane rolled out over a beautiful long runway until it came to a stop at the end of it.

"There to the side," Rafa announced. "Under the nets, by the Citation. That's one of Juan's jets. Park the plane there."

Martin saw the Citation jet hidden under the camouflage nets and parked the Cessna beside it. He powered down and watched all the gauges die, but his ears were left with a weak hum and ring in them.

"Eh, Compadre!" Rafa exclaimed, patting Martin over the back. "Welcome to Colombia!"

"Great," Martin said unenthusiastically. "Now what?"

"Now we get out and have a big lunch. After lunch we get into that Citation over there and fly to Bogotá. We'll be there two or three days, I don't know."

It couldn't have gone better if Martin had planned it. He knew Liliana was in Bogotá and this afforded him the best time for contact. "Where are we staying?"

"You'll be staying at the Tequendama Hotel. I'll be somewhere else," Rafa said evasively and saw Martin's face questioning him, so he added, "Business. I'll get in touch with you at the Tequendama in a day or two. Come on, let's go eat lunch!"

On that Tuesday afternoon, November 18, 1996, in his Washington D.C. office, Alfred Stevens worked through a mountain of paperwork that had collected over the past several days. The room was cool and it bothered him that he could never feel just right no matter what season it was. It was either to cold or too hot, but those were trivial matters that were far from his present sphere of thought. Dusty was there beside him, trying to arrange the chaos into some semblance of control and order. It was then when Harkin knocked discreetly on Alfred's office door.

"Any word yet?" Stevens asked without looking up.

Harkin laid a coded computer disk on Steven's desk.

Stevens looked up. "When did this come in?"

"At precisely nine o'clock this morning, sir," Don replied

Stevens moved the paperwork aside and turned on the power on his video-terminal. Then quickly he gained the necessary access into the mainframe and typed in the coded message. The computer decoded the message almost instantly and then scrolled it back onto the video screen.
DRUG-BUSTER

Stevens stood up without saying a word and walked towards the window. "Drug-buster," Stevens said, but Harkin looked at him with puzzlement. "It means Mister Black is in Colombia."

"Dear Lord, but we've never been this close to the cartel before, Don. Do you realize what we could accomplish if

Black is successful? We could bring the cartel down like a house of cards."

"I hope, for everyone's sake, it's not a trap," I said gravely.

Stevens nodded. "God help Martin Black, because he's going to need it. Thank you, Don. Keep me informed if there are any new developments."

Harkin knew Stevens had dismissed him and left his office.

Stevens stood by the window and Dusty watched how his eyes fell upon the city. He wondered if his mind were spiralling backwards in time, trying to recall the life of the man who had bedeviled the law for a quarter century, Juan Calderón, the most wanted man in the world.

# CHAPTER 6

The antichrist.
The first time Dusty had heard Juan Calderón referred to in that way, he laughed. At the time he had believed that it was a word for an unearthly creature, one of the fallen angels, but certainly not a word for a mortal man; although he was never quite sure about Adolf Hitler, but Juan Calderón...no chance. He would say this much later to the Congressional subcommittee to emphasize how much he had underestimated Juan Calderón, his satanic majesty.

The first time Dusty had ever seen the man the cartel called El Patron was on a video-tape. His image on the tape was so beguiling Calderón seemed incapable of hurting a fly, but that was before anyone knew anything about him.

Dusty's education on Juan Calderón began with the Santander Case, strangely not because Martin Black was flying at that moment into the land of fallen angels, but rather due to the fact that Colombia's F-2 police were closing in on Calderón at that precise moment in an operation they had aptly called El Rey: The King. The F-2 had never informed the DEA, which went to show just how cooperative Colombia and the United States were getting along. It was from the F-2 report on El Rey however, that the investigating sub-committee had been able to reconstruct what had happened -- if not in fact, then in spirit, to the Santander Case. It all began...


...The Toyota Land Cruiser rolled over the deeply rutted, unpaved track like a lumbering beast. The fallen trees and the uneven way strained the axles within inches from their breaking point, the woody vines having been forced aside as the jeep made its way through the dense vegetation, smashed back against the windows and made spider-web configurations on them. And above everything was the sound of the whining of the engine. The jeep was dying.

Hundreds of explosions reverberated in the rain forest and drowned out the angry shriek of birds. Two helicopters in pursuit of Juan Calderón flew above the jungle canopy and saturated the area with machine-gun fire. Juan Calderón had decided the police would not catch him and, therefore, leaned out of the jeep and fired his MAC-10 at the helicopters.

Suddenly there was a clearing and Calderón became exposed. He watched as a soldier leaned out of the Huey helicopter and swung the gun sight in his direction. The soldier peered through the sight, his aim was determined and his resolution was death.

The soldier fired and missed. Calderón returned fire and met with success. The soldier froze, his face twisting in an expression of agony as he realized he was going to die. He looked down, ripped his shirt open and found a red splotch in the center of his chest. At that moment the helicopter banked hard and the soldier collapsed. Then Calderón was back under the protection of the jungle canopy.

"Not much longer, Patrón," said the driver. "We're almost there."

Calderón knew his luck was under a test. He had sat down to have a quiet dinner when a phone call had alerted him to the impending military raid on his hacienda. It was all academic after that, because, without hesitating, he opened his strong-box and retrieved a million dollars in cash and then, with his two most trusted pistolocos got into his Land Cruiser and drove away. He ordered them to take the planned escape route that was built-in to every property he owned for such an eventuality, whether it be a house or an hacienda. The present escape route was now serving him well, even though the rain forest was claiming it back a little more each day.

"There it is!" the driver shouted and pointed at a power-boat tied-up by the side of the river.

The driver stopped the jeep and the men climbed out without bothering to turn off the engine. El Padrino boarded the power-boat as a pistoloco untied it from its mooring, letting it drift out onto the river's current. Calderón then pressed the ignition button and the twin 300 horsepower engines came alive with a bracing roar. Slowly he pushed the throttles forward until the power-boat was making fifty-knots down river.

"¡Mucho verraco!" Calderón shouted gleefully over the roar of the engines. Again he had escaped the mad clutches of the law and he would live to tell the tale. He would exact some careful and precise retribution from those who had betrayed him. Oh, how the poor bastard who informed the authorities of his whereabouts would suffer, he thought. And the good thing was, he knew exactly who the poor bastard was; Carlos Romero, his very own finance minister.

Why, Carlos? Calderón asked himself. We were like brothers! What caused you to betray me? Did I not take care of you always? Can you not remember our first business deal eighteen years ago and how...

*The truck moved slowly uphill in the morning twilight of Medellín. Twice the engine had overheated and together they had waited for it to cool, until they could pour more water into the radiator. They had said nothing since leaving the cemetery and Carlos was taking the situation badly. There was a repressed anger in both of them, but right now all they cared for was to get to their destination.*

*Their attention had to be fixed on the road ahead. The eyes had to be strained into sharp focus, looking for a military road-block or a tell-tale light of a guerrilla ambush in the pre-dawn light.*

*The sky was changing now, but the mountainous land was still shrouded in darkness. They did not use their headlights; they traveled only with the intermittent light of the Colombian moon.*

*It would not be long now, ten kilometers at most and four of them downhill. It took daring, but daring had been part of their lives since the fifth grade. But this was different, they were actually going to realize a heavy profit this time.*

*"How far are we?" Carlos asked.*

*"Two, maybe three kilometers," Calderón replied.*

*"I can't believe we're doing this, Juan. It's a bad omen to mess with the dead, you know that. We should've brought some flowers and left them on the graves."*

67

"What the hell for?" Carlos shrugged, but Calderón pressed him. "Why should we have left flowers?"

"My grandfather used to say that, whenever one went to a cemetery you had to bring flowers. That the spirits had to be kept happy while they awaited entrance into heaven or hell, because the air above the cemetery is like a waiting area and by bringing flowers we acknowledge their existence in our world."

"Shit, Carlos, sometimes I think you're insane," Juan said. "Anyway, what's done is done and it can't be undone."

There was no going back for them. They had desecrated the cemetery and, if caught, a Colombian would not take pity on them. And Carlos Romero was a superstitious boy of fourteen, just a year younger than Juan, and he was not one to forget about the spirit world and the bad luck that could be brought down on him by the spirits themselves. He would have to visit his grandmother and ask her for a remedy for protection against the spirits.

The truck gained speed as it entered Medellín from the north. The sky was changing rapidly now, but the sun was still well below the cordillera. The narrow mountain road then widened out into a wide city street. They made a set of turns until they were traveling quickly on narrow back-roads.

Finally, Juan pulled the truck up to a warehouse and leaned on the horn. The warehouse door opened immediately and he drove the truck into it.

"You see, Carlos," Juan said, patting him on the back, "nothing to it. Come, let's unload the truck."

For the next hour Juan and Carlos would unload thirty-two gravestones and shave the names, dates and endearments off of them, so that when they finished working on them the stones appeared as if they were new and non inscribed. The owner of the warehouse then surveyed the work and nodded his head. He would pay.

"Two thousand dollars, Carlitos. Not bad for eight hours work, eh?"

Carlos laughed. "Juan, we better hurry home. If my father finds out I'm not home when he wakes up, he'll give me a beating I won't forget any time soon. By the way, have you finished your math homework?"

*Juan shook his head gravely. "No, Compadre. I didn't have any time."* Carlos shook his hand to indicate Juan had been a bad boy. *"Why didn't you ask your mother for help? She's well educated, she must know something about math."*

*"Not to worry. I'll get someone to let me copy their homework."*

*"What happens if no one lends it to you?"*
*"I'll hurt them."*
*The silence was brutal.*
*Juan thought he'd gone too far, even though he had meant what he had said, so he tried to lighten the mood. "Carlos, you take me too seriously."*

*"Sometimes I wonder what you would do if the devil owed you a favor and he couldn't return it?"*

*"The devil, Carlos, is in all of us. Sometimes it manifests itself to us through girls, cars, or whatever our vice happens to be on that day. If you are tempted by something you know you shouldn't have, because you know it's wrong and you still fall to its temptation, then there is where you will find your devil."*

*A chill shook Carlos and he tried to pretend the morning was chilly, but Juan wasn't fooled.*

Calderón slowed the motor-boat and slipped quietly into the marina. He anchored the boat to a slip and climbed onto dry land. 'I will, by the end of the day, send you to the devil Carlos,' he thought, and then he got into his Mercedes and ordered his pistolocos to take him to the safety of his plane, which would fly him out of harm's way.

# CHAPTER 7

The Avianca building in the international sector of Bogotá was an imposing 48-storied-monolith of concrete and glass, whose twenty year existence had been a tortured one. In July of 1973, a fire had raged from the twenty-eighth to the fortieth floor and had nearly brought the building's four year existence to an abrupt end. Then, after its resurrection from the ashes it became the most frequented target for the guerrillas in which to place their bombs. By the mid-eighties it was hard to say how many times they had evacuated the building because of bomb threats. The more pessimistic bogotanos said that working in the Avianca building was flirting with disaster, while the more optimistic said it was the only building that extended one's vacation by several days.

And it was in this building, on a cold and rainy Wednesday at half past two in the afternoon, that Liliana Santander was staring at the clock in the offices of the Colombian Board of Tourism. She couldn't stare out at the vista which working on the top floor afforded her, because the low clouds that encircled the vast plateau of Bogotá had only offered her a view of several inches. She was closed in by a wall of gray, which she also determined to be an accurate assessment of her life. Gray, dull and boring.

Her job was to answer telephones for one of the lower-level bureaucrats who worked for the Ministry and, in her opinion, he was a pig. She had been offered the job because she could speak English and because she had once been married to a wealthy Chileno.

Lili had not kept in touch with Alejandro's family. They lived in Chile and that was too far for her to think they could be of any help to her or her to them, but she still managed to send a Christmas card every year.

She began to think on whether she should take up Guillermo's offer for dinner, but that meant she would be sending him a clear signal that there was interest on her part. There was not, but it was Guillermo who had found her the job and she felt slightly indebted. Maybe, she would go to the Centro-Colombo Americano and pick up a few more English tapes, except she would have to go out of her way before going home -- and on a day like this that was an ordeal.

She settled for ringing Lucía. She would try to convince her to go see a movie, maybe even do a little shopping at the Unicentro Shopping Mall. Lucía was one of her friends she could count on to do things, even though she became a little annoying when she tried to fix her up with men. It was not that the men she had been set up with were unattractive, but it was more a case of young men trying to impress. The men she dated always wanted her to know that they were part of what made Colombia run, the players. They were boys, really, and she could not go back to boys after having been married for two years to Alejandro. He had been twelve years her senior and she had never felt a difference in their age. He was mature and kind, but he was also very extravagant, which in the end had been his death sentence. She pictured his charred remains on the morgue's slab when the coroner had wheeled it out for identification. How could they have possibly thought she would have been able to identify him? But the corpse had a gold necklace, the one she gave to Alejandro for Christmas, in what she assumed was his neck.

Lili shook the ugly images away and looked at the clock, but found that the minute hand had only moved a few minutes. She began to think of things she should do before the weekend. First, she had to pay the electric and telephone bills, and then she had to give her doorman a nice tip for taking care of her Renault.

Today, there was no area in the city safe for a car, even if the neighborhood had its own security patrol looking out for their interests. And, even though Lili lived in one of the city's more lucrative places, Los Rosales -- thanks to Alejandro's last will and testament -- her car was still not safe. Unfortunately, car theft was Bogotá's biggest art form, which was second only to muggings. But she could live with that, because she learned not to wear expensive jewelry in the street or leave a car out in a bad area without a complicated alarm system.

Suddenly Lili noticed that the telephone console on her desk was blinking, so she cursed herself for daydreaming and lifted the receiver.

"Haber," she answered, forgetting to use the standard telephone protocol, which her bosses demanded she use.

"Señora Santander, please," the caller asked.

"Hablando." Speaking, Lili replied.

"Señora Liliana Santander?"

"¿Con quién hablo, por favor?" Who am I speaking to, please?

"¿Puedes hablar en Inglés?" Can you speak in English the caller asked.

Lili heard the American accent in the voice and relaxed, because it sounded like another New York travel agent calling for information on Colombia.

"Yes, I speak English, sir."

"Excellent," said the man's voice. "I'm calling because we have something in common..."

"You have still not told me your name, sir."

"Damn! that's right. Sorry. Well, my name is Martin Black. I received your letter you passed through a mutual friend of ours at the embassy...Hello? Are you still there, Señora Santander?"

"¡Ay, Dios mío!" Lili gasped. She felt as if the building were collapsing and she was falling, and everything around her was coming down along with her to.

Martin was caught off-guard. He had not expected such a reaction and in his scramble to stabilize the situation he became tongue-tied. "Well, uh...are you all right? Maybe I should call you later on, eh? No, what if I stopped by?"

"Yes, no, wait!" Lili stammered, confused by his barrage of questions. Mierda! she thought. The man is an idiot; he'll get us all killed and never know why.

"Listen," he said. "I'm at the Tequendama Hotel. Why don't you give me a call later on, okay? I've just arrived in Bogotá and I'd like to look around, okay? Why don't we meet for dinner, okay? Or if you'd like you can just stop by. They have a great restaurant in the hotel, okay? I'll leave it up to you, okay?"

Lili was shaking, but she anchored herself to Martin's constant use of the word okay. It seemed to settle her somewhat. "I will meet you at seven," she said.

"Seven, when?"

"Tonight!"

"Okay, where?"

"I don't know."

Martin waited for her to set the place, while thinking, damn it! The woman is a bimbo!

Lili began to calm herself and she let her mind think of places she could meet him. It's for my Godson I am doing this and he will die if I don't help him. "Meet me at the top of Monserrate Mountain. There's a restaurant at the top."

"I don't know where it is."

"Find out!" Lili said angrily and hung up. Then she walked to the ladies' room and was violently sick. She had not expected the call, at all! She had given up on the John Whitney letter; after all, it had been nearly three weeks.

By the time Lili reached her apartment she had recovered some of the color in her cheeks and her breathing had steadied. Fortunately, her boss had not asked many questions when she had asked to leave a little early. She had looked sick enough at the time. Now, quickly, she changed into her exercise sweats and settled herself on the soft couch in her living room. She reached for the telephone and dialed the Casa San Isidro restaurant and made reservations for seven o'clock, but seven o'clock was booked up and the earliest they had was eight-thirty. She agreed, knowing that she would have to sit around for an hour or so with the American and make small talk.

Then, dreading the next phone call, she dialed Medellín. It was a telephone number Ernesto had obtained for a small office he had rented and in which he had connected an answering machine specifically to take Lili's messages. And only Ernesto and Lili knew of its existence, because her brother wanted it that way. He had even made her memorize the number, so that nobody ever would find it in some address book lying around.

She thought about what Ernesto had said to her less than a month before. "This is dangerous for you, Lili," he had informed her. "If they find me out then they'll find you. They will kill us all, so you must do this because you want to and not because I am family. I must warn you that they might kill you anyway. It's how Medellín is these days -- life's cheap."

Lili heard the telephone ring on the other end and then the message machine pick up. She heard the signal to begin speaking and she said, "Hello, it's Lili. He's in Bogotá. Call me soon."

Lili then stretched out over the couch to catch a nap. She had developed a headache since Martin's call and she was hoping some sleep would alleviate it. She tried to picture what Martin was like, but she could only picture him as a bumbling fool who said okay to everything. She shook her head pitifully, wondering how she had involved herself in a plot to turn against the cartel, a plot which would be run by a norteamericano! But she trusted her brother, despite what he had become!

The rain abated shortly before dusk. The streets, still wet from the day's downpour, glistened under the taxi's headlights. Martin sat in the back seat of an old Renault 21 and watched as he drove through the streets of Bogotá. Huge buildings and giant avenues had been created in the city, if only to make the auto traffic worse.

"Meet me on top of Monserrate Mountain," she had said. Martin looked at his watch, it was five-fifteen in the afternoon and he told the driver to take him back to the hotel, knowing that John Whitney would have set up his men in and around the restaurant.

Martin recalled what Alfred had said to him before he left Miami. "John Whitney, is your contact man in Colombia. John Whitney is not his real name, but that doesn't matter. The less you know of the players, the safer it will be for everyone."

"Is he DEA?" Martin asked when they had laid the operation out for him.

"Ten years," Alfred said. Then he added, "Listen to what he says. If he offers you advice, take it. He's the best agent, by far, in Colombia. He will be around you constantly, although you won't see him. If you get into a bad scrape and he's able to get you out, he will."

Now, as the taxi drove Martin through the streets of Bogotá, he wondered if John were behind him in another taxi. Perhaps, John was even thinking the same things Martin was thinking about; maybe not, John was probably thinking about how Martin Black, the new man in town, was supposed to solve the American drug problem single-handedly by forcing him to endure a tour of Bogotá. Martin laughed and noticed the driver looking at him with a curious face.

"How do I get in touch with you people?" Martin had asked Alfred just before leaving Miami. "Do I just pop around the embassy and spill the beans?"

"No! For God sakes, don't even come near the damn place. Once we find out where you're staying we'll be in touch, or, I should say, Whitney will be in touch. He will make his approach early, so don't get rattled."

Finally the taxi stopped in front of the Hotel. The driver turned around and said, "I'm with the DEA, Mister Black. You should check in. Mister Whitney is expecting you in room 625."

Martin gaped in disbelief. Then he asked, "Are you John Whitney?"

"No, sir, he's my boss." Martin nodded and stepped out of the taxi.

The Tequendama Hotel, as the Avianca building, was also in the international sector of the city. It is still the most reputable hotel in Bogotá and the prices reflect it. It also boasts the best nightclub in town, on the seventeenth floor, and its restaurants are among the city's more respectable.

Martin showered, shaved and at ten minutes of six he walked down the hall and knocked on room 625. The door opened and he was met by two men who waved him in.

"This is my assistant, Special Agent Camilo López. I am John Whitney."

Martin shook hands with both of them.

Camilo seemed to be barely out of his teens, but the hard look in his eyes said he was close to thirty. He was a small man of average build and had the look of a costeño, the nickname Colombians use for people who come from the coast. Camilo had that mulatto look to him, which was prevalent to people from the northern coast. His voice was silky, like the singer Johnny Mathis, but his actions and movements were clipped, abrupt. There was also an economy of movement to everything he did. Martin at once recognized the signs of a man living undercover. His entire personality and concentration were honed to the one fact that mattered most, survival.

Martin told Camilo and John about the trip from the Everglades. He described the planes, the weapons, the people he saw in Ríohacha, the people who had come along with him to Bogotá and especially the man who called himself Carlos Romero.

"What about Romero?" John asked.

"I don't know," Martin replied, "but there was tension between Romero and Rafa. I asked Rafa later on, but he said nothing."

"Take off your shirt," Camilo said.

Martin did so and Camilo taped a recorder to his middle. "It's voice activated."

"I know," said Martin. "I've used them in the past."

"Do you want a vest?" John asked.

"A what?"

"A vest, a flack jacket, a bullet proof..."

"You're joking! Do you expect the girl to pull a gun out on me? Didn't I tell you about the phone call I made to her? For God sakes! The woman started to cry!"

John came close to Martin. "Listen, Black, I have been here for ten years, and I have seen things that would make you wet your pants. I have seen ten year old girls walk up to restaurants and lob hand grenades into them. Don't give me any fuckin' talk about what you know from some fly-by-night training you received. Here you know nothing, got it?"

"What is it that you don't like about me? Is it my deodorant, or is it my breath you don't like?"

"It's you! I read your file and it says you're a bum pissing in the wind. And let me warn you, if you screw this up I could lose ten of my men in a single night. Just remember that, every time you screw up, someone will die."

"A bit melodramatic, aren't we?"

John gave Martin a cold stare, but if Martin was thinking of saying something else he kept it to himself.

Martin put his shirt back on and then covered it with a tweed coat. "I thought we were in the tropics. Isn't a tweed coat a little heavy?"

"You're at 8,600 feet. Some nights in Bogotá the temperature can drop to below freezing," Camilo said with his matter-of-fact voice. "It will also hide the bulge of the gun."

"Will you be on Monserrate?"

"The less you know the better."

Martin checked himself in the mirror. He'd come a long way from Key West. He actually looked respectable. He wore a tweed coat, white button-down oxford, gray wool pants and cordovan loafers on his feet. He was pleased with his appearance, he admitted to himself. Now all he had to do was entertain a stupid bimbo and get the ball rolling. He began to sing because he knew it would irritate John.

*"I'm a Yankee Doodle dandy,*
*A Yankee Doodle do or die;*
*A real live nephew of my Uncle Sam's*
*Born on the Fourth of July."*

# CHAPTER 8

Monserrate Mountain was a place of pilgrimage for bogotanos who swarmed up its great flanks to pagar una promesa -- to keep a promise -- to the Fallen Christ, which was a colonial figure sculpted by a man whom the church house had been dedicated to. Some of those who made the pilgrimage did it on their knees, while others, during Easter week, made the climb with wooden crosses on their backs. But most, like Martin, made it up by cable car they called the teleférico.

The rain clouds had blown away, leaving behind a clear and unobstructed vista of the plateau. The city's lights shimmered and the outlines of the distant mountains stood silhouetted against the starlit heaven. Radiation cooling had begun and the air became cold and crisp, forcing Martin to lift up the collar of his tweed jacket. The tourists who had come up with him in the cable car, now gazed over the city from the looking-terrace. They nodded to each other, said a few words and then hurried into the restaurant.

From the terrace, Bogotá looked so beautiful that Martin could hardly believe that Colombia was 'murder central'. He remembered the DEA report Alfred had given him to read, which stated the principal cause of death among Colombian males was murder. The nationwide homicide rate already had exceeded the peak in the years of La Violencia, the period between 1948 and 1958 when 200,000 people died in an undeclared civil war between the Liberal and Conservative parties. Madness.

Suddenly she was talking to Martin, and asking him whether he'd had any problems coming up the mountain. Yes, it was cold, and yes they should move inside, but the view was spectacular and a few more minutes wouldn't hurt. His eyes looked into her eyes and tried to read the unreadable. Liliana Santander made small talk while she took stock of him. She was surprised by him because she hadn't expected him to be so tall. How tall? Six feet she decided. How much was that in centimeters, she asked him. No clue, he replied. They shared a nervous laughter.

The wind gusted, spilling Lili's hair into her face. She swept it back with a movement that Martin believed only women possessed. He took the moment to appraise her. She stood in front of him, all five feet seven inches of her and legs that seemed to run all the way to Tierra del Fuego. Her hair, which tousled down her shoulders, was the color of walnut leaves, setting off her smoky and sultry eyes.

As meetings go, John had later reported, things had gone as well as any initial covert meeting could go. They had established greetings and laughed a little, a man and a woman on a date. Normal. Lili was dressed well, in beige slacks and white blouse, partially covered by a long black overcoat.

They were very close, enough for Martin to feel one of her stray strands of hair touch his cheek. Lili looked around and when she satisfied herself that nobody was following her, she invited Martin into the restaurant.

He walked behind her, measuring her gait, watching the swing of her hips and realizing that she was an extremely attractive woman. His desire caught him off-guard and felt his face flush with heat.

The restaurant was tastefully decorated. The Spanish Colonial architecture blended well with the rustic setting of a French villa. It was also a restaurant with a French menu that did not have the gaudy translations at the bottom. She liked French food she told him. He did, too; they smiled. A waiter stopped by and informed them of the house specials and then left them to their menus.

"How have you found Bogotá?" she asked.

"Big," he replied. "I feel totally displaced, without roots, so to speak."

A silence came to them, because neither of them wished to approach the subject. They pretended to look around the restaurant with interest, as if they shouldn't miss its architecture. Thankfully, the waiter appeared and took their orders.

Lili ordered for both of them, filet mignon and a bottle of red wine.

Just come out and say it, Martin told himself. Do it! "Obviously we received the letter," he said.

"Obviously," said Lili, but Martin thought he detected some note of reproof. It angered him.

"My dear girl, the problem is this: the authorities don't believe Ernesto." There, he said it.

Lili stared back in silent shock. It had never crossed her mind that the Americans might turn down her brother's offer, and all the risk would have been for naught.

Martin continued, "It's not that they would be adverse to helping him out, but the people I work for would like some proof...first. Do you understand?"

"Please, do not treat me like a girl." Martin nodded and felt like an errant child. Then she asked him, "What kind of proof?"

"Everything, the whole megillah."

"Megillah? What is this word, megillah?"

Martin chuckled. "I'm sorry, it's a stupid American expression. It's a slang word that means everything."

"Has he not already stated that in his letter?"

"Yes, he has. However, the authorities would like him to deliver the information before they help him out."

Lili looked confused. "I will have to ask him, I am not sure what I may tell you. I must talk to him again."

"By all means, talk to him. Talking is the best thing for the soul; at least, that's what all the talk shows say."

"Please, Mister Black, do not make fun of me; I am very frightened."

Martin felt a pang of guilt. He liked her and he hated her. This woman who had stupidly involved herself in something that was, without question, beyond her control. She was beautiful, but a loser and, in being so, he was attracted to her. He was her only salvation now, he told himself, because even if Ernesto pulled out of the deal the DEA would blackmail him and she would become a victim of the fallout. He was her only hope, because he, too, was the champion of lost causes and she was in the biggest lost cause of them all. He was the king of failure, because he had never lasted at anything. The Marines, the DEA and now this, because this was only supposed to be a one-shot deal. Get in and get out.

"I'm sorry, I didn't mean to make light of your problems."

"You are forgiven," she said with a slight smile.

The waiter brought the food and set it out carefully on the table and then poured into Martin's glass a little wine for him to taste. Martin sipped it and nodded in approval. He hated the little dining courtesies and remembered once having shaken his head at a waiter who had only stared back at him in disbelief, and would have stared back until he had nodded fully and appreciatively.

"What do you do, Lili?" Martin asked, as he ate his first forkful of filet mignon.

"I work for the Ministry of Tourism. I am a secretary. The job is not very interesting. I answer the telephones."

"Where did you learn your English?"

"At the English School here in Bogotá."

"You mean, the American school, don't you?"

Lili shook her head. "No. The English School. It's out by the tercer puente, which means you take a right on the third bridge on the north highway. The school has a British Charter and when a member of the Royal Family comes to Bogotá, they visit the school. After I graduated I took some courses at the Centro-Colombo Americano, but I have a Ph.D. in archaeology."

"Your English is flawless; I wish I could speak like that."

Lili gave him a strange look. "Please, I do not understand what you mean?"

Martin loved to hear her speak; it was as if he were listening to an upper-class British society lady who had a perfect.pitch and enunciation. It also afforded him a time in which he could stare into her big sultry eyes.

"I mean, the way you speak; it's the way most educated people would like to speak. I speak English, but American English, which entails, to some extent, the accents, slang and bastardizations we've added to the language."

"I was thinking of learning how to speak Italian. I like languages, because people have told me I have a talent for them. They say I should become some sort of linguist."

"Whoever gave you that advice was right."

"How about you? Do you speak any other languages besides English and Spanish?"

"I suppose, I can speak my way through any language if I'm ordering a Big-Mac from McDonald's." Martin then said Big-Mac in five different tones of voice that sounded a lot like foreign language accents.

Lili laughed and was surprised that he had been able to make her do that.

"Are you registered at the Tequendama under your own name, Mister Black?"

"Martin. Please call me Martin. And yes, I am, Mrs. Santander."

"What do..." Lili was about ask something and then changed her mind.

"What do I do when I'm not in Colombia?" Lily nodded timidly. "Well, lately I've been on an extended sabbatical."

"Ah! You are a professor. What is it that you teach, please?"

"No, no, you misunderstand me. I haven't been working. I've been living on my boat for a few years."

"A boat?"

"Yes, I have a steel-hulled sloop that sleeps six. I call her Windraider."

She laughed, but then became serious as she tried to find the right words. "It sounds fabulous. Are you a good...I do not know the word...navegador?"

"Navigator?" She nodded. "Ah! I think you mean sailor, don't you?"

She thought and then nodded in agreement. "Yes, I mean sailor."

"I guess I am. I charter her out to wealthy people and sail it to the Bahamas, Jamaica, St. Croix or wherever the paying customer wants to go. I would like to sail her around the world some day, though, but I don't think I could."

"Why not?"

"I'm not sure I could sail her across by myself. It's a big boat and, to be honest, I'm not sure I'm that good a sailor to take her across the Cape and the Horn. I've seen the sea rise in the Gulf of Mexico and that was scary, and most of the time that's just a big lake. I don't know how I'd cope with a full gale sailing around the Horn."

"I think you would be able to do it if you set your mind to it," she said and meant it.

"Do you think your brother will want to meet me?" Martin watched her put her fork down. He had jumped too fast and now he tried to salvage. "That way, you wouldn't have to be involved."

"I am involved, but I do not know if he would be willing. I will have to talk to Ernesto. I will call you tomorrow and let you know."

Dinner was over; she'd made up her mind to leave. Martin called for the bill and left the money on the table. As he walked her out of the restaurant he caught sight of John talking to two women as they looked out over the city and he wondered if John enjoyed the work.

Lili was quiet on the way down from the mountaintop. The teleférico was swaying lightly under the heavy gusts, but she didn't seem to notice. She was a sad woman, Martin thought, and the thought saddened him. He saw her rubbing the wedding band on her fingers and wondered if she thought about her husband often. Suddenly he felt like an intruder. He wanted to rip away the hidden recorder from his midriff and send it flying out of the cable car, letting it smash on the rocks two-thousand feet below.

Finally the teleférico came to a stop at the bottom station. The doors opened and she was the first one out. Martin was forced to keep up with her. He could sense that she was running from him. She wanted him gone. Why?

"Can I call you tomorrow?" he asked.

"No," she replied as they walked together to the parking lot.

"Will you call me?"

"I don't know. I don't know what Ernesto will want me to do."

"Will you call me even if Ernesto doesn't call you?"

She turned sharply and faced him. "What for?"

"Because I'm a stranger in a strange land, because you're beautiful and I would like to see you again, because..."

"Okay!" She said, laughing. "I will call you."

Martin smiled and said, "Good."

He watched her open the door, start the engine and drive away in her Renault. He turned around and realized he wasn't sure of what to do now. He couldn't see a taxi for miles and the Tequendama was not quite nearby. He knew also he couldn't just walk to it. He was stranded and the neighborhood wasn't what he would call well-lit. Behind him he heard a car start its engine and he turned around, only to see it coming towards him. A terrible dread washed over his body as the car took aim on him. He stood stark-still, rooted to the ground. Then the car swung to the side and came to an abrupt stop. The window rolled down and Camilo stuck his grinning face out of the car.

Lili drove fast, slowing only at intersections, but not bothering to stop at them. There was an unwritten code in Bogotá; you didn't stop at traffic lights after midnight. To do so was to take your own life into your own hands. Gamines, the city's street urchins, lurked at stoplights with a brick. The brick would smash the car window, giving the gamine easy access into the car and, before the driver could react, the robber was stealing whatever was on the seats.

Lili sped down the wide lanes of Avenida Séptima until she reached the Los Rosales turnoff. She began the steep climb up the hill until she pulled up to her apartment's garage. She parked the car and set the alarm on, then ran towards the elevator.

Damn him! she thought. He was so casual; he didn't care about Ernesto, about her, about any of them. His condescending superiority drove her mad, because she had had it with the I'm-better-than-you attitudes from her working colleagues. Where was the damn floor? He was good looking, though, but he was cocky about it. Wasn't he? How could he be so casual when so much is at stake, or was it his way of masking his nervousness? Maybe. He's funny and he thought I was beautiful, too. Does he really think I am beautiful? It doesn't matter because he also thinks I'm stupid.

The elevator stopped on her floor. The doors opened and a man got in. She had not seen him in the building before. He nodded at her and he pressed an elevator button. The elevator doors closed. She turned and walked into her apartment and when she entered she turned on every light. Finally she collapsed on her bed and began to cry.

Lili did not remember when she stopped crying except that she did. She had fallen asleep and by the time she had awoken the sky was changing to a slate gray. It was the rainy season in Colombia, so the cloudy sky did not surprise her. She wondered what had awakened her and tried to hear any extraneous noises in the apartment, but all she could hear was the buzzing of the refrigerator in the kitchen. She had forgotten to get it repaired, because it really did make an awful racket. The telephone began to ring and she froze. She lifted the receiver.

"Lilita?" a voice asked tentatively.

"Ernesto?" Lili asked.

"It is. Have you spoken to him?"

"Yes," she said and felt a huge weight lift off her shoulders. The cartel still did not know and everyone was still safe. Ernesto, his wife, his children were all alive! She felt the exhaustion hit her hard and suddenly she was yawning, trying to keep herself awake, trying to keep his directions and comments in her head. Yes, she would do this and yes she would do that. And yes, the American seemed like a decent man. Yes, he was a big man and he was solid as a rock. Things were fine.

Finally she hung up and crawled into bed fully clothed, despite the fact the sun had risen over the mountains and the plateau was glittering like an emerald sea. Her last thoughts before falling asleep were of Martin, telling her she was beautiful and how he had made her laugh when she was nearly out of her wits. "Gracias, Martin," she mumbled and nodded off to sleep.

Martin listened to her sobs, the fear sobs. He recognized them, because he had suffered enough of them in the

Marines. Great heaving sobs that would not end until sleep extinguished them. He felt like a peeping-tom as he listened to her from five miles away via wireless microphone.

"Great timing! Come on in," John declared. "She's just arrived."

"Who's crying?" Martin asked.

"Lili. We've bugged her place silly. We could hear a rat fart in her apartment if we turned up the sensors. The phone lines are hooked up to ours and we even have the fucking door bell and call boxes hooked up."

But, for all the high technology they inserted into Lili's apartment, all they had managed to hear was the faint squeal of what sounded a lot like a cat meowing.

"What's that?" Martin asked John.

"It's Lili. She's...sobbing."

For twenty minutes Martin listened until it disgusted him. How had he allowed other people to let him sink to such a low? He stood up from the chair he'd been sitting on and headed for the door.

"Where are you going, Martin?"

"Out."

"Camilo will go with you."

"No thank you."

Suddenly Camilo was at the door blocking Martin's exit.

"I'm going for a fucking drink in the bar. If Camilo wants to go that's his business, but I'm having a drink by myself!"

John nodded and Camilo moved out of the way.

The Salón Monserrate was on the seventeenth floor of the Tequendama Hotel. Its ambience was not Martin's style, but it would do. It had a big band, subdued lighting, forties music and a cloud of cigarette smoke that looked like a fog bank rolling in from the unknown. He sat at the bar counter and ordered a scotch and soda, while he looked at the young tight bodies of women who swirled around the floor. They all seemed to be laughing and he wondered if he would ever laugh for laughter's sake again. Lili had made him laugh, though, but then she had scolded him for treating her like a schoolgirl.

Martin watched a woman at the edge of the bar eye him carefully. She was as old as he was, maybe older. Dark lighting in a bar always made people look younger. He ordered another scotch.

Lili was beautiful, Martin thought. She hated me. I hated her. I am the Walrus. I am him and you are me and we are them together... I'm nothing. I am not the Walrus and I am not together with her. She hated me. She was looking for salvation and she found a train wreck. I am Voznesenski's, Goya:

*I am Goya*
*of the bare field, by the enemy's beak gouged*
*till the craters of my eyes gape*
*I am grief.*

Martin ordered another scotch. The woman who had been eyeing him was now on the dance floor with a younger man. Her figure wasn't bad, he noticed. Her legs were chubby and she had a roll on her stomach, but that just made the woman more real and not like those brush-painted women in Playboy. He wondered what Lili looked like in the nude. God, was she beautiful! Here's to you, Lili! He toasted and swallowed the scotch.

The room was beginning to go soft and the sound didn't seem to be so loud anymore. She's the best thing I have ever seen. She hates me and I hate her. Why can't I stop thinking about her? I hate her and I want her. She's going to get me killed.

Why do I want her? I have met and made love to women as beautiful as Lili, so why do I need to possess her? She is not a genius, but she isn't stupid either. She is savvy. She is street smart. She is a survivor. She is true to herself. She is exactly what I am not. I am untrue to myself. I live for nothing and for no one. I am envious of her unselfishness and for having something to risk her life for, if that is what she is doing. IF. Are you lying to me, Lili, to all of us?

Martin was drunk.

Lili was here he thought, putting his hand over his heart. She had quickly peeked inside the real him and found a vast wasteland of spent conviction. The river of idealism and principle dried up. He was like a garden of morality and virtue that was decaying like a dead vine in a bone yard and just waiting for a strong wind to scatter it into oblivion. Then she moved away. Ran away, more like it! I want you, Lili, and I don't know how to stop wanting you, because I can offer you only misery. I am way past salvation and too late for redemption. I am past the point of no return, flying solo on a one way ticket to the Everlasting Register. But if you are for real...

Camilo came into his field of vision and flashed him a look of sadness. He motioned to Martin from across the dance floor to quit drinking and to go to bed.

Martin ignored him and kept on drinking.

# CHAPTER 9

She called him at his office, because he said he had the place swept daily for microphones. He had reassured her that if someone was listening to his conversations he would know of it immediately. Full discretion was assured.

They had met several years before, and she thought themselves as lovers; in fact, she began to wonder if he would ask her to marry him, because she certainly loved him. He was tall, striking and handsome. He had a Latin American look about him which she thought was quite becoming. He had jet black hair with the widow's peak, the rugged olive skin and the easy smile that made her knees go weak.

He, on the other hand, had no illusions about her. He didn't love her and didn't hate her, but their relationship was business and that's why he continued with it. For him it was like that with all women. He knew that women had found him desirable since he was a young man, but it made no difference to him because he did not find them desirable. He would sleep with them and pretend that their bodies and lovemaking enraptured him, but in the end he would still go out looking for a man in the streets, or if things got desperate enough -- an adolescent boy. And he knew that the woman was obsessing on him, partly because of the little gifts he made to her every two weeks grat's, but mostly because, when he had first met her he knew she was borderline insane. He knew now that he possessed her in a way most men would envy, especially whenever their sexual trysts occurred, even though he received no satisfaction from them. But lately, he began to receive a singular pleasure by playing with her mind.

He had met her because the cartel had ordered it so. He had become a rich man with the cartel. They had paid him well. He had five million dollars in a Swiss bank and yet he lived a frugal lifestyle. His home was a rented apartment in the Chapinero section of Bogotá. He drove a navy-blue 1975 Renault 4 and spent his weekends playing pool in a bar downtown. The wealth he had obtained from the cartel had given him access into the exclusive clubs not listed in any telephone book or Michelin guide. He would never have been able to obtain those privileges under a mere police captain's salary. He entered the clubs that catered to certain sexual needs with discretion that insured practical anonymity, so long as the money was there to pay for it.

"Did you get my gift?" he asked her on the telephone.

"I did. Thank you," she replied.

"Anything for you, my love."

"When will I see you again?"

"I'm working on it, but work and all... I'll see what I can do, but no promises. I know I'm overdue for a vacation. How was your day, by the way?"

"The usual."

He never pressed her. If she had nothing to say, she usually meant it.

"Same here," he said and then added, "but the days are boring without you."

Silence.

"I love you," she said.

"Did you get the package."

"Yes."

"Good. I'm sending you some photographs and some fingerprints of a man I need to know who he is. His name is Martin Black. If you do a quick job, I'll be able to get that vacation that much sooner."

"Promise?" she asked, forcing him to commit in a way she had never done before.

"I promise."

"I love you," she said again.

"I know. Good-night, sweet dreams."

The woman hung up and opened the package that was forced through the mail slot of her front door the day before. She had found it when she had returned home from work. She knew it was a quarter kilo of pure cocaine powder wrapped in saran wrap and locked into a sandwich zip-lock bag. It would last her exactly four weeks, by which time her next package would arrive. The schedule told her that she could control the habit, because she consumed neither more nor less every four weeks.

She sliced the kilo bag open with her long pinkie fingernail. Then she used that fingernail as a miniature shovel, scooped some of the crystal powder and brought it level with her nostrils. The powder disappeared with an intake of nostril breath. Then she scooped some more and kept on scooping until she had snorted five grams.

Control, she told herself. It was all a matter of control. Five grams a day would make her quarter kilo last four weeks. She would be a little short for the last few days but she could live with that, because that was just more evidence of her control.

Five grams was nothing. Her little itsy-bitsy, wafer-thin medallion watch weighed nineteen grams. Five grams weighed next to nothing. Yet, in the back of her mind when she was free from the euphoric spell of the drug, she knew she was snorting over seven-thousand dollars up her nose every four-weeks. But what did it matter? She got it for free, didn't she?

Yet, it mattered to a crew in a Blackhawk helicopter. To them it was life and death, because it was a war and those who perpetuated the demand were as good as traitors.

The Blackhawk helicopter climbed to four thousand feet and turned South over Florida City. It was an ugly night; rain spattered against the windscreen and the Hawk was bouncing in the sky like popcorn in a popper.

The helicopter crew was quiet, busy, involved and intent only on their jobs. They were the best and they knew it. They possessed the record for bringing in dopers during the last thirteen months.

Ray Sullivan, was the pilot flying the Hawk. It was a beastly machine powered by two 1,560-horsepower turbine engines and designed by the Sikorsky Aircraft Company in Connecticut. It was one of the more complicated aircraft in the world to fly. For every instrument there was a back-up, but, even then, Ray knew, there were systems and there were systems and some of them couldn't be backed up; like the stabilator, the flat stabilizer at the end of the tail which kept the Hawk from going into an out-of-control power dive. And then there was the transmission; if the transmission failed, the crew and the Hawk would become a ten-million dollar hunk of metal falling from the sky.

Tonight Ray was hoping that the lightning, which was flashing all about, would not come knocking on his bird of prey, because then he would probably have the ultimate "tango uniform," which was pilot's lingo for saying, 'fuck-up'. But for now the Hawk was moving fast at 135 knots per hour with five-hundred gallons of fuel left in its tanks.

It would be a close call, Ray knew, because the target was moving a little over one hundred and forty knots.

Ray, a former Gulf War and Panama Incursion Veteran pilot, had joined the Customs Air Branch after leaving military service. He was a tall, squarely built man who exuded strength of body and mind, yet he struggled every day to keep his temper in line. He was a divorced man, with two children and both of them lived with his ex-wife.

"What's it look like, Chet?" Ray asked over his intercom.

"If we turn south we should catch him as he comes over the coast," Chet replied. He was the radar man who sat in the rear of the aircraft and was responsible for targeting the doper. "It looks like he's heading for Everglades City."

"Do we have a positive I.D. on him?"

"Negative, captain. It could be a Cessna or a Navajo, by the speed she shows."

The weather turned for the worse and Ray began to fear a downburst. Downbursts were a pilot's worst nightmare. They were unexpected vertical winds that could reach speeds of two hundred miles an hour and usually preceded a downpour. They had brought down jumbo-jets -- which had a hundred times more power than a Hawk.

"Two minutes to intercept," Chet said calmly over the intercom.

Ray kept his eyes on the horizon, but it was like looking into a strobe light when lightning flashed. It ruined his night vision and made it harder to sight the enemy. And that was what all the unknown aircraft were to him, the enemy.

There was nothing that would give Ray more pleasure than to shoot a smuggler in mid-flight, but he hadn't always thought that way. He had believed in trapping and forcing them down and subjecting them to the full rigor of the law, but that was before his Katie.

Katie had been two months shy of her sixteenth birthday when she had overdosed on cocaine. She was now in a state the doctors called, "permanent vegetative." Coma. Ray had thought his daughter to be the ideal daughter, until a dark and sinister picture emerged in Ray's ensuing investigation. According to Katie's classmates, she had been smoking marijuana from the age of twelve and had graduated on to cocaine. Her friends had nicknamed her Snow White for the amount of cocaine powder she snorted up her nose. She had snorted close to a thousand dollars a week for two years, a habit she maintained with the only thing she had: her body. She had developed early in life and by the age of thirteen her body had matured into that of a graceful woman. In the process, however, she had discovered that she could sell herself to every perverted tourist who frequented the Miami area.

Everything with Ray had changed with Katie. Now he believed what he had never thought possible, that he and every other American were losing the war against drugs and that nothing was being gained by interdiction. It was all a wasted effort.

Suddenly his co-pilot shouted, "There it is!"

"Fuck!" Ray said when he caught sight of the smuggler.

"What is it?" Chet asked.

"It's a converted Navajo."

Chet knew that a converted Navajo could fly faster than a Hawk, but in this weather it would be a little trickier for the Navajo to escape. They could probably chase it until the smuggler's tanks ran dry, which was quite possible if the smuggler was coming in straight from Colombia, unless, of course, it had landed and refueled in the Turks or Caicos.

"She's dropping, guys," Chet said and then added. "She knows we're around."

"We've got him," Ray said calmly, but he was nervous. The lower the smuggler dropped in altitude the worse it would be for the Hawk if caught in a downburst. "Hold on! He's going into the soup. Chet keep your eyes on the target."

"Shit!" Chet's voice said over the radio.

"What is it?" Ray asked.

"You're not going to believe this, but either my screen's gone haywire or..."

"Or what?"

"The doper's got defensive measures."

"Say that again?"

"He's got defensive measures. My screen's lighting up hundreds of targets."

"Talk to me, Chet! I can't see shit in front of me. Its pea soup out there."

"I'm sorry, Captain. He's gone. I've lost him."

"Fuck!" Ray shouted into his radio-mike. He had had the doper in visual and then just like that he had lost him. "Call base, we're coming home."

Tonight the cartel had won, Ray thought, 350 kilos of grade-A cocaine valued at twenty-two million dollars had made it through. The day after tomorrow those same kilos would be in public schools going up kids' noses.

Tonight America had lost. Again.

Ray and his crew entered the room on base they used for debriefing and found two men were already sitting down beside the long table. It was his boss, Doug Mallum, head of the Air Wing for U.S. Customs Service in Miami, and, strangely, Wiley Dobbs, the man who liaised with the DAS, the Colombian version of the FBI. Ray motioned to his crew to sit down and they did.

"What happened?" Doug asked.

"I Had him in sight and I lost him," Ray said easily.

"Just like that?"

"It was a converted Navajo. Had thirty knots over our top speed."

Doug nodded in understanding. "So what is this about the defensive measures?"

Ray asked Chet to explain.

"I thought the system had gone tango uniform, but I ran a systems check and it was working fine. I think the doper had electronic countermeasures."

"On a Navajo, you're joking?"

Chet shook his head and then said, "No."

Doug looked at Wiley and said, "We just got word from Bogotá that the cartel is on the move. They've also gotten a new pilot to replace Tom Campbell. Show them the pictures, Wiley."

Wiley searched through a folder and retrieved two photographs. "We haven't sent them to the FBI, yet," Wiley said as he handed the pictures over to Ray. "We just got them."

Ray's face went pale. In the first photo he had recognized Rafael Sanchez and in the second photograph he saw a picture of Ernesto Camacho's sister. He didn't see the face of the guy in the third photograph, but he could bet the body belonged to Carlos Romero. It was the fourth photograph he saw which shocked him. He hadn't seen that face in nearly six years.

"You know him, Ray?" Doug asked.

"His name is Martin Black. I knew him in the Gulf." Ray could even remember the day the photograph was taken. "Jesus! I can't believe he would be piloting for the cartel."

There was a small silence and then Ray with sudden anger declared, "I want him. I want to break the bastard's legs."

"Take it easy, Ray. You'll have your chance. He'll be coming up your way soon, but don't give me this vengeance shit or I'll transfer your ass back to Oklahoma...got it?"

"Got it."

"I'll call the IRS on Black and see what they've got on him. By the time they're through with him, he'll regret the day he began working for the cartel."

Ray Sullivan smiled, because he knew what the IRS could do to someone if they found they were cheating on their taxes. But if a potential drug smuggler came under IRS scrutiny they made certain the smuggler had nothing left when they carted him off to jail.

# CHAPTER 10

It was customary for a cartel member to throw a party in honor of another cartel member if one should happen to stop by their home-town. Therefore, Fabián Pacha was obliged to entertain Juan Calderón at his home when he came into Bogotá. Fabián did not resent this tradition, because, as he put it to Rafa, "It legitimizes me as one of the players." Although Fabián was a wanted man by the Colombian military he still managed to entertain at home, thanks in part to the DAS Captain who would advise them the moment the military were moving against him.

The dinner party given by Fabián Pacha was a lavish and catered production that was bussed by a small army of waiters. His fifty-six chair and single table dining room insured an almost regal ambience to the meeting. The conversations held in the room were seldom boring, due to the fact they sat in a splendiferously decorated room. On the walls hung half of the world's stolen oil painting masterpieces, some of which had been recently stolen from museums around the world.

Martin Black, as luck would have it, was as good at socializing as he was at flying aircraft. The fact that his Spanish was halting, he still managed to keep people smiling, no matter how trivial or boring the conversation. But when Martin had been shown into the dinning room he felt a faint cold fear run through him.

"Señorita Santander," said the Señora Pacha, "you're over there, across from Don Rafa, in the gray suit, next to his wife, Victoria. You know, don't you, that Señora Sanchez is expecting?" Then she added, "Oh, Señor Black, you're to the right of Señorita Santander and beside El Patrón."

Except for Rafa and Lili, Martin didn't seem to know anyone, even though he recognized quite a number of them from the pictures Don Harkin had displayed in Miami. But Martin was only interested in one man, El Patrón. His recent acquisition of a Colombian textile company, legally transacted, had put him on a list in Forbes Magazine as one of the ten wealthiest men in the world.

Martin took the seat beside El Patrón and exchanged courtesies for a few moments. Then, aware that Lili was sitting beside him, he turned to her. "You look spectacular this evening Señorita Santander," Martin said, taking a look at her beige and white outfit.

"Thank you, Señor Black, you are very kind."

Suddenly Martin was staring into Ernesto Camacho's eyes as he took a seat across from him. He was of average height for a Colombian. Five feet five inches with close-cropped dark hair and a complexion that was fairly white. He was a weak man who spoke with a nasal and whiny voice. The man had no air about him, Martin thought, but at least he did not disclose through movement or gesture that he was selling out the House of Cocaine.

The dinner was long and elaborate. The last course was served at ten and people were growing tired of each other. Throughout dinner, Martin, frightened of El Patrón, sat in silence and listened to pieces of other people's conversations. He felt out of place, not only because he was dining with some of the more notorious criminals of the twentieth century, but also because it felt a lot like a high society dinner. He had tried to speak with Lili, but when an opportunity arose, Carlos Romero, the finance minister for the cartel, would quickly fill in the lull in the conversation. Only once had there been some meaningful contact between Martin and Lili, and it occurred when the waiter had come to remove their plates and they had dropped their hands to their sides and accidentally touched under the table. They glanced at each other and looked away quickly as if afraid of being found out, but, to Martin's surprise, she held his hand under the table and squeezed it softly before letting it go. It was a fleeting gesture that brought forward a rush of emotions in him.

Later in the evening, the men moved off into a large library and the women went to look after their kids, who were running about on the upper floors.

The kids, for Martin, as everything about the night, surprised him. He had never thought of drug runners with families before; now he could say he had met the next three drug running generations.

"A toast!" Rafa declared as he uncorked a champagne bottle. "I just had word from Miami that they received the shipment. They say the new electronic stuff worked like a dream."

Across the room and out in the hallway, Martin could see Lili watching him with an almost predatory look, as if ready to pounce on him at his first wrong move. She could not sit beside him to make sure of it, though, because they kept the women away from the room until the men conducted their business. Except for a few women, Martin realized the cartel did not employ women into their ranks. Although Lili was not in the room she easily could have overheard everything, but she did not give any indication that she had done so.

Lili was an enigma to Martin. She seemed aloof to his presence and whenever he looked into her eyes they said nothing of what she might be feeling. His instinct was that she was tougher than she appeared to be, because he watched her brush off Carlos Romero's sexual advances rapidly and efficiently. The cartel's finance minister, on the other hand, didn't like being turned away, but there wasn't much he could do.

Lili was 'familia', a woman in the family, and as such she was revered as a saint when it came to respect. Their jobs -- as most Colombian women, were strictly defined: cook, have babies and run household matters. In everything else they were expected to keep their mouths shut and be loyal, or at least pretend to be.

It hadn't always been that way, because when Juan Calderón began his empire, women were considered as transient and disposable. Nothing except immediate gratification mattered and in the old days of the business nothing was permanent. Then money had had happened and Juan Calderón began to seek permanence and respectability, but in order for him to gain it he would need a family which could command respect. Therefore, the women in his family would have to become above reproach.

"¡Perfecto!" Calderón declared as he listened to Rafa explain how the electronic countermeasures worked on their aircraft.

Lately, Calderón reflected that Rafa seemed to be solving all the little problems which kept the organization running smoothly, like the hiring of the new pilot, Martin Black. Rafa was coming through when others seemed to be falling apart. El Patrón would have to reward Rafa, because it was time and because together they had been through a lot. He could still remember the time they had first met...

*The concrete walls held the moisture and the foul smells inside the jail cells. Sometimes it was sweat and other times it was the smell of urine that prevailed. The smell was whatever the latest prisoner would have on his person when thrown into the lock-up with them, but this time Juan Calderón smelled stale sweat.*

"What are you in for?" Juan asked the new prisoner.
"Car theft. How about you?"
"Cocaine. Was it a good car?"
"The best. Mercedes."
"What happened?"
"I didn't see the fat woman in the back seat when I stole it. Her chauffeur was in the store buying some cigarettes. I had just happened along when the car was beside the street curb."

Calderón laughed.

"At least, I'll be out soon," Rafa said acidly, believing Calderón had been laughing at him. "Cocaine...wait a second! Are you the one DAS caught with twenty kilos in a spare tire?" Calderón nodded. "¡Mierda! They're never going to let you out." Rafa said happily then stood up and stuck out his hand. "By the way, I'm Rafael Sanchez."

"Juan Calderón." They shook hands. "I bet you, Rafa, I'm out of here before you are."

"I have no money with which to make a bet."

"Then let's just say you'll owe me a favor, okay?"
"Deal."

Calderón's arrest charges had been dismissed within a week, to the behoovement of the guards. The biggest criminal in Medellín, that year and his arrest had been rescinded. At the jail's exit Rafa smiled and said, "Paisa, luck runs far with you. I'll surely come by and see you some time. I could use some good luck."

Twenty-four hours later, Juan Calderón posted bail for Rafa and obtained his freedom.

"Rafa," Juan said after making a toast, "I need you to go to the big lab tomorrow. Take Martin and Carlos with you, and Ernesto. I'll be here when you get back. Pacha wants to throw a party tomorrow night."

"S', Patrón," Rafa replied.

"Patrón, why..." Carlos began to protest, but Calderón cut him off.

"Because I want you to go. It's time you saw the other side of the business and you, too, Ernesto."

"Martin, you better get some sleep," Rafa said. "You heard the man, we'll be flying tomorrow."

As Martin began to leave Pacha's home to return to his hotel, Lili followed him into the foyer. "Martin," she whispered.

Martin looked up and then checked to see who was nearby. "Yes?" he asked tentatively.

"Please call me if something happens tomorrow," she said. Martin was about to ask her what she meant, but she cut him off. "It's a death flight, Martin. Everyone knows it. One of you on that flight won't be coming back. If it's my brother, will you call me if you have a chance?"

Martin said nothing, but managed to nod his head. Later on, Martin would write in his report to Donald Harkin, how he had felt a few drops of urine run down his legs with the fright Lili had instilled in him, because he was sure it was he who was going to die.

# CHAPTER 11

To Bolivians it is known as the Beni; to others, it is the western edge of the Amazon Rain Forest. To Rafa, Martin, Ernesto and Carlos it was a place to land. The Beni Wilderness was the area Juan Calderón kept his cocaine processing labs. A few years before, Rafa told Martin, -- as the Congressional Sub-Committee later heard through Martin's hidden tape-recorder -- Colonel Juan David Uribe, head of the Anti-Narcotics Unit in Bogotá, Colombia, had nearly bankrupt El Patrón by setting in motion a chain of events that would culminate in a raid in the Beni. The most surprising fact was that Uribe was a Colombian and the Beni was in Bolivia.

Through know-how and reputation Colonel Uribe had convinced Bolivian authorities to go along with the raid. This would not have been possible if Uribe had not enjoyed the reputation he did. In a single year he had seized thirty-seven tons of cocaine and, with herbicides, destroyed ninety percent of Colombia's marijuana crop.

The runway they landed on was a plowed field and nothing more, but the Twin Turbo-Prop had taken it well. The area around the strip was green and lush and it looked almost impenetrable.

"Ernesto!" Rafa ordered, "take Martin along with you to lab number three. I'm going to number one with Carlos. We'll be back by two this afternoon. It should give you enough time to check things out."

"What do I check out?" Ernesto asked.

"Tell the boys that El Patrón wants 1,500 kilos in Ríohacha by Thursday." Rafa then turned to Martin. "Don't wander into the wilderness, Martin. Here, take this." Rafa handed Martin a MAC-10.

"Do I need this?" Martin asked.

They laughed.

Rafa then became serious. "The codeword for today is Cocaloco. Now, go."

Martin and Ernesto climbed out of the Turbo-Prop and then stood to the side of the runway and watched Rafa take-off for lab number one.

The moment the Cessna was in the air, Ernesto Camacho got down on his knees, crossed himself and burst into loud sobs.

Martin looked on, bewildered, and not knowing what to say, asked, "What does Cocaloco mean?"

Ernesto wiped the tears from his face, as if he had suddenly realized Martin was standing beside him. "It means coke crazy."

"Are you all right, Ernesto?"

"Yes, I am now. Come, we must move, because the lab is an hour into the wilderness. There is nothing we can do for Carlos; he is beyond hope."

"What do you mean?"

"Wherever Carlos is going, he is never coming back. It's his death flight."

The heavy, motionless air made their shirts cling to their bodies. The path to the coca lab was nearly run over by the wilderness and the going was slow. For the better part of twenty minutes they had remained silent, until Martin, bored by the walk, decided to engage Ernesto into a conversation.

"Did El Patrón ever get back at Colonel Uribe for destroying the labs?"

"Yes," Ernesto replied.

"How?"

Ernesto stopped and looked at Martin, then shrugged as if deciding that by telling him he wouldn't be putting himself into jeopardy.

"By the end of 1985, Colonel Uribe...

*"Uribe must die," El Patrón declared. "He's caused us a billion dollars in losses. He's seized thirty-seven tons of co-*

caine and 116 airplanes, seventy-four boats and three thousand trucks. Intolerable! Uribe must die."

"You want to take a contract out on him?" Ernesto asked.

They were sitting beside the pool in El Patrón's hacienda. The one that cost fifty million dollars and had twenty man-made lakes. The main house, El Patrón would brag, could sleep the Colombian Congress and on a good day they could be seen doing just that.

Carlos, who had been fixing himself a drink, but who had heard El Patrón, now returned to his seat. "The repercussions could be devastating," he said, without being disturbed in the least by killing Colombia's top cop. "It could also cost us some money."

"How much?" El Patrón asked.

"I would say, about a quarter of a million dollars, I don't know. He's also been promoted to general and that means some people will probably become our enemies, that's if we go ahead with it."

"I don't care, just do it."

General Juan David Uribe had learned of the Juan Calderón contract, on April 16, 1990, when a man who had been informing on a band of M-19 guerrillas told him that Marcos Pacheco, alias, Paco or Jefe de Ejecuciones (Chief of Executions), of the Alberto Cortés Brigade for the Medellín cell, had picked up the contract. The price was 110,000 dollars.

Uribe knew it was no bluff. The guerrilla splinter group of the M-19 (Movimiento 19 de abril) was the most violent of all the guerrilla groups. They would come for him, Uribe knew.

For eight months the Uribes had lived in the General Santander Police Academy in Bogotá. His wife Isabel, after a few weeks became ill from nerves, his sixteen-year old son Pedro had learned how to handle a MAC-10, and on family outings he rode shotgun with a pistol between his legs.

After eight months the strain had begun to show and General Uribe was nearing the end of his patience. He was thinking about leaving Colombia when finally a break came.

In Medellín, General Uribe's second in command informed him that Calderón had rescinded the contract. It was the best news Uribe had received in nearly a year and he decided to make the most of it. He drove with his wife and children to his brother's farm in Cali, where they would spend a weekend holiday.

The holiday had been the best days for the Uribes in the last two years. Juan David had seemed reinvigorated and soon his wife Isabel knew he would throw himself back into the fight. Her husband was a good man in a land where the cartel cowed good people. Fear had subdued the nation.

During their last night in Cali, Isabel sat staring into a cup of black Sello Rojo, the best coffee in Colombia. The coffee was laced with brandy and, as she sipped it, she wondered when she had become an alcoholic. Everyone had gone to sleep early, the day had been an exhausting one and much alcohol had been consumed. The children had worn themselves out in the pool and, when put to bed, hadn't complained. Isabel looked at the digital clock over the liquor cabinet; it was nearly three in the morning. She shivered again as thunder rolled over the horizon.

Isabel was a fair-skinned, soft-spoken woman who had somehow retained the aristocratic blood from conquering Spain. She wore her bathrobe that was one size too large, but that was her preference because it hid the small pistol she carried in its pocket. Underneath the bathrobe she wore a nightdress that was too hot for Cali weather.

In the last two years, Isabel could not remember when was the last time she had slept through a night. Ever since the cartel had driven by their home and left a sign that said, Death to the Uribes, she felt unsafe, exposed. And, although her husband was not to blame, he had not been around since his promotion to General. She loved him; he filled a need in her that had been with her since her father had died. She knew it was also part of the reason she had married Juan David, because he was so much older than she. He was her father figure.

Lightning flashed in the sky, but this time she caught a shadow move across the room. They had come, she thought, as she knew they would. The story that Calderón had dropped the contract had been a lie, a trap. Her husband, for all his military and police training, didn't understand the basic concept of vengeance. She did; it was ingrained into her from childhood, but it wasn't unusual either. It was the way people were brought up in that part of the country. She was a Paisa, a citizen of Antioquia, born and bred in Medellín.

The thunder rolled again. The figure stepped out from the hallway and walked towards her. Isabel curled her right fingers around the pistol and brought it level against the shadow. This was it, she thought, they had come for her family.

"It's me, querida," Juan David said, knowing that if he made a wrong move his own wife would kill him.

"I'm sorry," Isabel replied, but she didn't feel the need to explain why she had pulled a gun on him.

Juan David sat down on the couch and put his hand around her. Everyone in the family was jumpy, he thought. A week ago he had caught his son Pedro looking out the window with a shotgun in his hands. Pedro said he had heard noises outside.

"How long have you been up?" he asked.

"Two years."

Juan David felt like crying instead of laughing. The cartel had crushed him. They had effectively locked him up and rendered him useless. "I think I'll get some coffee and join you," he said and stood up to go to the kitchen. He returned a few moments later with a piping hot cup of coffee and sat down beside her. "El sol sale para todos." 'The sun comes out for all,' he said, because he was determined to bring his wife out of her dark mood.

"No hay rosas sin espinas." 'There are no roses without thorns,' Isabel countered.

Juan David knew his wife would not give up. "Come to bed, querida. We have a long drive tomorrow."

Isabel relented and followed her husband to bed.

"Querida, I think sometime this week we can begin to go out a little more," Juan David declared as he drove his Toyota back to Bogotá.

*Isabel had awakened that morning with a brighter outlook than the one she had fallen into the night before. She was determined not to spoil the last day of their holiday.*

*They left Cali early, knowing that the traffic on their return to Bogotá would be heavy if they didn't get a jump on it.*

*Isabel looked at her husband skeptically. She had lived under the threat of death for so long she couldn't believe the cartel had forgiven them. "You think that's wise?" she asked. "I mean, going out and all?"*

*"I don't mean you should go out all the time, but maybe once or twice a week. Would you like that?" Juan David shifted gears as they entered the plains of Bogotá.*

*Isabel took his hand and squeezed it reassuringly.*

*He gave her a wink and pulled his hand back from hers, because the bridge over the Río Bogotá was coming up and he had to concentrate. Although the city traffic was light at that hour, it was also notorious for bad drivers, but Juan David knew he had made the right decision in leaving early. He slowed his Toyota to let the green Mercedes -- that had been behind him for the last several miles -- pass him, but the Mercedes kept pace at his side even though it was now traveling in the wrong lane.*

*Juan David then heard his son say something and he glanced at the Mercedes beside him in time to watch the tiny spits of fire. It's bullet fire from a MAC-10, he thought, just before it went completely black.*

*The contract on Colombia's top cop had been carried out.*

"Did they kill the whole family?" Martin asked, bile rising into his throat.

"The woman had been shot through the knee by a stray bullet," Ernesto said. "Somehow she got out of the car and begged for the life of her children. One boy had been shot through the legs and the other had been shot in the hand. All of them except for General Uribe survived."

"¡Alto!" a voice cried out in the thick wilderness.

Ernesto and Martin froze.

"Don't move," Ernesto told Martin. "Don't say anything and do exactly what I do."

"Pongan las manos sobre la cabeza." Put your hands over your heads.

Ernesto raised his hands over his head and Martin followed suit.

Four men emerged from all sides of the compass. They carried Uzi's in their hands and grenades on their belts.

A dark, small man, no taller than five feet, who Martin realized was a real Inca, spoke to them curtly. "¿Diga?" Speak.

"Cocaloco," Ernesto replied.

The Inca smiled and the men put their weapons down. The Inca suddenly became a humble man, bowing to everything Ernesto and Martin said.

Yes, Don Ernesto. But, of course, Don Ernesto. Would Don Martin like to relax in the hut? Would Don Ernesto and Don Martin like some cerveza?

Ernesto said no to everything and turned to Martin. "Have you ever seen how cocaine is made?" Martin shook his head. "I'll show you."

Ernesto took him behind the hut, where the four men obviously slept, and showed him a bunch of oil drums and vats.

"Is that it?" Martin asked with genuine surprise.

Ernesto laughed. "What did you expect? Beakers and bunsen burners?"

"I suppose. How is it made?"

"Well, the coca leaf grows on the Andes, usually at about seven thousand feet. El Patrón has some coca fields in Putumayo Province in Colombia, but the fields are not high enough to produce good quality cocaine. Those fields produce a yellowish coke.

"Anyway, the coke leaf is harvested three times a year by Incas on two acre plots. The plots are known as cocales. After the leaves have been picked they are carried down a couple of thousand feet and spread out on a small area that is exposed to the sun. The sun dries the leaves and then they are packed into costales, potato sacks, and then brought down to a lab like this one. Here is where the leaf becomes coke.

"First the dried leaves are put into this vat and are treated with lime, because it is an alkaline solution. The coca leaf has fourteen alkaloids, but we are only interested in one of those alkaloids. Then we transfer the treated leaves into this drum which is filled with kerosene. The kerosene will extract the alkaloid we want from the leaf. The leaves are them removed and thrown away, but we keep the kerosene which now contains the alkaloids. We add sulfuric acid to the kerosene mix which turns the alkaloids into little rock salts. The rock is cocaine sulfate. You then strain out the kerosene and add an alkaline solution to neutralize the sulfuric acid. Once you strain it all out you're left with a paste at the bottom of the barrel.

"The paste is then refined through another round of kerosene and potassium permanganate which destroys all alkaloids that have managed to survive the process except for the cocaine alkaloid.

"You filter out all the junk again and you add ammonium hydroxide, which in time is filtered out. What is left is cocaine base. Bazuco. To get it to look like what people put up their noses you have to put it through a round of ether, hydrochloric acid and acetone. When that's filtered out you have cocaine hydrochloride. The white powder."

"Good God!" Martin exclaimed. "I never knew. I wonder how many people know exactly what they're putting up their noses? I mean, its all chemicals."

"I know, and yet the demand is so big we can't keep up with it. It's our modern day plague, if you ask me."

"How much is the overhead?"

"The biggest expense is the ether and acetone. You need seventeen liters of ether to make one kilo of coke. We use a couple of hundred thousand metric tons of ether a year."

"I didn't know Colombia was an ether producer."

"It's not, Martin. We buy it in the United States or Europe. The same goes for the acetone." Ernesto turned to the Inca and said something in Spanish. The Inca bowed and hurried away.

"What did you say?" Martin asked.

"I told him that eleven hundred kilos should be ready for shipment tomorrow." Ernesto then glanced at his wristwatch. "It's time we get back to the strip. Rafa should be on his way back. We'll take the horses."

The Inca led them through a series of trails which didn't look like trails, but had to be, because a horse could navigate them at a gallop. The long walk that had taken them two hours, took them twenty minutes by horse.

Ernesto then thanked the Inca and gave him some American currency. The Inca bowed and quickly disappeared into the wilderness.

One hour later, Martin and Ernesto heard the sound of Rafa's Turbo-Prop and they began to search the sky. The plane appeared as a little dot on the Eastern horizon and then grew to the size of a fly, until it seemed to be a flying behemoth.

Martin stood behind Ernesto and saw how his legs became unsteady. Carlos was not in the plane, Rafa was flying alone. Ernesto's breathing became irregular. Good God! Martin thought the man was becoming undone in front of him.

In the four hours that Martin and Ernesto had spent together, Martin hadn't been able to get a feel as to what made Ernesto tick. It worried him because his life and many others would depend on him. Yet, he knew he had to make contact with Ernesto if he was to move the operation forward, and the thought of it was turning his stomach into knots.

"Ernesto," Martin said calmly. "I have something to tell you."

"What is it?"

"We got your letter?"

Ernesto was about to say, what letter, when he caught himself. Instead, he turned; his face washed from all color and said, "You?"

"Me."

Rafa touched down and rolled towards them.

"Lili told me they had sent someone, but I didn't think it was you! How? When? I mean..."

"I'm with the DEA," Martin shouted over the engine noise. "They have agreed to your proposal. Full immunity plus health care for your son in return for your testimony."

Ernesto held his breath, fidgeted with his hands, and, as he exhaled, he let out a long, loud laugh. He laughed loudly because Martin had said he was with DEA and Ernesto had heard him.

# CHAPTER 12

"Do we assume he's dead or merely unable to contact us?" Alfred Stevens, the Administrator for the DEA, asked us. Don, Lisa and Dusty sat around his office wondering about Martin Black's whereabouts.

"I need to know! The President's Chief of Staff personally called me this morning for an update. I felt quite stupid telling him we didn't know where Martin was. We followed him to Bogotá, Norman, and then lost every trace of him; I've never been so embarrassed in my life."

"We have to give him time, sir," Don said. "It's still pretty early in the operation. We'll hear from him soon, though. John Whitney will be at his post through the night."

"Dusty, what do you think?"

"Let's give Martin some time," Dusty replied. He was sitting with his briefcase unopened in the corner of the room, and hoping to avoid having to speak at all.

Alfred didn't like his answer, so he turned to Lisa. "What do you think, Miss Mejia?"

Lisa was stunned. She had only gone to the meeting as a matter of formality, because she hadn't expected the director to ask for her opinion. She looked over at Don, but he avoided any eye contact with her as if to say 'you're on your own.'

"I think Don is right, sir. Mister Black is probably being watched and is unable to contact us, but, other than that, I wouldn't know."

"God Almighty!" Stevens said angrily, "tell me who the hell knows and I'll talk to him personally."

Alfred then pressed a button on his intercom and said, "Send in Mister Lewis, Please."

Don and Dusty looked at each other and wondered why the White House Chief of Staff was coming in, but their answer was not long in coming because, at once, he let them all have it.

"The Colombians want in all the way," Lewis declared.

The tension in Alfred's office suddenly became thicker three day old gravy.

Don and Lisa sat in the office scowling like two school kids listening to a headmaster go on about detention. Dusty, on the other hand, sat in one of the two sofa's as if he hadn't heard a word of it. He had buried reports on operations where as what Lewis was proposing had happened all the time, so he didn't seem surprised in the least.

But in the dead silence of the room it became evident that something needed saying, so Dusty boldly said, "Oh?"

"The President has agreed to it," Norman Lewis stated in a tone that left no room for discussion. Lewis was a man of medium height, but heavy through the middle. He wore thick reading spectacles, which looked more like magnifying glasses that warped his eyes into grotesque bullfrog orbs.

"Why?" Dusty asked again taking the bull by the horns.

"Dusty! He's the President," Alfred declared as if Dusty had just committed a mortal sin in front of the Pope.

"So what? The man doesn't know shit from shinola when it comes to the drug trade."

"That's not fair, Dusty. He's a busy man trying to do his best. He simply wants the information shared with the Colombians, perhaps, because he doesn't want to look like he's not cooperating."

"Bullshit! he's worried about his personal image. I read The New York Times yesterday. Didn't the editorial say he was full of hot air when he spoke about the drug problem?"

"That has nothing to do with it, Dusty. And what in the world is wrong with sharing the information with the Colombians? It's their country, isn't it? And won't we need to tell them anyway to get Calderón extradited from Colombia?"

"That's right, but that doesn't mean we have to let them know before we've got him. And what about the Colombians cooperating with us? We had no idea about the El Rey operation. Where was the cooperation then? Don't you people know the cartel has men everywhere in the Colombian Justice Department?"

"Well," said Lewis, "that's the way the President wants it."

Alfred said nothing. He sat there as if he were a spectator, not really involved in the argument at hand, which angered Dusty all the more.

"You know," Dusty said to Norman, "why the chicken is the craftiest animal in the world? Because it doesn't cackle until the egg is laid."

Dusty had become quite animated, because he believed Alfred had never given a moment's thought to the half dozen people whose lives depended on the decisions he made. Dusty realized, although not at that moment, that Alfred was not a man given to deep introspection. Ideas and self-assessment were of such a nature to him that he consigned them to the area of the brain which he determined as 'unexplainable.' The que será será philosophy.

Alfred was a political machine, born and bred. He had run for a Senate seat twice and lost. He had been an outspoken Attorney General for the State of Massachusetts, but during the presidential campaign he had been a mouthpiece for the President's War on Drugs. He was rewarded with the top DEA job. He was a master of his own political survival and cared little for anyone or anything else.

At that moment Alfred had the hottest thing going in Washington, because of blind man's luck. He was the man in the cat-bird's seat and the players were now deferring to him for the first time in his life. Perhaps, if he'd just taken a moment to consider all the angles of the case, he would've seen that he was sitting in the political hot seat and that his future would depend on the man he had so easily put into harm's way. Alfred was the start of a domino effect in which he was unquestionably the dominant piece. It was Alfred who became the catalyst in the disaster.

Finally, Don moved forward in his chair and said, "So this argument is really academic?"

"Of course not!" Lewis replied. "We value your input and we've considered it in good light..."

"What light is that, Norman?" Lisa interrupted. "Political light?"

Norman was angered and stood up.

"Come now," Alfred said in his broadcaster's voice, "let's not bicker. Listen, Norman, why don't you and I go down to the Oval Office and have a talk with the President, eh? Maybe we can work something out."

Dusty put my hand over my mouth to try to stop himself from laughing, because he knew Alfred had no intention of backing the President into a corner. He had just wanted them to hear him intimate that he had some influence with the Big Guy, that he could just pop around the White House and have a small chat with his Excellency and convince him that the boys down at HQ didn't think too much of his idea. Balls! Dusty thought. The bastard was glorying in his own shining star.

"That would be a good idea, Alfred," said Lewis looking at Dusty with an evil eye. He had his number, he was saying through those enormous orbs. Start packing, he was aching to tell Dusty, but obviously he didn't know who he was, because Dusty had seen the likes of him come and go like the many tides that had washed up on Chesapeake Bay.

"Alfred's an ass-kisser," Don said when Alfred and Lewis cleared out of the office. "A freaking Ph.D. in the art of ass-kissing."

"Yep," Lisa said and then added, "but that isn't going to change the fact that the Colombians are going to be in the operation from now on."

"The Colombians and everyone's grandmother," Dusty said. "If the Colombians get into it and if we get the information from Camacho, we'll also have to bring in Justice to get him extradited from Colombia. And I'm sure some treaty will be involved and that means State will get into it, as well. Christ, Almighty! We might as well advertise our intentions to go after Calderón."

"Why State?" Lisa asked indignantly.

"We can't extradite someone without State getting into it, because it concerns immigration laws. We'd better let Martin know the shit is about to hit the fan, so he can start watching his back."

"John Whitney is going to blow his top," Don declared. "He might just quit on us."

Later that night Dusty went home to Elizabeth, but she wasn't home. She had left a note saying she had gone to see her mother in Alexandria, and that she would be back tomorrow. Dusty crumpled the paper and wondered whether this time her lover would be young or old. It had been a long time since he had stopped believing in Elizabeth's little lies, because he had once called her mother on the pretext of asking Elizabeth something and discovered that she hadn't slept in her mother's house since the day she'd left for college. And for the past seven years he had said nothing when she told him she was visiting her mother.

It happened twice a month. At first he would inquire about her mother, but then Elizabeth would shrug and say, "The usual," and, soon after, he stopped asking altogether. At the time he made himself believe that as long as she came back to him it was all that mattered.

Alone in his house Dusty let himself rest in the dark and somber room that acted as a study. He let his thoughts wonder about Martin and how he was getting along. He missed Martin's companionship, and during the day he found himself turning his head several times expecting him to be standing right behind him. What had Alfred done? He asked himself. What had they all done to Martin Black?

They sold him out to politics.

# CHAPTER 13

Martin was moody when he touched down at El Dorado International Airport. He had switched planes in Cochabamba, Bolivia, from the Turbo-Prop to a Citation jet. The flight from Bolivia had been done with less than a dozen words exchanged between them. Rafa had said nothing about Carlos, and Ernesto and Martin had not asked him, but Martin had had Carlos on his mind ever since leaving the Beni.

Suddenly, as Martin landed the aircraft and reversed the thrust on the engines, he asked, "Rafa, what happened to Carlos?"

"He had to stay back in Bolivia," Rafa replied without flinching.

"Did you kill him?"

Rafa turned and faced Martin. "Why would you ask that, eh?"

"Come on, Rafa! You left with the guy and he didn't come back."

"And that means I killed him?"

"If the shoe fits..."

"Calm down, both of you!" Ernesto said trying to appease each of them.

Rafa's stare was ice cold. "Martin, I don't have to tell you this, but I will, because I like you. Carlos Romero had set El Patrón up for a fall. He was involved with the U.S..."

"DEA?"

"Worse, CIA. His contact was Tom Campbell, the man who used to fly this plane before you did. That's all you should know."

"There's more?" Martin could not help himself from asking. "Someone else is involved, right?"

"Martin, don't ask. The less you know, the better."

Martin brought the aircraft to the area the cartel had reserved in the name of some dummy corporation and brought it to a complete stop. Then he turned to Rafa as if he hadn't heard his warning. "Did he say who?"

"No!" Rafa said angrily, but immediately he realized he had overreacted and modulated his tone. "Look, Martin, we're tired; why don't you get some sleep and we'll talk in the morning. I'm going out towards Zipa to talk with the Mexican. You go check in at the Tequendama. The Presidential suite has been reserved for you."

"What about Ernesto?"

"I'll stay with my sister," Ernesto said, standing behind them. "She has an apartment in Los Rosales. I usually stay with her when I'm in Bogotá. You should call her, Martin, she's beautiful. You've met her, right? You know she speaks very good English. Isn't that right, Rafa?"

Rafa replied, "Uh-huh, but I don't think she's been out on a date since Alejandro died." Then he turned to Martin and added, "Her husband died two years ago."

"I know this is going to sound crazy, but I don't have any money on me," Martin said apologetically.

"What about the money we gave you?"

"I still have it, but I've wired it into a bank. I don't have small bills."

"Come with me," said Rafa. Martin unstrapped himself and followed Rafa to the rear of the Citation.

"Here, Martin," Rafa said, handing him a clear plastic bag full of money. "This should cover any expenses."

"Shit! How much is in here?"

"Ten, maybe fifteen thousand dollars. Spend it all. I have to go. They're waiting for me. Go find a girl, Martin, or take Lili out and have some fun. I think the day after tomorrow you might have your first mule ride. If you want I could have some girls stop by your place, real girls. Blonde, brunette, whatever, they all fuck." Rafa checked to see if Ernesto was still behind him. Then, in whispered voice, he said, "Lili is class, man. You can't just wine and dine her and get her into bed. She's smart when it comes to that, but I also don't know of any one who's been to bed with her. That's why I didn't mention her to you before; she's bad luck, Compadre. I can get you some girls, if you prefer; twenties, thirties, whatever age is okay."

Martin was shocked, but he didn't want to let it show so he laughed. "I think I'll look around on my own, Rafa," he said and gave him a knowing punch in the ribs.

"Eh, Compadre! We should do the town one night. We'll have the women going crazy for us. You and me," Rafa said and, feigning like a pugilist, added, "the old one-two combination."

Rafa and Ernesto then said their good-byes and stepped out of the Citation and ran to their waiting Mercedes.

Martin closed the Citation's hatch and took one last look at the plane before he walked away. Once he was outside the airport's main terminal, he flagged a taxi to take him to the Tequendama Hotel. During the ride to the hotel he began to think about contacting Whitney at the U.S. Embassy. But what should he tell him, he asked himself. That Ernesto Camacho was a wimp and was having second thoughts? Or that, in his opinion, Ernesto couldn't be trusted to carry out the operation? Maybe he should say that he had seen a man go to his death, or better yet, that he might be flying to the States in the next few days with hundreds of kilos of cocaine.

It was out of control, he would tell them. He knew nothing, while the cartel seemed to know a hell of a lot more than all of them put together. They even seemed to know that the CIA was up to something, while he knew nothing. He was working in the dark, while the cartel was working from knowledge. It was a recipe for disaster. Damn it all! They could have told him that the CIA had a man in the cartel!

Martin checked in at the Tequendama, realizing he had no change of clothes.

The concierge had smiled when Martin checked into the Presidential suite, because not too many people could afford its price.

"I realize that it's dark outside, but would I be able to find some clothing stores open at this hour?" Martin asked.

"It is only seven in the evening, sir. The stores are still open, but, if you prefer, I could have my assistant take your measurements and go out and buy you some clothes."

"Can you do that?" The concierge nodded. "That would be perfect."

The concierge lifted the phone and spoke rapidly in Spanish. "He will be in your suite in a few minutes, Mister Black. If you need anything else, please let us know at once."

Martin thanked him and left a hundred dollar bill on the counter, which the concierge removed unobtrusively. Although it had seemed natural to leave such an enormous tip, Martin would later tell Dusty that he had never tipped anyone so much in his life, but, what the hell, he had said, it wasn't his money and Rafa had ordered him to spend it.

John Whitney closed his office door and pulled out the fold-out bed from the couch. He had had to leave the Tequendama because one more day there would have looked suspicious, and he didn't dare leave his office telephone when he had an operative running on the frontier. The bed, however, was too small for his frame. He was five feet nine inches and the bed was only five feet, but it was better than sleeping on the floor.

John was spreading the sheets over the bed when the telephone, rang. For a moment he stared at the telephone thinking he might have imagined the ring, but then it rang again and he lifted the receiver.

"Hello?" Whitney said. He never identified himself on the telephone. He had learned from his predecessor that sometimes the cartel would send a high-pitched sound over the line, blowing out one's fragile ear drum.

"John Whitney, please?"

"Who wants to know?"

"The frontier man," Martin said using his code name.

"I'm Whitney. I'm glad to hear you're all right. What have you got?"

"What would you like to know?"

"That good, eh?"

"Yes, but I'm on a public telephone in the hotel lobby. Let's meet."

"Where are you?"

"Are you being watched?"

"No, I don't think so. They've pretty much left me on my own."

"Okay, that's good, but I'll make sure. Go to the Sal—n Monserrate, I'm sure you recall it. It's on the seventeenth floor. When you see me enter the room get up and go to your room, then come back and sit down. It will give me a chance to spot any tails."

"Okay."

"I'll be there in twenty minutes."

"One more thing," Martin said hurriedly.

"What's that?"

"I want a gun."

Martin saw Whitney come through the entrance of the Sal—n Monserrate as he had promised. Martin worried for a moment, because Whitney's gaze passed over him without a flicker of recognition. Martin wanted to wave at him to make sure, but he stifled the urge and began his pre-arranged exercise.

The process took fifteen minutes, but John approached Martin on the dark side of the bar. They sat at different but adjacent tables. When they spoke they had to lean on their backrests, so that the backs of their heads nearly touched. However, Whitney knew that, from a casual observer's point of view, it would seem as though they were strangers.

Finally, Martin told him about the flight to the Beni, about the tension he felt between Rafa and Carlos Romero and how Carlos supposedly had stayed behind in the Beni to do business. He told him of his afternoon stay in Zipa, where he had come face-to-face with Calderón, Contreras and Pacha. He told him about the Beni and the coke labs, the aircraft, Rafa's remark about the CIA and Tom Campbell, and he told him about Ernesto Camacho.

"He scares me," Martin told Whitney who was wired with a microphone and a tape-recorder. There was fright in Martin's voice, but everyone at DEA said it was normal. Whitney, however, had picked up on the nervousness and pressed him.

"How so?"

"He's committed to his son, but I think his nerves will give him away. He was knocked out when I told him I was DEA. His sister had told him that she had made contact through the pre-arranged plan, but she never told him it was me. It's hard to say how Ernesto will react from one moment to the next. One moment he's happy and the next he's falling apart. The man seems to be coming undone, but, whatever he's up to, the next move is his."

"Don't pressure him, Martin, because it'll make him jittery. Let him come to you. He's the star of the show, he calls the shots. If he wants his family out, I'm sure he's thought of a plan. Tell me about Lili. Is she straight up or is she dirty? Can she be trusted?"

"I don't know, but she's not like him. She's good-looking, but I don't know about the rest of her. I can't tell if she's scared or she's leading us all down the proverbial path." Martin let out a small chuckle. "She's like any other woman, you can't tell what they'll do next."

"How much do you think she knows?"

"A lot, John. Sometimes she sits close by and hears everything the cartel says. I think, if she sat in a meeting, no one would complain. I think she doesn't because she'll hear it from Ernesto anyway."

Whitney nodded. "Anything else?"

"A shipment is being prepared," Martin said with amusement. "I think I'm the designated pilot."

John let out a small laugh. "The flies certainly don't settle around you, do they? When will you be flying?"

"I don't know; the next few days, probably."

"We need to know, Martin, or you'll be flying through a shooting gallery."

"If I knew I would tell you. It's not very easy to take timeout to make a phone call. Someone is usually with me."

"Do your best," John said as he stood up from his chair. "Don't look now, but I've left a paper bag beside your seat. It's the best I could do on such short notice."

"What is it?"

"Your gun."

# CHAPTER 14

Martin could smell Lili's perfume as they walked through the wide alleys of the Unicentro shopping mall. The boutiques and modern shops were displaying their wares and exclaimed their half-reduced prices and special offers. At every four or five shops Martin would stop and look into a shop's window and he would say something like, "That's nice or I wish I had that," then he would use the window's reflection to check behind him. On the last occasion he had seen three young girls and a boy flirting with each other and an old couple who had walked slowly past him.

Martin marveled at the shopping mall. The place was enormous, full of shops that boasted names like: The Leather Shop, American Boutique, Burger King and every other name one would find in a similar mall in America.

"You're surprised, aren't you?" she asked. She seemed sharper now, alert, the confusion of their first meeting gone.

"I am surprised," Martin replied, "but I don't understand why most of the shops have American names."

"Glitz."

They fell into a silence as they entered a small restaurant on the second floor. They ordered drinks, Martin a scotch and soda and Lili a Chardonnay. Martin had expected the menu to be Colombian, but found it to be Continental.

He eyed the people in the restaurant and especially the couple who had entered after them. Then he felt the tape-recorder, which was taped around his midriff, chafing his skin, and he wondered if the machine could pick up the sound of his hammering heartbeat. He turned his attention to Lili and found her staring at him. Would you run away with me, he thought crazily, have my children, live in sin, forget all the cartel nonsense and live the life that dreams are made of? She blinked.

No, he heard her say with her eyes. He was too immature, a man without a future and a terrible sense of humor; but she did not say so, because she only looked back at him and said nothing.

"You are mad at me, no?" Lili asked.

"Of course not!" Martin said hurriedly. "What makes you say that?"

"The way you treat me. The way you talk to me. I am twenty-two years old. I have been married and seen my husband buried. Do you think I'm still a girl?"

"No. I'm sorry."

"Stop saying how sorry you are! I just want you to believe me, to believe Ernesto. I don't want to play games."

Anger flared in Martin. "I'm not playing games!" He said in a controlled whisper. "I'm risking my fucking life here. Believe it or not, I had a life before this, I..."

"Who is that man, please?" Lili asked, cutting Martin off.

"What?"

"That man, who is he? I saw him on Monserrate Mountain when I had dinner with you."

Martin turned around and gaped. He'd never seen Whitney come in. How had he done it? Had he entered through a back door?

"He's with me," Martin said and reached for his beer. He drank the contents in one swallow and signalled for the waitress to bring him another.

The meeting was going badly, Martin thought. If he had been a better operative and this meeting had been their first, he would have walked out on her. Then Lili would have been termed an adversarial contact by Washington and that would have been the end of it. He would have been removed from the area and the contact would have been marked for blackmail. It was all a fantasy, he knew, because in this case he had an adversarial contact who desperately needed his help, except that she didn't trust him.

"Why can't Ernesto get the treatment in Colombia?" Martin asked Lili.

"It's not available."

"Who is his doctor? Where was the diagnosis made and when?"

"Why is that of any relevance?" Lili asked.

Martin leaned over and said with thinning lips, "Because the people who've sent me don't believe him."

Lili clasped her hands together tightly, until they began to turn white. "Bogotá. The diagnosis was made by an old friend of the family. His name is Alvarez. Doctor Héctor Alvarez. His office is in the Chico section of Bogotá. Do you know where that is? He also works at La Samaratina Hospital."

"Thank you," Martin said with meaning.

"I should be the one apologizing. We have involved you in something that was not your concern. I am sorry."

"Apology accepted." Martin paused and began a new tact. "Lili, why don't I ask you some questions and we'll see how things go, okay?"

"Okay."

"How did Ernesto get involved with the Cartel."

"It began in Medellín. He was working for a bank when he noticed large monetary transactions that were not making it into the books. He took the matter to the bank Vice-President and he was told to forget about it. Ernesto knew enough by then to realize what was going on in Medellín, so he turned in his resignation and went home. Later that night two men stopped by his apartment and told him that if he left the bank he would be killed, but if he didn't leave he would be amply rewarded."

"Did he know the two men?"

Lili shook her head. "No, not by name, but he did know their concern's name. They were the group that controlled a sizable interest in the bank and went by the name of Los Calderones."

"Juan Calderón's group?"

"Yes, El Patron's group. At first they didn't ask him to do anything, but then one day they invited him to a party. They treated him like a king, deferred to him when possible and sought his banking advice. At first Ernesto thought they were being kind, but he's like that. He is numbers smart, but stupid when it comes to common sense. One day El Patrón called him on the telephone, as if they had been old friends and asked him what he thought of American stocks and whether he should buy some. Ernesto told him that the big investments should be done in real estate. They talked a little more and then El Patrón told Ernesto that he was having a party and asked Ernesto whether he would like to go. Ernesto told me he hesitated, but then El Patrón told him who was going to be there and convinced him. Ernesto later told me that members of Congress were there, financial big wigs, judges and lawyers. The important people in Colombia."

"The players," Martin said. "The people who make things happen because they have power and money."

"Exactly! The players...is that a slang expression?"

"Yes, it is. Go on, please."

"Well, there is not much to tell. Two months after that, Ernesto began to receive huge presents. A Mercedes sedan, a penthouse apartment in the city and they were all gifts! Cards would be signed with little phrases like: Thanks for the advice. Even by then, Ernesto believed no one had a claim on him and that he was still his own man, because he was clean. He truly believed he merely advised people, as if he would advise any person on the street. He truly believed he couldn't be held accountable for what someone did with his advice, after all, it was only advice. I suppose, with all the gifts and the important people he met, everything got blurry for him, which is no excuse. The fact that Calderón smuggled cocaine was not Ernesto's fault, so long as he worked for his own money and Calderón stayed out of his job -- he would be okay."

"What got him into the cartel?"

Lili sipped on her Chardonay and Martin could sense her ease as the wine spread its warm glow through her body. He also realized that he liked watching her green eyes, her small delicate nose and the shape of her chin. Then he began to wonder how she would look undressed and whether she was a tornado between the sheets. When she began to speak again Martin was astonished at how he had lost his concentration.

"Ernesto fell in love with Helena Campos," Lili continued, "who happened to be a cousin of Juan Calderón. How he met her, I cannot say and I have never asked. Perhaps, I don't want to know because he really loves her. The rest is academic. Ernesto was told that he could not marry Helena, because he was a danger to her and to himself. They told him that they respected him enough to leave him alone at the bank and not involve him in their business, but if he were to marry into the family he would have to accept the other part, too."

Martin drank some of his beer and wondered if he had been in Camacho's place and the girl had been Lili, whether he would he have done the same. Yes, probably, he told himself. He would risk hell for Lili's love. My God! Why am I thinking like this? She hates me! I hate her! "Are you prepared to do what I say, Lili?" he asked her. "Has Ernesto told you that you will have to leave the country, as well, if you wish to live after his departure?"

"Of course! He has explained the dangers and has said that the odds are not in our favor."

Martin shook his head. Something was wrong, something didn't feel right. She had told him the truth, as she knew it; he was sure of it. He knew the truth when he heard it and her eyes had been wide and honest in the telling.

"You don't believe me?" Lili asked. "I have told you the truth, I swear it."

"I believe you, but that's not it."

"What then?"

"I don't know, that's just it. I believe that his son needs special treatment and he's willing to do just about anything to see that he gets it, but..."

"But what?" Lili asked, her voice rising. "Isn't that enough? What else do you want? He's risking his entire family and myself included to save his only son..."

"Bingo!"

Lili stared at Martin with open hostility and for a moment he thought she might throw the wine in his face, but she remained still.      Finally she stood up and said, "I'm tired. Perhaps, this has been a big mistake..."

"No, wait!" Martin declared, grabbing her left wrist. He saw her wince in pain and he let go of it immediately. "Please, stay and listen to what I say...please. I will explain."

Lili looked at him for a moment and then sat back down. "Okay, but this is the last time."

"I will explain the doubts I have and the doubts my superiors will have. Your brother has joined a bunch of ruthless killers and he did it by choice. He knows the price of betrayal, death. But in Ernesto's case it would be worse, they would kill him as well as his family and that also includes you. Correct?" Lili nodded. "His son has cancer and it's terminal. The death of his son would be a tragedy if it isn't already, but risking his whole family for a medical treatment his son will never outlast is insane. So, why does he take that risk? Is he incapacitated? Does his son's cancer have him so totally distraught that he can't think straight? What is it?"

Lili looked into her wine glass as she held it by the stem and slowly swirled its contents. Her eyes became watery and she fought for control of her emotions. She had no more room for tears, because she only had room for resolve.

"I believe my brother seeks redemption," she said at last. "He is being tortured by his conscience and believes that God is now punishing him for his sins." Martin raised an eyebrow in skepticism. "He has done something terrible and it is driving him to madness. I think he wants to atone."

"Because he laundered money for the cartel?"

Lili shook her head and then softly said, "The plane."

"What plane?"

"The jet-liner that blew up over Soacha last July. He had the bomb placed in the cargo hold, at El Patrón's orders. The plane blew up in mid-air, killing hundreds."

Martin was revolted. He tried to say something, but he found himself speechless. He wanted to ask her more questions about why Ernesto had done what he did, but, instead, he signalled the waitress for another scotch. He waited for the drink. He watched Lili's eyes turn away from him when she saw the revulsion spread over his face. Now, sadly, he understood her crying. My God! he thought. Who wouldn't cry if someone had discovered such a monster in one's family, and what did that say about America, which was going to give him a new life for switching sides?

The waitress appeared and Martin asked for the bill as she left the drink on the table. Lili was looking at him and he guessed she was wondering if he was just going to get up and leave her there. He drank his scotch and paid the bill.

"Come on," he said, "let's get out of here. I need some fresh air."

Lili grabbed her purse and followed him out. She was hard put to catch him, but she managed. They emerged from the confines of the Unicentro mall and began to walk along the wide street that was carrera 15.

They walked fifteen blocks in silence when Lili, exhausted, said, "Please, stop. Say something! I cannot keep following you around like this..." Then she broke down and cursed herself, knowing she had broken her promise not to cry. But, this man! This stubborn man! She hated him, so why did she care what he thought? Who was he to pass judgment? And yet, she desperately needed him to believe in her.

Martin stared at her for a moment, as if realizing she had been walking beside him all along. He saw that they were standing in front of an ice-cream shop, and when she burst into tears he reached out and brought her close to him.

"You're okay," he said, running his fingers through her hair. "It's all right. You are not to blame. You had nothing to do with it." He took her hand and led her into the ice-cream shop. He sat her down in a chair and ordered strawberry ice-creams for both of them. He wanted to talk to her about what her brother had done, but he needed time to get himself under control. He decided to steer the conversation away from the exploded plane.

"How many times have you seen Ernesto since he gave you the letter?"

"Once. El Patrón's dinner; you were there, too. I usually see him three times a year. Sometimes he comes to Bogotá, but most of the time I see him in Medellín. I'll hop on a plane and spend a weekend at his house."

"What do your parents think?"

"They died when we were young."

"Who did you stay with when you were growing up?"

"My godparents," she said gladly that the subject was not her brother or the cartel. "They live here in Bogotá. They were heartbroken when they found out what Ernesto was doing. They are old now, but I still love them as if they were my parents. I married Alejandro when I was nineteen. I met him at a wedding party. Alejandro was new in town, so when he met me he wasn't thinking about taking me to bed. He was lonely and he needed a friend, so I gave him my telephone number. He called me and soon we were seeing each other regularly."

"Then you married him and he got killed." She nodded. "Was he really just a target for the guerrilla or was someone in particular gunning for him?"

"I don't know. His death has never been investigated fully, but the more you complain to the authorities the more they see you as the problem. I know that the guerrilla rarely targets foreigners, because it's not the kind of publicity they are looking for. Alejandro, however, was an arms dealer from Chile and he negotiated with the Colombian government, so, in that sense he was probably a marked man by the guerrilla."

Suddenly both of them were silent and aware that they were holding hands over the table, and neither of them knew when they had joined them.

"What did Ernesto say to you last night?" Martin felt her hands tighten around his before she withdrew them away.

Lili became cold, remote, as if she were no longer allowing him to view her emotional side. She was hiding and he knew that she knew, but they remained silent as the afternoon turned to dusk and the black walls of fear closed in on them "He told me it was a death flight," she said, her voice flat and devoid of emotion.

"What exactly is a death flight?"

"When someone takes you up in a plane and they throw you out."

Martin was silenced. It seemed that every time he heard something shocking about the cartel, there was still something even more shocking to be heard.

"Ernesto has agreed to your conditions," Lili said and paused before continuing. "He says you will have to go to Medellín. If he leaves Medellín for too long he will immediately come under suspicion. He says that you two should meet in Medellín."

"When?"

"I don't know."

They were together most of the night, both of them tense and weary of each other, but afraid to part. They were each other's touchstone, holding out against the tide of fear threatening to crash over them.

They had dinner at La Fragata, a restaurant which had its seafood rushed in fresh from the seacoast every day. Their conversation was dull and infrequent and Lili would not help him with the big silences. Martin had wanted to pledge his loyalty to her, to let her know that he would do his best for her or go down trying. He wanted to protect her, but he realized how meaningless the thought was, in view of her self-sufficiency. He wanted to tell her, as best he could, that he cared for her. He wanted to make love to her and the thought itself frightened him. He wanted to tell her how great life could be if they were just together, but he could see that she saw in him what he had seen himself: The broken spirit of a man who had given up on chasing his dreams. Instead, he told her about America and asked her if she had ever been there. Once, she replied; Washington. She didn't like Washington. He didn't either. It was why he had moved to Florida, he told her, but he had lost her and she was only pretending interest in his conversation in order to pass the time.

Eventually they agreed that they must go home and he saw her out into the street where he hailed a taxi for her. Then, as a taxi drew to the curb, she did something so unexpected that it shook him to the bottom of his soul. She turned around and, against all odds, stood on tip-toes and kissed him on the mouth. Then she gave him a smile that he had seen only once before and then she was off. He stood there by the side of the curb grinning until he could no longer see the taxi.

He then hailed another taxi and headed for the Tequendama, but now he was restless, because all the energy he had been trying to summon up to entertain Lili was now bursting out of him.

He arrived at the hotel and entered his suite, only to find John Whitney crouched over a radio set, listening to Lili's every move. Martin would have none of it. He declared he was tired and that he was going straight to bed and then saw Whitney out. Whitney puzzled, wished him a goodnight's rest and left.

John Whitney would later testify to the Congressional Sub-Committee that Martin had done as professional a job as he had ever seen from an operative in the field, but that he had never mentioned what had happened between Lili and him later that evening.

# CHAPTER 15

Martin awoke with a start and reached for his gun. Someone was knocking on his hotel door and it was nearly one in the morning. He got out of bed, walked towards the door and looked through the peephole. His heart skipped a beat when he saw Lili.

He opened the door.

She stood in the hallway, waiting, smoking a cigarette, nervous. She wore a linen skirt and a white coat over a white blouse, and her hair was up in a chignon. It was the first time he had seen her with her defenses down, alone, looking her age and he felt so protective of her he seemed to feel inadequate.

He moved towards her, but she stood still and they said nothing. He nodded for her to follow him, but she didn't move. He shrugged and moved back into the suite, remembering what John Whitney had said: "Don't pressure her, because it will just make her more jittery. Let her come to you. She's the star of the show; she calls the shots."

She followed him, closing the door behind her.

"You're the only one I can't figure out," Martin said. "You seem to be ambivalent to the whole matter. In fact, you look more like one of them."

She shook her head and said in exasperation, "Ernesto and his wife told me about their son and I summed up their chances, that's all. It's suicide, but he's the only family I have."

"Have you told him what you think?"

"Every day." She feigned laughter. "He doesn't have the...metal for it, I suppose. His wife does, though. She's the one who got him to do it."

"Do you think he'll change his mind?"

"I don't know. They would shoot him anyway. He's scared as everyone else is of being found out. He could be tortured like the ones who've been caught by the cartel."

"You think I'm scared?" Martin asked suddenly.

Lili measured him with a cold gaze. "You'd be an idiot if you were not scared."

"He's going to kill himself," Martin said without emotion. "You know that, don't you? The odds...well, you can figure it out."

Martin felt removed, outside the loop of reality. He looked into her eyes as she scanned his and he realized she was feeling the same way. She was meeting friend and foe alike and treating them on the same terms, indifferently. She had figured out that both sides would disavow their knowledge of her if things went to hell in a bucket.

It had been a long time, Martin told himself, since he had felt that peculiar sensation of a spreading warmth in his solar plexus which made him feel light. Something was happening to him and to her, because they looked at each other and didn't say a word.

Suddenly, Lili reached up and touched his face, surprising him and herself.

They were almost swaying now, holding on to each other. The air was warm, the scent of her perfume around them. They stood still with their chests pressed together and both feeling their arousal. Then he put his hand behind her head. She looked up and let him kiss her.

Then she pulled away and opened her eyes. "Let's go to bed."

Martin lay in bed, waiting for her with the light turned off. He heard her fumble for the light switch and then the room flooded with light. He looked up, squinting in the glare of the lights. Then Lili moved towards the bed and lay beside him.

Finally, when they coupled, neither of them could remember a time when life had been as sweet and joyful. It was meant to be, they told themselves, and everything was for the best.

It was time out of mind.

It was just after five-thirty, morning twilight coming in through the window when Martin awoke.

Lili Santander slept comfortably with her mane of hair spread across the pillow, her face at rest, innocent to the harshness of the world. A thin, white sheet covered her legs, but kept her stomach and breasts exposed. Martin thought of the passing night and of the slow way they had made love. Now the sight of her naked body began to arouse him once again, but he did not want to disturb her, so he let her sleep.

Martin stood up and walked towards the shower when he heard a knock on the door. He wrapped the bed's cover around him and tip-toed quickly to the door, wondering who would be knocking at such an indecent hour. He looked through the peep-hole and forced himself to become alert.

Martin opened the door. "What the hell, Rafa?" he whispered.

"We got to go, Martin," Rafa said as he tried to push himself through the door, but Martin blocked him. Rafa gave him a questioning look.

Martin nodded with his head into the room. "I'm sorry, Rafa. I have company."

"You got lucky, Compadre?" Rafa asked, as a huge grin spread across his face.

"Why don't I meet you in the lobby in fifteen minutes, okay?"

"Sure, but hurry. We've got a long day in front of us."

Martin nodded and closed the door. He turned and walked back into the room and saw that Lili had brought the sheet up over her shoulders and was curled into a fetal position. He smiled and headed for the shower. The cool jets of water from the nozzle had sharpened his senses. He had dressed quickly, mentally preparing himself for whatever the cartel had planned for him.

Suddenly he noticed her standing by the window, wearing one of his long shirts as a nightshirt. She was pale in the gray dawn breaking.

Martin walked towards her. "You look beautiful, Lili," he said.

"It's been a long time since I've felt beautiful, but last night you made me feel wonderful."

He smiled. "I think you just stole my words."

They stood holding each other, a meaningful silence between them.

"Where do we go from here, Martin?"

"Let's just take it one day at a time."

Lili nodded and then kissed him.

"Who was that knocking at the door?" she asked.

"Rafa. He says there are things to do." Martin lowered his voice and whispered, "Tell Ernesto I need to know what he has in mind as an escape."

Lili tilted her head back and mouthed the word 'okay.' Then she added in a louder voice, "I love you, Martin."

"I love you too, Lili, and I won't let you down."

Lili tightened her arms around him, holding on for dear life as rain clouds swept across the plateau and blocked the rising sun.

"Who was she?" Rafa asked Martin as he got into the Mercedes-Benz.

Martin thought about lying, but he knew Rafa would find out sooner or later. "Lili," he answered.

"No!"

"Yes."

Rafa gazed openly at Martin. "How? When? I don't understand. Everyone that I have ever known and has tried..."

Martin gave him a grin. "I'm not everyone."

Rafa laughed and said, "I can see that, Compadre."

"Where are we going?"

"Medellín, but we're driving because we have business along the way. You'll like the drive. It's beautiful country, even though some parts are dangerous. That's why were carrying weapons. Do you have a weapon?"

"No," Martin lied. He didn't want Rafa asking where he got it.

"It's okay, I'll give you a relic."

Martin looked at the duffel bag in the back seat. "Are those the weapons?"

"No, its a uniform."

Martin wondered what kind of uniform, but he thought Rafa might not tell him, so he let it pass. "Why is traveling to Medellín dangerous?"

"The guerrilla hide in the area known as Medio Magdalena. The military is also a little trigger-happy because of the guerrilla. If the military stops us at one of their unexpected road blocks and catch us with the weapons, they'll drag us out of the car and shoot us. On the other hand, if the guerrilla ambush us, they'll shoot us, too -- for sure, except they'll take their sweet old time doing it." Rafa sighed. "The guerrilla is a pain in the ass in this country."

Martin was horrified, because if the army searched him, how would he explain the weapon in the small of his back? Perhaps he could pretend to make a pit stop and dispose of the weapon.

"Why are we going to Medio Magdalena?" Martin asked.

Rafa said nothing as if he had never heard Martin.

"How about some breakfast before we leave Bogotá?"

"We'll have it on the way."

"Is someone coming with us?"

Rafa turned and leveled a cold stare at Martin. "You ask too many questions, Compadre." Martin looked away. "Look, Compadre, it's not that I don't trust you, but..."

"I haven't proved myself."

"Exactly."

"Then let me ask you one question?"

"What's your question, Compadre?"

"Where am I going to be tonight?"

"Why?" Rafa asked angrily.

Martin managed a smile and said, "I would like to see Lili tonight, if that's no problem."

Rafa laughed. "You're in love, Compadre! I'll see what I can do."


It was just after eight o'clock in the morning when Rafa turned off the main road and entered Puerto Salgar on the banks of the Magdalena River. The Magdalena River was Colombia's Ol' Man River and Puerto Salgar was a river-port town, as Vicksburg was on the Mississippi, Martin thought, except around Puerto Salgar hundreds of people had died within the past year.

Rafa pulled off the main road and into a small, deserted side street.

"Where is everybody?" Martin asked.

"It's Sunday, Compadre. No one in Colombia gets up before ten or eleven," Rafa replied as he slowed the Mercedes and turned into a small gasoline station.

Suddenly a two-car garage door was opened and Rafa drove right in. They parked the Mercedes-Benz beside a military jeep as the garage doors closed behind them.

"What gives?" Martin asked.

"Business," Rafa said. "Let's go."

Martin instinctively knew he was in over his head. He recognized the two men in the shop as El Patrón's pistolocos. Hard, cold men who killed people on Calderón's command.

"Come on, Martin!" Rafa shouted. "Put this on, hurry!"

Martin looked at the uniform Rafa was handing over to him. It was an army uniform with a captain's bar on its shoulder sleeves.

Rafa's uniform had the bars and rank of a lieutenant's.

Martin acquiesced, but he felt his stomach going hollow and his legs turning to jelly. Thankfully, he was able to remove the weapon from the small of his back along with his pants and hide it under the seat, before Rafa or the pistolocos could see it.

"¿Viene ahora?" Is he coming now? Rafa asked the pistolocos.

"Salió hace una hora con el comandante." He left an hour ago with the commander, the pistoloco answered.

Rafa turned to Martin and said, "Are you ready?"

"Yes."

Rafa checked the action on his pistol and nodded for Martin to get into the jeep. The pistolocos opened the garage door as Rafa turned the ignition on the jeep. The engine came to life with a sputter and then settled.

Martin watched Rafa adjust the driver's seat and put on a pair of military aviator glasses, then motioned for Martin to do the same. Then he shoved the gear-column forward and stepped on the accelerator, causing the jeep to lurch forward.

Dear God, help me! Martin said in prayer.

It was almost nine o'clock when Rafa parked the jeep by the side of the road. They were on the autopista Medellín, the highway that connected Bogotá with Medellín. The humidity was overwhelming, and the road had been deserted until they spotted a car coming towards them.

"Grab that M-16 and put it between your legs," Rafa commanded, as he climbed out and stood in front of the jeep.

"What's going on, Rafa?" Martin asked.

"Shut up!"

Martin watched the blue Mazda slow down as Rafa waved him down. The two men in the Mazda looked at each other, their looks telling Martin that this was unexpected.

The Mazda came to a stop and the driver rolled down the window. "Buenos d'as, mi teniente. ¿Cómo puedo servirle?"

"¡Papeles!" Papers! Rafa ordered.

The driver handed Rafa two laminated cards, which Martin guessed was their identification. It was the other man who surprised Martin, because he was handing over an American Passport.

Rafa looked the papers over and said, "Muy bien."

Relief spread quickly over the men's faces as Rafa handed them back their identification.

The two men busied themselves by putting their papers away and, perhaps, it was why they never saw Rafa unholster the weapon. Rafa shot the American in the head, killing him instantly. The other soldier sat back with brain tissue and bone fragments stuck to his face and clothes and began to pray. "¡No! ¡Por el amor de Dios!" the soldier cried before Rafa shot him too.

"God has nothing to do with this. Its business. El Patrón said you would understand," Rafa said and then shot the man between the eyes.

Martin's mind reeled as Rafa got into the jeep and drove back to Puerto Salgar.

"Who were they?" Martin asked, unable to conceal the range of emotions he was feeling. They were driving to Medellín after having changed clothes and cars.

Rafa smiled. "The Police Commander of Medellín," he said, completely unaffected by the killings.

"And the other guy?"

"Stupid bastard, you know. He showed me his American Passport. Did you see? Actually, if I had been him I would have done the same, because the military have orders not to mess with any Americans. The guerrilla are also not stupid enough to antagonize them either. Unfortunately, he didn't count on me being from the cartel. A few days ago Calderón discovered the American was a CIA spy who had penetrated the Cali Cartel. That's why I was picked for the job, because the man didn't know who I was. ¡Ay! Madre m'a! Cali is going to owe Calderón a huge favor and they're not going to be very happy about that."

Martin and Rafa entered Medellín late in the afternoon. The city looked magical, with the sun casting a golden light over the eastern mountains and from afar it looked like a city in the middle of a huge bowl, a scene from the movie "Alice in Wonderland."

"It's beautiful, isn't it?" Martin nodded. "Medellín used to be called La Taza de Oro. The Golden Cup."

"What do they call it now?"

Rafa let out a laugh and said, "La Ciudad de Bala. The City of Bullets. Or they call it La Taza de Plomo. The Cup of Lead."

"What's so funny about that? It's sad."

"Things change, Compadre. The moment it gets dark in Medellín you can hear the bullets being fired around the city. It's a desperado town."

"What about the police?"

"They are too afraid to do anything. If they go and check out a report they might get ambushed, but if they don't they'll be fired the next day. So they have friends call the station and claim that someone is choking or something and the men on duty go and assist them, which makes them look as if they're really doing their jobs."

"Doesn't anyone complain?"

"Everybody complains, but it doesn't get the police out of the station any faster. The people of Medellín feel lucky that anyone in this town still wants to be a policeman. If you were a policeman in Medellín and you knew that thirty-eight people died every night by bullet wounds, would you go out? Of course you wouldn't! Because the real figure is more like sixty."

"So how does the city survive? Why would anyone stay here?"

"Because there are rules, Compadre. Medellín Rules. Sálvese quien pueda."

"What does that mean?"

"It would mean something like survival of the fittest. This is a cartel town, Compadre. If you're not with the cartel you're against it, simple as that. Those are the rules. Medellín Rules."

"I'll try to remember," Martin said sarcastically.

Rafa drove the Mercedes off to the side of the street and stopped. His face was cold and serious. "Listen, Martin. I told you before that I like you, so I'm only going to tell you, even though I shouldn't. Calderón said to me, Rafa, kill these two guys. I said okay, because if I had said no he would have ordered someone else to do it, but in doing so he would have said, by the way, kill Rafa while you're at it. Kill or be killed, Compadre. Got it?"

"Sixty people a night, Rafa?"

"Maybe more. The coroner's office is so swamped that they ask the local university and the neighboring cities to help them out. You have to remember that the cartel, Martin, is not just Calderón, Pacha and Contreras. It's two hundred different groups, although most of them are smaller operations than Calderón's. The little two hundred are loco, Compadre. They are always trying to eliminate each other, because they want a bigger market, and a bigger market means more money, and more money means more power. El Patrón doesn't care because its small-time." Rafa paused. "I could have let you take the flight to Medellín and spared what you witnessed today, but my boss was insistent and he ordered me to take you. I protested, but he ordered me. I don't know why he did, but he did and that was that. You know what I mean?"

"Why do you think he did?"

"Maybe he wants you feeling the way you feel right now. You have those men on your conscience now, don't you?" Martin nodded. "Then you've been touched, or as Calderón would say, 'you've been put into a frame of mind that encourages you to follow orders.' You see, he doesn't really trust pilots, at least not since Tom Campbell."

"Who was he?" Martin asked

Rafa put the car back in gear and drove on through the city streets. "Kevin Mitchell was a lot like you," Rafa said, checking into the rear-view mirror and making sure no one was following him. It was the first time Martin had seen him do anything that showed Rafa ill-at-ease. "Tom was a beautiful, wonderful, bastard of a pilot who betrayed us all. El Patrón hasn't trusted a single pilot ever since."

"How did he betray you?"

"He used to be a pilot with us, but he was working for the CIA. Are you working for the CIA, Compadre?"

The question rocked Martin.

"God, no!" Martin answered with feeling. "I think spooks are crazy." Rafa smiled.

"Did Campbell testify?" Martin asked, making a mental note to ask Alfred about it.

"No," Rafa said icily. "We took a contract out on him and got him."

Martin raised his eyebrows, but said nothing. Instead, he watched Rafa pull into the Inter-Continental Hotel's driveway and come to a stop. The thought of Tom Campbell being targeted for assassination in America brought back the fresh memories of the assassination he had witnessed in Puerto Salgar. He thought again whether he could have been able to stop the killings, but the answer was again no. He thought of different scenarios and how he might have been able to stop the killings. It had happened so fast. Maybe he chickened out, he told himself, which was the idea that worried him the most: Because how could he help Ernesto's family if he was going to

146

chicken out when push came to shove? God help him, he was scared.

Suddenly, Martin realized Rafa was speaking to him.
"Excuse me, what did you say?"
"I said, what have you to say about that?"
"About what?"
"Tomorrow night, your flight to Florida."
Martin looked at Rafa, his eyes widening. "Tomorrow?"
"Yes, tomorrow night you run the gauntlet. It's your vuelo de prueba. Your test-flight. Ríohacha to Florida, non-stop. You lose the cargo and you pay."
"What do you mean, I pay?"
"Bang, you pay!" Rafa said, mimicking the action of a gun. "I brought you in Compadre, so if you mess up, I pay as well. If that is any consolation to you."
Martin was too excited to care. "Where in Florida?" he asked.
"You're given the landing coordinates during the flight, that's why all our planes have High Frequency radios. Forget about it, just concentrate on having a good time tonight at the fiesta."
"What fiesta?"
"El Patrón is having a fiesta at Los Caracoles. It should be great. I'll have a man come by with your pass. Don't lose it or you'll be in trouble. There's a room reserved for you in the hotel. Why don't you wash up and get dressed. You can even invite Lili to come, I'm sure that she will be more than welcome."
"Excellent, I'll do just that. I'll see you tonight, Rafa." Damn! Martin thought. He had to get in touch with John Whitney and fast!

# CHAPTER 16

"I thought you might not be in," Alfred said on the telephone, as if Dusty were in the habit of skipping off early from work. "Come on up then and we'll have a talk."

It was only nine in the morning, but it looked more like five in the afternoon. The sky was the sort of gray that washes out all traces of color and threatens to do most anything, except rain or snow. Dusty was not worried by the lifeless sky, but rather by Alfred's tone. Whenever he affected a tone of old camaraderie, it was because he was having doubts about something. And if he were having doubts, God help them all, Dusty thought.

The first thing Dusty was surprised to discover in Alfred's office was a tape machine, the type that had huge tape-recording reels. Long ago he had been told by experts in surveillance that those ancient looking contraptions could tape six to eight hours on a single reel. At any rate, the second thing he was surprised to see was Alfred's state of dishevelment.

"John's fucking pissed off," Alfred said as Dusty strolled into the office.

There were a million things John could be angry about, but, for the life of him, Dusty couldn't think what could have incurred his wrath this time. So, he said in his usual forward way, "Oh?"

"He says he heard the Colombians tapping into Ms. Santander's line early this morning." Then Alfred affected a smile that looked more like a barracuda moving in for a kill. "He said it was like listening to a train wreck."

"Oh, that!" Dusty said with evident relief as he sat on the comfortable paisley couch Alfred kept in his office, just in case he wanted to have old Dusty up for a talk, he thought meanly. "He'll get over it, Alfred."

"My thoughts exactly, Dusty. I mean, it's not like I had any choice, did I?"

Dusty remained silent, because he damn well knew Alfred had had a big choice and in his opinion he had taken the wrong one.

"You think I jumped the gun allowing the Colombians to get into it this early?"

"I think we could have waited a few more days before letting them in, sir." Alfred raised his eyebrows, as if Dusty had sucker-punched him. "The problem now," he continued, "is to keep the Colombian list down to a minimum. If we can press them on keeping the access to the case on a restrictive basis, then we'll probably be all right."

"Yes, of course. They've assured me a maximum restriction. The President has seen to that. He asked them to produce a list, because if anything happens we'll know who did the blabbering." Alfred then shuffled through a sheaf of papers and produced a stapled stack of papers. "Here it is. The list of people with access, including our team. Good people, Dusty. Real good people, trying to do some real good in this world."

Alfred handed Dusty a stack of stapled sheets he hefted in his hands and later would confess on weight alone had already scared the living daylights out of him. He looked through the list quickly and was surprised to see sixty-seven names on their team alone, but he was truly shocked to see fifty-one Colombians.

Alfred must have read Dusty's facial expression, because he immediately asked, "You think it's too long?"

"Long?" he said sarcastically. "Of course, it's too fucking long! A couple of more names and we'll have the entire hemisphere on it. For God sakes, Alfred! You have people risking their lives out there!"

Dusty began to rub his forehead until his impatience got the best of him and he began to pace the office. Then he looked at the list again.

"Who the hell is Humberto Santa Rosa?" he asked.
"He's the Police Commander of Bogotá."
"And Marcos Del Cano?"
"He's head of the F-2 police. Colombian Intelligence."

"Miranda Cabrera?"

"Hmm. Oh, yes, that's right. She's the F-2 chief for the Province of Antioquia."

"Oh, God!" Dusty said and began to shake his head in despair. Antioquia was the name of the Province whose capital was Medellín.

It was at that moment, Dusty knew, that Alfred was firmly in control of the Titanic and had just sailed into dangerous waters. It was now just a matter of time before someone called out, "Iceberg!" and everyone would be running for the rafts, trying to salvage whatever might be salvageable.

"At any rate," Alfred continued, undeterred. "The Colombian Minister of Justice will be here later on, as well as the United States Senior Trial Attorney."

Dusty didn't say anything. His anger was beyond words.

"A pleasure to meet you, Dusty," said the Colombian Minister of Justice. Her voice was articulate and precise. "This is my assistant, Carlos Bustamante." Dusty shook the Minister's hand and then the assistant's.

The Minister was a fragile-looking woman who appeared capable of crying at a moment's notice, but, as Dusty thought this, he knew he was wrong. She was taking on the cartel single-handedly and had been marked for death for her troubles. She was a woman of delicate features. Medium sized forehead, small nose, wide mouth with thin lips and two big beautiful brown eyes. She had long and light brown hair wrapped into a bun at the nape of the neck. She was dressed in a white blouse, blue suit-coat and a small skirt that came just below the knees.

"Mrs. Fernandez was just filling us in on what they have on Camacho. It really is quite interesting," Alfred said motioning at everyone to take a seat. "She also has a bit of bad news, I'm afraid. Nothing serious, though."

Dusty felt a pang of fear, because he knew every little thing was serious, no matter what. Lives were now hanging in the balance. The Minister must have seen me him wince or something, because she volunteered to tell him.

"Miranda Cabrera was an agent for the F-2. She was found dead last night on the Autopista Medellín. Unfortunately, that is all we have."

"How much of the present case did Miss Cabrera know?" Lisa Mejía asked.

"Señorita Cabrera was cleared for the case, but had not yet received any material on it."

Lisa smiled. "Excuse me, but what material is that?"

"The blueprint to the operation. No names are mentioned, of course, just logistical support."

Lisa looked at Dusty and he thought he could hear her shouting through her eyes, "Jesus H. Christ!" as she often said, especially when things were flowing against the current.

Alfred broke in at last and changed the subject before the tension in the room got any worse. "The Minister has been informed that Ernesto Camacho is seeking complete immunity from prosecution and she was telling us, Dusty, that it might be a problem for her. Is that not so, Minister?"

She nodded and said, "We cannot offer immunity to Camacho; at least, not total. Maybe we could work out a reduction in sentence, but we could not give him immunity. For Colombia that would be out of the question."

"We'll give him the immunity," Elaine Fitzgerald stated. She was a hard-nosed woman with nearly sixteen years of experience in prosecuting the hardest criminals in America. She was also the United States' Senior Trial Attorney and she would be the woman in charge of taking Calderón to trial.

"Unfortunately, I am sorry to say it is not possible," replied the Minister's assistant. "First we would have to agree to let him out of the country and, since he is a wanted man in our country, that would be impossible. Under Colombian law we would have to try him in a Colombian Court before we allowed him to be extradited."

"We'll smuggle him out," Dusty said.

"Then we will be forced to serve papers of extradition on your government, Mister...Dusty. He has technically committed the crimes in Colombia, not in the United States. Since he is the one responsible for the murder of one-hundred and seven people in Colombia, the public outcry in our country would be considerable. I'm sorry, but we should be the one to put him on trial."

"And you think you could successfully do that, put him on trial?"

The assistant shrugged.

"What if we tried him for a crime in America first?" Elaine asked.

"What crime?" the Minister asked. "He has committed no crimes in America."

"He'll just have to commit one," Dusty said and everyone turned to look at him. "We smuggle him out in a plane and fly him to Florida and give him some cocaine to carry along. When he lands in Miami we arrest him for trafficking or possession. We can then offer him immunity and he becomes a witness against the cartel."

The Minister pursed her lips as she thought it out and then said, "It could work, but you would have to return him to Colombia when we bring Calderón to justice. Mister Camacho would be a state witness."

"That wouldn't be necessary. Calderón and the other members of the cartel can be brought to America to face criminal charges under the present extradition treaty. They have committed crimes in this country. In fact, Calderón is currently under indictment for murder and extortion. We can even throw the RICO statutes at him."

"RICO?"

"Racketeer Influenced Corrupt Organizations Act," Alfred said, displaying some of his legal knowledge. "It provides for the seizure of assets on any criminal organization. Title 18, U.S. Code, Section 1962."

The Minister looked at her assistant and both exchanged looks that said, "Why not?" Then the Minister turned to Alfred and said, "My assistant will prepare the papers."

And just like that a plan for bringing in the most dangerous criminal in the world had been worked out. But a working basis was a long way off from actually arresting a criminal, especially if he was as cunning as a fox.

The meeting broke up after they worked out some of the cumbersome legal aspects, then, as he was about to leave, the Minister asked him if he'd like to have lunch with her.

Dusty looked past her shoulder and saw Alfred give him a dark look, because he had intended to be the person with whom she shared that lunch.

"Yes, I would be delighted, Minister," Dusty replied ignoring the malevolent stare from Alfred.

She smiled and it seemed to make her a different woman. Then she said, "Call me Virginia, please. Shall we say, twelve-thirty and I will meet you in your office, if that is okay with you?" Dusty nodded happily. "Good because I still have to pay a visit to my embassy."

"That would be perfect...Virginia."

Two immediate problems presented themselves to Dusty after having accepted the offer for lunch, namely, where to go and how to get there. He had not been out on a lunch date in years. The city's restaurants were now a complete mystery to him, but he was lucky. Don Harkin was able to arrange a reservation in a fashionable restaurant near the Capitol and it was there where he took the lovely Virginia Fernandez.

She dazzled him with her knowledge of American politics and, to his amazement, she genuinely made him laugh, but while she kept him entertained Dusty noticed that she was a woman fraying at the edges. She had a constant preoccupied look about her.

"How do you go on and not let the cartel get under your skin?" He asked her, catching her off-guard.

"They have gotten under my skin," she replied sadly. "I am constantly frightened, but more so when I am away from my family. Every time I go on a trip I think, is this the last time I'll see my children?"

"How old are your children?"

"The oldest is six, he's just begun his schooling. The youngest is three, and she has a nanny who takes care of her."

"What does your husband think of what you do?"

She was silent, unsure of how to respond and, for a moment, he thought she would not.

"It's been very hard on him. He is a businessman, but his partners are afraid of him. They realize that my husband is a target and because they are always near him, they believe they could die by their proximity to him. I cannot blame them, if the cartel were to lob a grenade in my husband's direction, anyone within forty feet could die."

"I'm sorry, I didn't know."

"No one does, but it's the little things that really get to you. We have our telephone number changed every week, but someone still manages to call up and say, you're going to die! My son goes to school with twelve bodyguards, our house has a military platoon surrounding it and our cars, as you know, are bullet proof. While I'm traveling between my home and my office I wear a bullet-proof vest and my mail is checked for letter bombs. I haven't had friends over for dinner in six months and I have not visited my brothers and sisters since I took over the Office of Minister." She became silent again as she stared at her empty plate. "I am the prisoner and the cartel are the jailers."

Dusty reached over the table and took her hand and squeezed it softly. He couldn't say why he did so, but it seemed natural. "It will not be like that forever, Virginia. It will end someday."

"Dusty," she said gravely. "I will tell you something that I have only told my husband. They are going to win."

"You really believe that? Even though we've got them on the run now?"

"Now more than ever. If Calderón is brought to justice, someone else is going to take his place. The person who takes his place might or might not be from Medellín. He could be from Cali or Bogotá. The demand for cocaine is too big." She paused and then consciously made an effort to change the subject. "Is Dusty your real name?"

"God, no! It's Joseph."

"That is a good name, Joseph. Do you have children?"

"No, I'm afraid I'm...we can't have children."

"Have you thought of adoption?"

"We've discussed it, but we decided against it."

The truth was that Elizabeth had decided against it. She used his sterility to remind him of his failings and how he had not been a proper husband to her, because he had been unable to provide her with any offspring. When she first used the statement, "You're not a real man," he had been devastated, but, with time, he learned to ignore it.

"What does she think of your work?" Virginia asked, lifting a cup of coffee from the table.

Dusty shrugged and said, "She's not thrilled about it." Then he purposefully changed the subject because it was hitting too close to home. "What do you think of the Santander Case?"

Virginia seemed to weigh the answer before speaking. "We've had two cases similar to it, but this one looks better than most. As always, it will depend on how much Ernesto Camacho decides to tell us."

"What happened to the other cases?"

"The cartel found out and they killed the witnesses, or so we think. We never saw them again; they disappeared."

"I think we'd better get back," said Dusty as he glanced at his watch.

Virginia then reached over and grabbed his hand. "Thank you for lunch, Joseph. It's the first time I've had lunch in a restaurant in four years. My husband would like to take me to one, but it would be too dangerous. I am sorry to have burdened you with my problems. You are a very decent man, thank you."

There was a note of desperation in her voice which stayed with him long after they had lunched together. It was only much later when he thought about her, that he was able to remember her voice and how it had sounded. She was a woman who had seen her fate and was living with that knowledge, and had resolved herself to the inevitable.

# CHAPTER 17

The skin had wrinkled and turned red, yet Martin remained under the shower nozzle and allowed the jets of nearly boiling water to splash over his skin. And even then he could not shake the feeling of being soiled in blood.

Martin had seen the killings and done nothing to stop them, and now his conscience was torturing him. Could he have stopped them, he asked himself over and over again. But the answer was always the same, who knows? Maybe. Maybe not.

He emerged from the shower, dried himself off and got dressed in the same clothes he had put on that morning. He felt akin to Pontius Pilate, because he was unable to rid himself of the affair, even after he had washed his hands of it. He knew something was happening to him at a base level, but he was at a loss to explain it. Life in Medellín, he realized, was worth whatever the cartel deemed it to be. He was losing touch. He was not controlling events anymore, because the events were controlling him.

He lifted the telephone and dialed the information operator. He asked for Lili's number. The operator gave it to him and he wrote it down. One minute later he was sitting by the side of his bed, smiling, coming out of a great dark.

"I've talked to Ernesto," she said quickly. "I..."

"Listen, there is a party at Los Caracoles tonight," Martin said, cutting her off. He didn't want her talking over the telephone. "Why don't you come to Medellín and we'll go together."

There was silence.

"All right," she said, but there was a feeling of uncertainty in her voice.

Had he misjudged last night? Had he been something for her to hold on to during the night? Didn't she feel what he had? Why was she hesitating? "Good!" he said, trying to keep his voice free from any suggestion of doubt. "I'll call the airlines and have a ticket waiting for you at the counter. See you soon...love."

"Bye," Lili said coolly and hung up.

Martin stared at the phone, trying to figure out what had happened. What had he said to her? Was she upset that he had cut her off? Or had Ernesto changed his mind? Dear God! I hope, for everyone's sake, he hasn't.

Martin dialed the concierge and asked him to arrange a flight for Lili. He would pay for it when he checked out the following morning. The concierge said he would have the lady in Medellín before the sun was down.

Martin then hung up and took stock of himself. He needed clothes for tonight and tomorrow, and he still had something upwards of ten thousand dollars Rafa had given him in Bogotá. His first priority, however, was to call John Whitney. He checked the slip action of his Hechler and Koch, and decided to make the most of it. Then he walked out into the Medellín streets, risking life and limb as he went looking for a public telephone.

His first surprise was the city itself. Whenever American news networks mentioned Medellín, he had pictured an old sleepy town where the cartel ordered men shot just to encourage the population, a city without running water or electricity, and the poor running barefoot on the city streets. It was, to his surprise, the exact opposite, except for the killings that occurred after sundown.

It was a city where sky-scrapers filled the air; wide, paved avenues criss-crossed the valley, and industry and commerce thrived at a vigorous rate. It was like any other modern city in the last stages of the twentieth century. If he had wanted to, Martin told himself, he could close his eyes and feel himself in Miami or Los Angeles.

Martin crossed Carrera 53, across from the Zea Museum and read a giant billboard that had been placed on the side of a modern thirty story building. "Medellín -- La Ciudad de Amistad, Flores y Juventud Eterna." The City of Friendship, Flowers and Eternal Youth. Then he wondered if anyone in Medellín believed the sign. Many, he decided, because it was a city of nearly two million people who seemed completely unaffected by the random violence that plagued it.

He watched people putting up streamers and signs along the major streets that advertised the upcoming Festival del Recuerdo; The Festival of Remembrance commemorating the city's past.

Finally, Martin spotted a bank of public telephones across the street and looked around to see if anyone was following him. He spotted two old women crossing the street, an old man selling flowers on the corner and a young girl wearing some sort of school uniform. The girl looked twelve, maybe thirteen years old, as she looked dreamily through a shop window. He found it odd that a schoolgirl would find a tobacco shop interesting, but this was Medellín and who knew what normal was.

Martin crossed Calle 50 and entered the furthest telephone booth, because it afforded him the best view around him. He dropped five dollars worth of coins and dialed John Whitney's number.

"Hello?" said the voice which Martin recognized immediately.

"I'm in Medellín. I don't have much time, so listen."

"I'm ready."

"I fly tomorrow night. I'm going to El Patrón's hacienda tonight for a fiesta. I saw something today..."

"I'm listening."

Martin tried to search for the right words. He didn't want an over-anxious operator trying to figure out what he was talking about.

"Hello, are you still there?" John asked.

"I'm here...I saw an American get cashed in."

John was silent.

"He was with another guy, a Colombian. He, too, got cashed in."

"Could you have stopped it?"

"I don't know. It happened too fast."

"Who was he, the American?"

"I was told he worked for the company," Martin said, using the nickname for the CIA.

"What is your destination and ETA tomorrow night?"

"I don't know. I receive instructions in mid-flight through an HF radio. There's more, though. The girl is unsure of our friend's steadfastness; she thinks he might back out. I'll find out more tonight. This will be my final contact."

"Understood. Good luck."

Martin hung up and was about to stretch his neck when he froze. In the glass of the telephone booth he could see the reflection of someone watching him. It was the girl in the school uniform he had seen across the street, except that she was no girl. She was a woman in her early twenties. He turned slowly to face her and, as he did, she knelt down and pretended to tie a shoe.

Martin shuddered. He could feel the onset of a panic attack, but he fought it and brought himself under control. Thoughts raced in and out of his mind: he should follow the girl and discover who she is; kill the girl before she tells anyone; trap the girl and find out what she knows and who she works for; kill, kill, kill. Sálvese quien pueda.

Martin decided on making another call. He called Rafa.

Rafa answered the telephone after three rings. "¿Diga?"

"It's me, Martin. I'm sorry to call you, Rafa, but I forgot to ask, how do I get to Los Caracoles?"

Rafa laughed and said, "Don't worry, I'll have a car sent to you. Did you call Lili?"

"Yes, she's coming."

"Ah! Compadre! It's love!"

Martin let out a feigned laugh.

"Where are you calling from, Compadre?"

"Somewhere downtown in a public phone booth. I have no clothes and decided to buy some, but then I remembered I hadn't asked you how to get there."

"Don't worry, Compadre. A car will pick you up. I'll see you later."

When Martin hung up and walked out of the telephone booth the girl was gone. Had he imagined it? Was she working for the cartel or for John Whitney? Was the girl able to overhear his conversation? Why did he keep thinking of her as a girl when she was plainly a woman? It was the uniform, he decided. It had fooled him completely. It was the everyday things like this that would do him in, he decided. If he didn't remain alert and suspicious he would die sooner than later.

Suddenly he felt as if walls were closing in on him and that his time was running out.

Rafa carefully explained to Martin how Paisas loved to throw a good party. He told them that it was in the blood, that Paisas had been born with a sixth sense of how a good time might be got at.

"Three live bands," Rafa declared as he showed Martin around the hacienda. "One for merengues, another for salsa, and the other for whatever else that might be missing. You see, Paisas love to dance. Not to your rock'n'roll music, but to real Latin rhythms. You know why, Compadre?"

"No, but I'm sure you're going to tell me all the same," Martin said, ribbing Rafa.

"Because it stirs the blood. It's sexy! It gets men and women in the mood, Compadre. Look!" Rafa said pointing at a buffet table beside an Olympic size swimming pool.

"Beluga caviar! A guy in St. Petersburg couldn't pay us in dollars, so he gave us Beluga. We made money on the deal, can you believe it? El Patrón sent some people to Russia to look into the caviar angle of things. "If people are thirsty look what El Patrón offers them, Dom Perignon and Krug."

Suddenly, Rafa switched topics. "So, you're in love!" he declared lowering his voice conspiratorially, "You're a crazy gringo, Compadre. Sometimes I think you're crazier than I am."

"I don't think so," Martin replied easily, and then added in jest, "I still haven't been diagnosed as certifiable."

Rafa laughed, but it quickly died when a man walked up beside him and whispered in his ear. The change in Rafa was instantaneous, from happy-go-lucky to cold-hearted-bastard. Rafa, Martin thought, was an emotional chameleon.

"El Patrón wants to see us," Rafa said in grave seriousness. "Business."

El Patrón sat like a lion in the jungle. He was master of all he purveyed and then some. He had come to know what was possible within and without the law and then stretch it some more. He played by his own rules; no other rules mattered. He was feared and respected and, in some cases, loved; no one dared to say otherwise. He had made his own kingdom and it grew exponentially with his wealth. "I am the law and the law is me," he seemed to say from his chair, challenging anyone to tell him otherwise.

Calderón motioned with his hand for Martin to take a seat in front of his desk. He watched Martin register the three pistolocos and reflexively feel for his own gun. This was a strong man in front of him, El Patrón thought, a man who would rather fight it out than go down in surrender.

"You are armed," El Patrón said. It was a statement not a question.

Martin, startled and caught off guard, said, "Yes."

Two pistolocos immediately moved towards Martin, but El Patrón waved them off.

"The movement of your hand gave you away."

Martin nodded.

"You are taking some of our product to America tomorrow, Martin. Did Rafa tell you?"

"He did."

"You will be taking an extra load, almost five hundred keys. We usually don't send more than three hundred, but we have to settle some debts in America."

"How much is it worth?"

"Forty or fifty million dollars."

Martin let out a soft whistle.

"Yes, that's why you will be flying. We need it to go through." El Patrón paused. "But we have a problem, and that problem is you."

Martin was able to keep his voice steady and without sounding alarmed, ask, "Why is that?"

"They know you're flying with us." Martin's heart hammered away in his chest.

"Who are they?"

"There's a pilot in Miami that keeps calling out your name. One of our other pilots taped it the last time he went in. Would you like to hear it?"

"Yes, I would."

El Patrón motioned at one of the pistolocos, who retrieved a small tape-recorder from a book shelf and placed it in front of Martin. Martin then leaned forward and pressed the play button.

The voice emerged eerily through the speaker. "...Martin Black, we've got your number. Can you hear me, Martin? We got you!..."

Martin was stunned. What kind of game was the DEA playing? Were they trying to make it look as if he really didn't work for them?

"Do you recognize the voice?"

Martin shook his head. "No, who is he?"

El Patrón said nothing, but when he saw that Martin was baffled he broke the silence. "The DEA photographs all our pilots, so they know who they're up against. They must have taken your picture in Bogotá and sent it to the U.S. I have ordered our people in Miami to take pictures of all DEA pilots currently flying in Florida. If they want to play games, so can we.

"Now, on to other matters, you will be flying out of Ríohacha tomorrow and given a map with flight instructions. Follow them to the letter." El Patrón leveled a stare at Martin, but, without altering his voice, added, "because, if you make a mistake don't bother coming back."

El Patrón closed his eyes. The meeting was over.

Martin made love to Lili that night in the hacienda, but his mind racing and made him get out of bed the moment Lili fell asleep. He put his pants on and walked towards the window. He thought about El Patrón's eyes: the cold, hard and black orbs that had ordered the execution of dozens of people and not blinked in the telling.

It was nearly dawn and the party was still going strong. Every now and then Rafa's voice would waft under the door and Martin would hear him telling lies to some woman he was trying to get into bed. He wondered about Rafa's wife and whether she knew his whereabouts. He remembered making the rounds with Rafa, being introduced to men and women whose names he tried to commit to memory. There was a Colombian Congressman who Rafa said would ground the entire Colombian Air-Force, so that the cartel could fly out its coke-loads unimpeded. Then there were the starlets. Some were powerful women, too; a mayor of some city where the cartel was allowed to operate without hassle, a judge, an attorney for the city of such and such. The list was endless.

Then Martin began to think of the conversation he had had with Lili when he had picked her up at the Medellín Airport. From the moment he had seen her he knew something had gone wrong. He asked her while they got their baggage and she had told him.

"It's Ernesto," she had said. "I think he's chickening out. He's imposed all of these strange conditions."

"What conditions?" Martin asked as he held his voice at whisper level.

"He wants to keep all of his money. He wants a guarantee in writing from the President of the United States that he will be immune from prosecution. He also wants his entire family, uncles, cousins, nieces, nephews -- in short, everyone he might be related to -- afforded the same conditions." Martin had a feeling of falling from a great height. He shook his head as if to clear it from dizziness. Then he looked up and said, "Why?"

Lili said apologetically, "He's afraid."

"Christ! So am I, but I'm not fucking trying to make it worse!" Martin paused. "Did he say how he planned to get his family out?"

Lili opened her pocketbook and handed him a thick brown envelope. "He said it was all in there, plus his conditions. He won't talk to you at the party tonight. He'll avoid you at all costs. Please do as he says."

Martin held the envelope in his hand as if weighing it. Then, deciding he could do nothing about it, he pocketed the envelope.

"What will the DEA say, Martin?"

"I don't know. They're desperate for any kind of break, but this...they might feel it's too risky for their agents. Christ!

What am I saying? It's all ready too fucking late for Ernesto. If he doesn't come through, the DEA will use him whether he likes it or not. He's a dead man, for sure, if he backs out."

A silence fell between them.

"What will you do if my people say no?" he asked her, feeling a great chasm opening up between them.

She put her arms around him as the baggage came through the conveyer belt. "I don't know. Ernesto's the only family I have left. His kids are my god-children, I can't just let go. I know what El Patrón would do to all of them. I love you, Martin, but I cannot betray my family."

Martin nodded as a lump the size of his fist seemed to lodge itself in his throat, his happiness ebbing away like a sea tide going out.

Now, as he waited for the dawn, Martin heard a rustle of fabric behind him and turned.

"What are you doing?" Lili asked him from the bed.

"Nothing, I couldn't sleep."

"Come back to bed, then."

Martin walked back and heard Lili reaching over to turn on the bed lamp. "Don't," he said. "The sun is almost up."

"What's wrong?"

Martin got into bed and, with his left hand, began to trace the line of her jaw. He saw her eyes, her face, oddly unfamiliar, but beautiful in the cold dawn light.

"You're going tonight, aren't you?" she asked him.

"Yes."

Silence.

"Whatever happens, Martin, I love you."

Later on, as thunder rolled across the valley and the sun began to rise, Martin watched her face take on a rose-colored hue as the light of day became stronger. Her eyes were closed and her breathing was as faint as a baby's. He heard a few rain drops splatter against the window and the guests using the john before going to breakfast. Then, with the gray, flat light coming through the window, he spied the room: white walls with oil paintings in fancy frames, dark antique furniture contrasting heavily with the white walls. In this room, with Lili in his arms, it seemed to him that he was a man without a country, a man of divided loyalties. The rain fell with a mighty crash and then settled into a rhythmic beat. He thought of Windraider, tied to the dock in Key West, waiting to be steered into the wide open blue. Lightning flashed and he began to count: One thousand one, one thousand two...thunder boomed. He thought of the girl he saw in Medellín the day before, wearing a school uniform, the one who had seen him in the telephone booth and pretended to be tying her shoe. Who was she and whom did she work for? Fear gripped him and he didn't know how to shake it off. He thought of Windraider slicing through the waves again and tried to recapture the freedom and happiness he had felt at her helm. But the fear stayed with him and began to grow like a cancer.

# CHAPTER 18

It was a cold night in Washington. The sky was spitting sleet and it was much to early in the season for it to be snowing, but a freak change in the jet stream had changed Autumn into Winter and everyone seemed to be unhappy. The people inside Alfred Stevens' office were no exception. Don and Lisa, along with Alfred and Dusty, had heard John Whitney tell them about his talk with Martin Black. Then they all watched Alfred place a call to the Director of the CIA, who swore up and down that they were not running an operation with the cartel.

"I don't believe Langley," Lisa said. "They have a pattern of not sharing information with us."

"But why?" Alfred asked. He was tense and it showed with the bags under his eyes. He hadn't been sleeping well. The operation, he knew, was the biggest thing of his political career. It was the operation to end all other operations. "It could bite them in the ass if they don't share the information with us."

"It's their way, sir. You know, National Security and all that."

Then Alfred asked Don, "What do you think?"

"I think Lisa's right, sir. They've pulled this routine before. I think they've tapped into something and they're not going to tell us, sir."

Alfred drummed his fingers on his desk. "What do we do if Martin flies into Florida with a couple of hundred kilos of coke. Do we bust him?"

"Let him come in, sir," Lisa said. "Then we'll put tails on their ground contacts. We could have a snowball effect."

Alfred shook his head. "That's a lot of people we're talking about. The more people who know about this, the more dangerous it gets for Martin."

"We could limit the number, sir," Don said.

"What happens if he flies in and our nearest agent is three hundred miles away?"

"We could call in the Customs Service for help," Lisa said tentatively.

"No! That's the last thing we want. They've asked Congress for a bigger budget to fight the cartel. We can't be seen to be asking for their help, because Congress might give them a good chunk of money that should come to us. We need a big bust and so do Customs, and sharing the information with them is just telling the people on the Hill that they're doing a better job than we are. And who knows what Customs man might leak this information. No, we keep Customs and the Coast Guard out of it. We'll have to go it alone."

"It'll be more dangerous for Martin, sir," Lisa put in cautiously.

"How so?"

"If he flies in and the Customs or Coast Guard don't know it, they could shoot him down to pieces. Then what?"

Alfred was ready for the answer. "What if we tell them and they leak it? The cartel will kill Martin straight off, probably torture him before they turn out his lights...What do you think, Dusty?"

Everyone turned to look at Dusty, as if startled to discover he was in the room at all. They had seen him, but he had been so quiet everyone forgot he was there.

"I think we should tell Martin," Dusty said evenly.

Alfred looked at Dusty, as if he had betrayed him and said, "He could walk right out on us and I wouldn't blame him. So, should we let him walk and lose the best thing we've had on the cartel, ever? Hell no! We don't tell him. If he gets forced down and arrested, well then, things could work out for the better..."

"What if he gets shot down and killed?" Don asked.

Alfred looked at Don, as if measuring him for retirement. "We're at war, Don. People get killed all the time in a war."

# CHAPTER 19

"She's a beauty," Martin said, as he looked down the tarmac and walked towards the plane.

She certainly had the lines, Martin thought, and then some. Her long sleek wings with winglets and tip tanks at the end of them, her elongated and pointy snout that housed a turboprop -- which belied an intense ferocity to the engine -- was beautiful.

"She's a converted Bonanza," Rafa said. "It has an Allison 250-B17C engine."

"What year is the airframe?" Martin asked.

"She has an '87 airframe. She also has less than two hundred hours on her engine and she won't need a water bed to take you to America. We've added an extra thirty gallon fuel tank besides the tip tanks she already carries. It should be more than enough fuel to get her to the States. I bought her in Omaha, Nebraska, for nine hundred thousand dollars."

Martin whistled. The wings to him felt almost like silk in their smoothness. Then he walked to the nose and put his hand on her windmill, which was slightly above the turbine intake. The prop was a Hartzell three-blade, deiced, reversible, 90 inch din that shone like silver. She was twenty-nine feet from nose to tail and she had a thirty-four foot wingspan. He also noticed the extra hatch above the pilot's seat and looked back at Rafa. "What's the hatch for?"

"We put it there just in case the pilot has to bail out."

"What's wrong with the regular hatch?"

Rafa grinned. "Compadre, you wouldn't be able to get to it. All the available space is taken up with cargo."

Martin then looked inside and what he thought had been seat covers were big army duffel bags stacked from floor to ceiling.

"Five hundred kilos, Compadre. That's why you're flying this baby and not the Cessna. It's going to be a little tricky for the first couple of hundred miles because of the weight, but after that you'll be okay. Good luck, Compadre."

The street lights in Washington were beginning to come on, even though there was still a good half hour of natural light left. Alfred Stevens loved this time of day best, because it seemed as if a blanket of tranquility descended over the Capital, a serene beauty in what had become America's killinground. Dusty had been beside him for most of the day and watched him receive frequent reports from Don and Lisa, who were in Florida waiting for Martin.

At one point during their lunch break, while Dusty ate his Pastrami on Rye, Alfred said to him, "I had a call from Langley this morning. One of their men was murdered in Colombia yesterday. The Director said they had an in into the Cali Cartel, but that's about as far as he would explain."

"It was probably the man Martin saw killed," Dusty said.

Alfred nodded. "Tell me again what the plan is?"

"We've staked out Florida into grids' sir..." Dusty began to explain for the second time. He knew Alfred had to be feeling alienated, because he was so far away from the action. He also knew that it had to be that way, because if someone spotted him in Florida the cartel might change its plans and the whole operation would become another fruitless exercise.

"What time do you think he'll be coming in?" Alfred asked after he finished explaining.

"Sometime after midnight, I suppose."

Martin closed the hatch above him and strapped himself in for the flight. He adjusted the seat and then let his eyes scan the avionics in front of him. The altimeter, air and ground speed gauges, loran, radar, auto-pilot control, transfer fuel pump knobs, and the u-shaped handle for the control column. He ran his right hand over the position of the switches, controls and circuit breakers, committing them to memory. He also noticed the radio control head in the center of the panel, the ice-protection, lights and ignition switches.

There was nothing left to do but fly.

He opened the small window on the pilot's seat and yelled out, "Clear!" and turned the ignition key. The turbine lighted up, a rising whine that reached a crescendo and settled before the whip-sounding snap and steam whistle toot as the fuel began to fire. He watched the crazy swing of the turbine outlet temperature needle when the flame caught. He was surprised at the smoothness of it. He had expected the vibration of the piston-driving engine coming to life as most prop's did, but the propeller twirled and passed the vibration stage easily as it spun up. Finally the power stabilized and he felt as if he were in a jet and not a prop.

Martin knew he needed a ground run of at least six hundred feet, which El Patron's runway had. In fact, it had a twelve hundred foot runway. He looked out his window and saw Rafa sitting behind a Toyota Land Cruiser giving him the thumbs-up. Martin waved back, increased the throttle and brought the Bonanza into the wind, then stopped.

He revved up the engine, slammed the throttle to the stop and simultaneously let go of the brakes. The Bonanza lurched forward and began its ground run. At seven-hundred feet Martin pulled back on the control column and hauled off the runway. He retracted the gear and the Bonanza increased her speed rapidly as she began her voyage to the United States.

The Cessna Citation jet is the U.S. Customs first line of defense against the drug smugglers. It is a jet with enough electronic equipment to detect and track any single or twin engine propeller the cartel might be using to smuggle coke. It has two Pratt & Whitney JT15 turbofan engines with two 2,900 pounds of thrust each, which can propel the aircraft at over four hundred knots. It is the Customs Service answer to the Air Force's AWACS, except that the Customs called their plane the 'Sensor Bird.' SB for short.

The SB was flown by a female pilot, a co-pilot and, in the rear on the starboard side was the Eye-Man. He sat behind the scanning airborne radar, FLIR controls, and the panels of switches and knobs that would help him track a smuggler to the ends of hell.

At two minutes after midnight, as the SB made it's final turn over what was known to Customs pilots as the Dead Zone -- the area west of Andros and east of Florida, because it was too far to be covered by conventional air-traffic control radar -- the Eye-Man saw a blip appear on his radar and then disappear. He fine-tuned the instruments and there it was again, the Medellín Express.

The Eye-Man pressed the intercom transmit button and said, "Bogey, bogey, bogey!"

"Check with C3I," came back the pilot's command.

C3I, stood for Command, Control, Communications, and Intelligence center in the old Navy blimp base in southwest Miami. C3I would verify whether the aircraft had filed a flight plan or he was a doper. C3I responded instantaneously. The aircraft flying out of the Dead Zone was a doper.

"It's a doper," said the Eye-Man to the pilot. Then he gave her the coordinates and she took over the chase.

"How fast is the doper moving?" she asked.

"One six zero knots."

"Cessna?"

"She could be."

"Okay," said the pilot. Her voice was cool and confident, despite the fact she was diving a jet-aircraft from fifteen thousand feet to four hundred. "We'll be coming up on its six. Call in base and let them know that we'll need the Hawks up and flying and tell them we don't have the fuel to keep up a long chase."

"Do you see it?" she asked her co-pilot.

"No. It must be running without navigation or clearance lights."

"How far?" she asked the Eye-Man.

"Three miles."

The pilot hit the air-brakes, lowered the flaps and brought the Citation from 380 knots to just over one hundred and thirty as she came up on the bogey.

"Bingo!" she cried. "It's a Bonanza. She's heading for Miami."

"I've already alerted Miami International, and the FAA people are aware."

"What about the Hawks? We need the Hawks! This bird's gonna be suckin' fumes in twenty."

The headquarters for the air wing of the U.S. Customs' Service is located in Homestead Air Force Base on Biscayne Bay. It was an old runway, decommissioned by the Air Force long ago, but was finding a new life under the Customs Service. However, instead of housing fancy jet-fighters and tactical nuclear bombers in its hangars, it now housed a different sort of fighter. Piper Cheyennes. King Airs, Titans, Citations, and Blackhawks.

In the main building, an old converted hangar, a row of offices and recreational rooms had become the nerve center for the Customs Air-Wing. It was the front line of the U.S. Government's interdiction effort and where Ray Sullivan was catching up on some overdue paperwork.

Suddenly the klaxons on the base sounded and Ray Sullivan scrambled from his desk. He turned the corner into the hallway and ran for the exit doors. He was out of the building as a voice on a PA address system said, "Launch the Hawk. Launch the Hawk. This is a scramble."

Ray reached the Hawk. His flying uniform was soaked in sweat after running across the tarmac in the stifling Florida heat and humidity. He climbed into the cockpit and found his co-pilot sitting and grinning at him from his seat. Ray strapped himself in as the rest of the team got into the rear of the Hawk. He ran down quickly through the pre-flight and turned on the auxiliary power unit, which would feed power to turn the 1,570 horsepower turbine engines. He switched on the boost and the rest became automatic.

Ray looked at Gus Bain, his co-pilot, who gave him a smile and he hit the starter switch, moved the power to idle and the rotor began turning. He checked the oil and transmission pressure and everything looked good. The rotor blades became a blur, rattling and shaking the Hawk.

Gus Bain radioed for take-off permission and received it immediately. He then turned to Ray, gave him the thumbs up signal and Ray rose off the ground with the grace of a bird.

Ray flew low and north, with the night air drying off his uniform. The Hawk was running fast at one hundred and forty-five knots.

"Where are they, Chet?" Ray asked.

"He just flew over Sands Key. He'll be crossing the coast just north of Perrine and south of Kendall. We'll be waiting for him."

Ray heard the Citation pilot tell him she was low on fuel and she would break off the moment Ray spotted the doper.

"Okay, fellows," Ray said. "Keep your eye-balls peeled."

Gus spotted the lights of the Citation bathe the Bonanza in light. The Bonanza banked hard to the South and then descended until it seemed it would touch down on I-95.

"Jesus H. Christ!" the pilot in the Citation cried out over her mike. "That bastard must have stretched those wings doing that. I've never seen anyone do that before!"

Ray followed the Bonanza down to one hundred feet, feeling the hot thermals coming off the cooling pavement of I-95. Suddenly, the Bonanza shot up to four thousand feet and merged into the commercial air-traffic of Miami International. Ray pushed the Hawk as fast as it would go and kept up a good chase.

But, unexpectedly, the Bonanza doubled back in a maneuver Ray hadn't seen since his combat days. Then the Bonanza flew south over Miami and Ray lost him. And, at that moment, Ray knew he'd been out-flown by a damn good pilot.

Martin was exhilarated. The adrenaline was coursing through his body as it had during Gulf War, but the exhilaration was short-lived because he was flying on fumes and he still had to land.

He pressed the buttons on the Loran and read the digital display. He was one minute out from his landing coordinates, but all he saw was blackness below him. He was flying level at one hundred feet and it scared him, because if an electrical or water tower rose in front of him he wouldn't see it until it was too late.

"There it is!" Martin said loudly as he saw a patch of land light up under two powerful lamps; the type of lamps used during World War Two to spot bombers.

Martin lowered his gear, lined up on the marker, checked his altimeter and touched down.

He powered the aircraft down and popped the hatch open as one of three pick-up trucks pulled up beside him. Eight men jumped out of the pick-up trucks and six of them began unloading the plane as Martin climbed out of the Bonanza. Two men approached him when he stood on Florida ground. One of them, by the pouch he carried in his right hand, Martin was able to tell that he was a pilot. The other man, however, was Rafa's underling.

"How much fuel in her?" the pilot asked.

"Six gallons," Martin replied.

The pilot turned to the men and shouted "¡Llénenla!" Fill her up! Then he turned to Martin. "We'll put some fuel in her and I'll fly her to the Caicos."

"Good luck," Martin said.

"No worries," said the pilot with an Australian accent.

"Señor Martin, this is yours," Rafa's underling said, handing him a briefcase. "Don Rafa said one million in cash. Inside the briefcase you will also find a paper with three telephone numbers. Please call them tomorrow at ten in the morning and verify your whereabouts. You have three days down time before you fly out again. The blue pickup truck is yours to use. The keys are in the ignition. Adios."

"Is that it?"

"That's it, mate," the Australian said. "Wham-bang-thank you ma'am. It's the easiest way to make a million dollars; of course, you have to be a damn good pilot to earn it, but you seemed to have managed. Good-day, mate!"

Unbelievable! Martin thought. He walked towards the pickup truck, briefcase in hand and one million dollars richer. He covertly tried to spot the DEA agents, but he saw nothing. He decided the DEA was either very good at surveillance or they were nowhere near the area.

## CHAPTER 20

Don Harkin had played his game more secretly than a grandmother in a bingo parlor on a wet Tuesday night. He knew that to catch Martin on conventional aircraft radar would be a crapshoot and we could all end up with nothing, but he had a feeling and that feeling was Lucio Bonilla.
The moment John Whitney reported that Rafa was still with Martin in Medellín, Don began to suspect that Rafa would not be taking care of the cocaine load when Martin brought it to Florida. So, he made a list of people in Florida the cartel would entrust with a planeload of cocaine and Lucio was the first person on the list.
Don and Lisa staked out Lucio's house in the suburb of Lauderhill, northwest of Ft. Lauderdale, before the sun was up. Lisa was behind the wheel, while Don spied through a pair of binoculars. They had watched Lucio collect his morning paper, seen how he had sent his kids off to the local public school and then watched him leave the house on foot. He had walked seven blocks to an old garage with a sign above it that read, CHUCHO'S TRUCK REPAIR. CHUCHO'S was a large shop and, by all appearances, it was doing quite well.
It was shortly after three in the afternoon when two Ford F-150 pickup trucks drove out of the garage. Lisa spotted Lucio in the first pick-up and began to follow him, staying far enough away not to be noticed.
Lucio's first stop was the gas station, where the pickup trucks were gassed and set in order. Lisa instinctively checked her own fuel gauge and saw that it read three-quarters full. Lucio then drove out of the gas station and headed south until he reached the Hialeah exit and turned off. He drove to a

small, white, single story house and parked in front of it. The second pickup truck pulled in behind him and did the same.

"Who do you think they're visiting?" Lisa asked Don as she stopped the car, carefully minding her position in order not to be spotted.

"Could be anyone," Don said as he peered through the glasses.

"You really think Lucio will meet Martin?"

"Uh-huh. It makes sense. Right now he's the cartel's senior man in the area."

"What happens if he isn't?"

"Then we lose."

"Just like that?"

"Just like that," Don said. "We can't go to Customs. It's too dangerous for Martin. They might have a leak somewhere and that would be the end of it."

"Isn't forty people a little weak to cover the Miami-Everglades area?"

Don put his binoculars down and looked at Lisa. "Weak is the understatement of the age, but every battle has its weaknesses. You can't be strong everywhere, you have to choose where your strong points will be and hope the enemy doesn't find your weak ones."

Lisa let out a chuckle. "You really do make it sound like a war."

Don looked at her. "It is a war."

"I know the facts and statistics, Don. I've been with the DEA for some time now, you know?"

"I'm sorry."

They fell into silence.

At four in the afternoon Lisa had to turn the air-conditioner off in the Ford Escort, because it was using up too much fuel. They were down to half a tank, and who knew where the trail might lead, so they opened the windows and let in the hot and humid Florida air and they began to sweat.

When the sun set and the temperature began to fall, Lisa and Don stopped sweating, but they felt sticky against their clothes and the smell of dried sweat permeated the air. They had spent fourteen hours in the car and the close, cramped quarters did nothing to alleviate their discomfort.

Don's pelvic bone was aching from sitting on it and Lisa began to tremble as if she were cold and a glaziness seem to come over her eyes. They were hungry and thirsty, but they dared not move.

At ten minutes of eleven, Don began to get nervous. Lucio had not left the house and, for a while, they pondered the idea of a rear exit, when the front door of the house opened and Lucio came out. This time seven men were following him.

"We're on!" Don said as Lisa started the engine.

The pickup trucks drove away and Lisa and Don fell in close behind them.

Lucio drove down to the Tamiani Canal and then turned right and sped towards the Everglades National Park.

Twenty-five miles west, alongside the Tamiani Trail, Lucio pulled off onto a deserted, unpaved road and made tracks towards Big Cypress National Preserve. Then, fifteen miles before Big Cypress, he turned into yet another dirt road.

It was at that moment that Don picked up the radio. "This is Papa Bear. Over."

"Go ahead, Papa Bear, over," a voice over the radio set replied.

"Goldilocks has pulled off the broken road to Big Cypress. Inform back-up they have to drive with the lights off or they'll be spotted. Over."

"What is your present location? Over."

"Don't know. We'll mark the turn-off with a white sweatshirt. Over."

"Roger. Out."

It was a seven mile trek and Don and Lisa now understood the reason for the pickup trucks. The road had deteriorated to such a condition their Ford Escort was almost unequal to the task. Fortunately, they saw the brake lights of the trucks come on and Lisa stopped.

"I'm getting out," Don said. "I'll take the camera and hitch a ride with the other group. I want you to wait by the Tamiani Trail and pickup Lucio's tail once he passes you. Follow him wherever he goes and call in your position. Okay?"

"What about the scanner?" Lisa asked him. "Do you want it?"

"No, it would make too much noise out here."

"What if I hear Customs bringing Martin down?"

"Then come and get me."

Forty minutes later, Don Harkin watched Martin land. He witnessed Lucio's crew unload the plane as he photographed it with infra-red film. The trigger clicked-furiously, but he was not concerned, because the click from the camera was indistinguishable from the creaking cicadas. Then he focused on Martin and watched him get into a pickup truck and drive away.

Don reached for his radio. "This is Papa Bear calling Mama Bear. Over."

"Go ahead Papa Bear. Over."

"Pickup coming your way. Follow, but do not intercept. Repeat. Do not intercept. Over."

"That's a copy."

It took Lucio and his men twenty-two minutes to refuel the plane, unload the five hundred kilos of cocaine and watch the aircraft take-off. It would take Lucio another hour to make it back to CHUCHO'S TRUCK REPAIR in Hialeah. However, it would be Alfred Stevens' decision to postpone the bust until they had met with Martin Black, which proved to be a big mistake.


Martin checked into the Miami Hilton. He felt the tension of the flight drain out of him and exhaustion suffuse him. He did not ask for the best suite, but, instead, he chose a double room and asked for an eight o'clock wake-up call.

Once he entered the room he threw his briefcase on the bed and picked up the telephone. He dialed Alfred in Washington and got him on the first ring.

"Working late, Alfred?" Martin asked as he lay down on his bed.

"Martin! Welcome back," Alfred said happily. "Don has tracked the coke to some town called Hialeah. You know it?"

"I do."

"How much did you bring in?"

"Five hundred kilos."

"Dear God! Where are you, anyhow?"

"The Miami Hilton. Don and Lisa must be very good at surveillance, because I didn't see them. How did they know where I would fly in?"

"Don had assumed that it would be Rafa who would supervise the unloading, but he changed his mind when he heard Whitney tell him Rafa was still with you. So, he asked himself who would be the next person to supervise the unloading."

"That's good thinking on his part."

"You talked with Ernesto, obviously. I'll be taking the first flight to Miami in the morning. I'll be there at ten o'clock, but can you give me an idea of how things are going?"

"Not good."

Silence

"He changed his mind?" Alfred's voice was quiet, strained.

Martin's voice wavered when he said, "Not exactly." He was tired and he yawned. "Lili thinks he's having a change of heart. I think she's right. Camacho has added some conditions to the deal."

Silence.

"I have to check in with Rafa at ten tomorrow and let him know where I am. He didn't say why, but I suppose the cartel is going to be tailing me. My suggestion is that you get Don or Dusty in here tonight."

"Don will speak with you tonight."

"All right, but get him in here fast. The longer I wait, the more suspicious it becomes, and the cartel is suspicious about everything."

"I'll give him a call right now. Hang tight...and Martin?"

"Uh-huh?"

"You've done a first-rate job; thank you."

"Good night, Alfred."

Don's face turned a shade rosier than usual in Martin's presence. He was embarrassed by the fact he had put an old friend into such a life and death situation.

"Hello, Martin," Don said as he entered the room. "You know Dusty. He'll be taping everything you say."

"It's good to see you again, Dusty," Martin said, shaking his hand warmly.

Dusty smiled and shyly set the tape-recorder down on the bureau. The recorder was the type most executives use to tape memo's or notes to themselves.

Don sat by the edge of a bed, while Martin rummaged through his coat and came up with Camacho's brown envelope.

"Alfred told me that Camacho has changed the rules," Don said.

"It's all in there," Martin said as he took the bed opposite Don. "I haven't read it, but Lili told me the basic outline."

Don tore open the envelope. He scanned it quickly, his eyebrows going up in certain places. Then he let out a soft whistle and said, "Impossible."

Martin shrugged. "I told her as much, but she said it was the way it was going to have to be."

"You think she's behind this letter?"

"Not at all. She thinks her brother is making a mistake."

Don glanced in my direction and then back at Martin. "So why does she ask for such a preposterous job?"

"What?"

"It says here, my sister is to be given a suitable job at a university commensurate with her talents in archaeology."

Martin snatched the letter away from Don and scanned it. His face seemed to collapse when he arrived at the passage in question. "She never mentioned it before. I don't know why she didn't tell me..."

Don leaned back against the bed's headrest and stared at the cheap print on the wall. His short, fat fingers stroked his chin as if he were pondering a philosophical matter. "Well, maybe she didn't know," he said at last, watching the relief spread across Martin's face.

"That's probably it."

Don smiled. Again he looked at the letter and stroked his chin with his fat fingers, knowing now something he did not want to believe. Martin Black had fallen in love. Don was the first to notice it. Dusty could see then what was coming from the moment Don had mentioned the word love.

"Could you trust Liliana?" Don asked Martin, setting him up.

"With my life!"

"Oh?"

"She's not cartel, Don. She's regular folk. You and me."

"She's a liability."

"What do you mean?"

"I mean that this operation is to dangerous to risk a DEA man. Camacho is now adding conditions, even though his son is dying a little more each day, not to mention that Liliana seems a little unbalanced."

"She's not unbalanced!"

"Oh? What makes you say that?"

"She's not! And leave it at that."

Don looked in Dusty's direction and signalled for him to turn off the tape-recorder. It was an old DEA ruse, because Dusty knew Don had another recorder going in his pocket. It was a psychological trick to get a person to open up by deceiving him that the conversation would take on an even higher state of confidentiality. Therefore, Dusty pretended to look puzzled and did what he was told.

"You slept with her," Don said, shaking his head. It was a statement. "You idiot!"

Martin said nothing.

Don paced the room and then stopped abruptly. His short, fat index finger pointing directly at Martin. "Are you in love with her?"

"Oh, come on, Don!"

"Un-fucking-believable!"

"Fuck you," Martin said in anger, spittle flying from his mouth. "Fuck all of you! I'm going back with or without your permission. I'm getting her out."

"And where will you go? Huh? Where in this tiny little fucking world will you go? Because they'll look for you and they'll find you."

"I'll find a place."

Don laughed. "You're right, but we own that place and from where I stand you don't have a snowball's chance in hell of buying into it. You know why? Because you're no longer in the game. What do you think Alfred will say? You think he'll just let Camacho waltz all over us with these demands? Of course not! He'll blackmail Camacho and his family, which is what we should have done in the first place! If Camacho gets burned, well, that's the price he'll pay for getting into the business."

Martin stood up and looked at Don. "I'll be on Windraider tomorrow. You can reach me there with Alfred's answer. Right now I'm tired and I'd like to get some sleep. Good-night, Don."

Don let go of his anger immediately. He had handled the situation badly. "Let's just think this through, Martin, I..."

"Get out!" Martin commanded.

Don looked at Martin. He had pushed too hard. He had blown it, even though he knew he was right. If Martin were a man of divided loyalties it would make him unpredictable and the DEA could not afford to have an unpredictable man in an operation.

"I'm sorry, Martin," Don said, picking up the tape-recorder and the notes. "You've done us a great thing and...I'm sorry. Let's go, Dusty."

Later that night Martin called Rafa. The DEA had tapped into Martin's hotel line and heard the conversation. The connection was awful and Martin had had to shout into the mouthpiece to be heard, but he told Rafa about going to Key West and would call him in the morning.

Rafa jotted down the telephone number in Key West where he could reach Martin and then asked him if it was a hotel. He didn't sound surprised when Martin told him it was the number to his boat. "What's your boat's name?" Rafa asked.

"Windraider," Martin replied and then asked, "where is Lili tonight?"

"Bogotá," came the faint reply. "The connection is a bad one, Martin. I will talk with you tomorrow. Buenas Noches."

Martin said good-night and spent the rest of the night wondering if he should call Lili, but he didn't. Instead, he suffered a nightmare because the DEA men listening in on his every move reported that he had tossed all night long.

Dusty would later think often of that late night meeting with Martin, not because of what Don said, but rather because it was the last time any of them would ever speak to Martin again.

# CHAPTER 21

The Santander Case began to unravel in earnest the moment Camacho's plan came to light. It was faxed to Alfred, and once he read it he passed it around to his subordinates. It was tenth hand news by the time Dusty got to read it, because Don hadn't let me read it in the hotel room. Camacho's plan was a good plan, Dusty thought, despite the stupid conditions he had added, but then again no one had bothered to ask him.

Dusty sat in Alfred's office in Washington early the next morning after having taken the red-eye from Florida. He explained what Martin had looked like, sounded like and acted like during the previous night's meeting. Alfred, however, didn't take his views too deeply. He sent the Camacho plan to the battery of psychiatrists, sociologists and 'crystal gazers' that he holed up in the darkest rooms of HQ. He seldom asked for their advice because he seldom took it, but this time he did not heed his own instincts and took their words as if they were coming from God.

Some of the expert opinion had determined that Mr. Camacho was under duress when he wrote the plan and, therefore, it was a trap, while other experts proclaimed the plan wildly imaginative and the product of a man teetering on the edge of sanity. In the end, there was only a small minority who believed Mr. Camacho's plan.

It was only after being unable to reach a consensus on Martin Black's loyalty that Alfred called in for outside help. It was there, perhaps, where Alfred steered way off course and, as in the Titanic's case, he did not realize he was sinking until it was already too late. "We need a fresh perspective," he had intoned with that know-it-all broadcaster's voice. "Dusty, you and I will go see the Chief of Staff."

The Santander Operation, which was really the Ernesto Camacho Operation, was one week old and already had the weight and feel of a case several years in the making. Alfred acquainted himself with every aspect of the case on their way to the White House -- which was to say that he skimmed the file -- from the people involved, to the logistics which made it what it was today.

He skimmed rapidly over the three hundred or so pages that contained detailed warnings by Don and Dusty, the facts and suppositions and the minute-by-minute history of the Santander Case which made it the dinosaur of all cases. In the file he had read Martin Black's background and knew him to be the type of man who would go to hell and back on command, and yet he must have believed Don when he had said that Martin was a man of divided loyalties. So, why Alfred needed to stop by the White House and ask for a new perspective was beyond Dusty. What he should have done was close down the case.

There was a photograph of Martin in the file. It was his high school graduation picture. There was a newspaper photograph of him as he emerged from the deserts of Iraq. Another photograph had him in front of the President being awarded the Medal of Honor. The most recent photograph had him emerging from Windraider; the one Lisa had taken before they had signed Martin on. The change, Alfred realized, was Iraq. His eyes were harder, colder and full of disappointment, as if to declare it wasn't worth it. He knew Martin was a hard nosed bastard if push came to shove, and yet he had fallen in love with a girl sixteen years younger than he. Alfred wondered if Don was right in his assessment that Martin had fallen for the pretty little face of Liliana Santander.

Alfred knew that if he flushed the case down he would lose the best evidence against the Cartel anyone had ever come across. If he continued and he lost, life would still go on. No self respecting bureaucrat -- in the political power game of Washington -- ever lost his job to the cartel. The bureaucrats never got blamed for the losses, and the death of one agent would hardly make a ripple in the on-going war against drugs. But, if he blackmailed Camacho, he would end up with some returns.

He peered out of the limousine's darkened window and began to weigh his options, again.

Alfred was a man who always had expected that his big break would come through hard work and interdiction, and not through a turncoat. He had imagined receiving accolades for making the big case, but never had he imagined having the big case with the possibility of it coming undone and receiving some minor negative publicity.

No damn way was he going to let go of this chance! He was going to try to make it work!

Alfred intended to tell the Chief of Staff that the operation was still a 'go,' and he was also going to try to get some support from him. In that respect Alfred was politically astute, because he wasn't going to hang out in the wind alone if he could have someone else with him. He knew that his ace in the hole, if things went sour, was the five hundred kilos of cocaine he had under constant surveillance in Florida. Those kilos could be used to make good copy in the morning papers and he knew the President would fall for it. It would also be good for 'damage limitation' if things went wrong, and it would probably also save his ass.

Alfred and Dusty listened to the assistant to the Chief of Staff. They sat in a White House basement office. If Alfred was disappointed in not seeing the Chief of Staff he had not shown it. Instead, he had acted as if he had intended to see the assistant all along.

"Let me summarize your case," the assistant said. "Martin Black has fallen in love with Liliana Santander, unconfirmed, but it might or might not compromise the operation. At any rate, the operation is running okay, except for the conditions Camacho has added to the deal. Customs, FBI and Coast Guard are uninformed of the operation, because to do so would endanger the OP itself, and Martin Black is still willing to go ahead if we give the okay. Is that it?"

"That's it, except that we still have the five hundred kilos under surveillance," Alfred replied.

The assistant frowned. "What do you think, Dusty?"

"I don't know, really. This romance might make Martin unpredictable, but, maybe not." When Dusty finished speaking he looked at Alfred, who gave him a look of pure hate.

The assistant nodded. "The Chief of Staff and I met with the Director of the CIA a half hour ago, Alfred. He asked me to speak with you. The CIA has an ongoing operation in Bogotá and that's all you need to know. However, they've come across something curious and they would like to know if... Here, I'll just let you listen to it and make up your own mind."

The assistant retrieved a small tape-recorder and pressed the play button.

"...Did you get my gift?" he asked. "Anything for you, my love...........................I'm working on it, but, work and all... I'll see what I can do. I know that I'm overdue for a vacation. How was your day?........................Same here, but the days are boring when I'm not with you...............................
.......I know. You'll be getting a package from me tomorrow.............. ...........................it's not that. It's something else. It's on Martin Black. You might be able to help me with it. If you do, I'll be able to get that vacation that much sooner............................ .........I promise......................I know. Good-night, sweet dreams."

"Who is he?" Alfred asked.

"The Colombian Captain at DAS," the assistant replied. "The voices are computer generated. It was the best they could do."

"Who is he talking to?" Dusty asked.

"We don't know, but the director says the man is a homosexual. It probably made him an easy target for the cartel to blackmail. Colombia isn't quite as liberal as America. At any rate, Langley believes it to be a man."

Alfred looked puzzled for a moment. "I'm sorry, but I fail to see the relevance."

"The call was made from your bureau." Alfred's face paled.

Dusty wondered what his face looked like, but he knew his mind was spinning and thinking who the traitor might be.

The assistant let the fact sit in and then asked, "How long can you sit on the five-hundred kilos?"

"A day or two, at most."

"The Chief of Staff wants you and Dusty to undergo a polygraph test," the assistant said and then paused when he saw Alfred wince. "It's that or I have to call in Customs and the FBI to investigate. I know it's neither of you, but there's a lot at stake."

Dusty was shocked. "Are you saying that the operation is still on? Didn't you just hear that the operation is compromised?"

"That tape doesn't say anything like that!" the assistant replied angrily.

"I understand," Alfred said placatingly. "We'll do as you ask."

"We have to do something, Alfred. We have to get off the fence with this drug war. The President wants the operation to proceed."

"I'd like to hear that from him," Alfred said quietly, with a note of resignation about him.

"Of course. I'll have him confirm it by memo. Good luck."

Alfred thought fleetingly for a moment that he was being railroaded, but he quickly convinced himself otherwise. Who could tell what machinations were being cooked up at the White House, Alfred would tell the Sub-committee later on, because even he couldn't even keep-up with the ones at DEAHQ! The only real truth that would emerge from that meeting, would be the dead certainty that Martin Black was on his own.

# CHAPTER 22

---

WARNING
United States Government Seizure
> This property has been seized for nonpayment of internal revenue taxes due from Martin Black by virtue of levy issued by the District Director of Internal Revenue.
>
> Persons tampering with this property, in any manner, will be prosecuted to the full extent of the law.

---

It was betrayal.

Martin read the sticker which someone had stuck in the most obvious places on Windraider. He climbed aboard with a rage he had not known since his military days in the Gulf. He first walked along the topsides and made sure everything was secure and battened down. He didn't want her slipping out of dock and smashing against something else and reducing her all to rubble. However, when he entered the cockpit, he felt violated.

The inside of the sloop had been broken all to pieces. The navigation table, or what was left of it, held nothing but the shattered remains of the Decca, SatNav and radar. Thousands of dollars of equipment had been smashed to bits and pieces, which had taken a lifetime to save for, but which now lay like shattered wine glasses on the cockpit's deck, and the aft master cabin's expensive teak walls had been destroyed as if with a battle axe. His clothes also had been taken out of their holds and torn to shreds. Nothing was spared. It was all gone.

Martin didn't need to see the rest; he had seen enough, but he went topside and, for a moment, he considered slipping her from her moorings and taking her out to sea, where he could scuttle and send her to the bottom. It would have prevented the bastards from laying their hands on her ever again, but if he scuttled her, he would be in violation of American tax law and the IRS was like the Nazi party when it came to exacting retribution. They had torn out Martin Black's soul.

Somehow there had been a leak and the IRS had caught wind of it. Whether the leak had emanated from DEA or the cartel was unknown and, perhaps, would forever be unknown.

Martin got off his boat and began walking up the long winding dock of the marina when he caught the sight of two men walking towards him. Instinctively, he knew that they were coming for him.

Bureaucrats. Two men in gray suits who enforced the tax laws of the United States. Perhaps, the men who had violated and disemboweled his sailboat. One of the men was tall and stooped, as if he had grown up with the complex of being too tall. The other was short, heavy and balding. They were men who sat behind computer video screens and carried out law enforcement by pressing buttons. There was no escape from them, because the IRS was single-minded in its purpose.

"Martin Black?" the small man said as they met on the floating dock.

Martin eyed the two men carefully and said, "Who wants to know?"

The tall man reached into his suit coat and retrieved a badge. "IRS. This is Special Agent Potter of the Internal Revenue Criminal Investigation Division and I'm Special Agent Delmo of the Justice Department. Okay? Now, are you or are you not Martin Black?"

"I'm Martin Black. Are you the assholes who wrecked my boat?"

"Mister Black, according to our records in 1976 you bought a single family dwelling in Georgetown, Washington D.C., for $107,000. Is that right?"

"Yes, but I sold it in 1986," Martin said nervously, uncomfortable with someone looking into his past.

"The sale price of said house amounted to $457,000. Is that right."

"Yeah, I made a killing in real estate, so what?"

Special Agent Potter ignored Martin's tone. "Therefore, according to our calculations you made a gross gain of $350,000?"

"Do we have to talk about it here?"

"Yes, we do."

"Christ, you guys are worse than the gestapo."

Special Agent Delmo bristled, but he kept his cool. On the other hand, Special Agent Potter went on ahead as if Martin were mute, because he said, "Your capital gain from the sale of said residence was $350,000..."

"It wasn't a gain!" Martin interrupted, knowing now where the conversation was leading. "I bought that boat right over therewith the goddamm money! So, I rolled over the gain as I am allowed to do according to the Tax Code. I'm sure two smart guys like you know the exact section, sub-section and what not."

"Section 1706. 'Postponement of Gain for All Taxpayers.' However, the section refers you back to Section 1034, which states: '...the gain from a sale of principal residence can be postponed (or "rolled over") if a new principal residence is bought or built within the period beginning two years before and ending two years after the sale of the old residence. The new residence must also be used by the taxpayer as a principal residence within this period.' This Section also applies to houseboats, such as yours."

Martin said nothing.

"According to our records Mister Black you sold the Georgetown dwelling in March of 1986 and bought the boat in September of 1988. The 'roll over' period already had expired. You broke the law. Normally, Mister Black, we'd ask you to pay a small fine since the oversight involves a period of six months. However, in the subsequent years you never claimed the gain from the sale as income earned, which leads us to believe that you willfully failed to make a return, keep records, supply the required information, or pay any tax or estimated tax. Fraud, Mister Black. Therefore, we're bringing criminal charges to bear under the Criminal Penalties Section 2895 of the United States Tax Code. Special Agent Delmo..."

Special Agent Delmo retrieved a pair of handcuffs and said, "You are under arrest for violating the United States Tax Code. You have the right to remain silent..."

Martin heard the men read him his rights, as if he were in a dream. The voice of Special Agent Delmo seemed to Martin to be coming from a long way away. He felt the cold metal of the handcuffs snap tightly around his wrists as they pushed him forward up the dock. Was this planned, Martin asked himself? Had Alfred put this into operation as a cover? No. It was too real. He was really being arrested.

There was no other explanation for it, he decided; the IRS had made an error. Computer error, glitch, snafu, whatever it was, it had to be the IRS' fault. Their bureaucratic machine had spit out another cyclopean botchery, for which they would never apologize. Madness.

Martin was taken to the Broward County Jail. It was a cold concrete structure painted in governmental gray that distinguished it from all other buildings in the area. The sheriff booked him and then had him arraigned for bail purposes. The judge heard the charges and ordered bail set at a quarter of a million dollars. He was then taken back to lock-up, asked to empty out his pockets and discard his jewelry into a small carton, which would be returned to him when he left, and finally he was asked to remove the belt around his waist.

"What for?" Martin asked.

"Rules," said the sheriff. "A lot of people use their belt to hang themselves, but some just dive nose first into the concrete floor. No one has done it since we put the cameras in the hallways, but it pays to be safe."

Martin removed his belt. Then he removed his watch and the two-thousand dollars he had in his pocket, causing the sheriff to raise an eyebrow.

"You always carry this much, Mister Black?"

Martin grimaced. "I just came back from the jai-lai game."

The sheriff chuckled and put an old black telephone on the counter. "You have one phone call. Please, don't be stupid. Call your attorney."

Martin stared at the telephone. Who should he call, Alfred or Rafa? If he called Alfred, this mess would be cleared up quickly, but the operation would be over, Camacho would be over, Rafa would be over and most of all, he would never see Lili again.

"We don't have all day, Mister Black."

Martin lifted the receiver and dialed the long distance number.

The mountains that surround Medellín are part of the Andes Cordillera, and in some instances the summits can almost reach ten-thousand feet. Compared to the Sierra Nevada of Santa Marta, they were small, but they were no less wondrous. Rafa had neither thought nor feeling about these mountains as he sat by his pool, because his mind was thinking about when to move the next cocaine load to the States. He would let Martin fly that one, too, although this time he would use the Mexican route and fly it into the border states. It was the safest route for everyone involved and especially for the pilots, because it afforded them a limitless border they could penetrate at will. Unfortunately, he would have to pay Pacha for the use of the landing strip in Mexico and that would mean at least two million right off the top. The thought irked him and, for a moment, he considered flying it out of Nicaragua or Panama, but that was riskier with all the American military activity going on in the area.

Suddenly the telephone beside him rang. He reached over and picked it up without looking.

"¿Diga?" Rafa said.

"It's Martin. Listen and listen well. I've been arrested by the IRS for tax evasion. I'm at the Broward County jail. Bail has been set at two hundred thousand. Rafa, get me out of here."

Rafa sat up straight. His mind took in everything at once. He was already thinking ahead of Martin. It had happened before and speed was of the essence.

"Hang tight and keep your mouth shut. I'll have you out of there by six o'clock." Rafa hung up. He called El Patrón and told him there might be trouble. Soon after, he hung up, then called Lucio on the beeper and hung up. Then he dialed Liliana Santander at her work.

"¿Aló?" Lili said.

"Buenas, Lili. It's Rafa. I have a problem and I need your help."

Silence. Then she gave a tentative, "Yes?"

"Martin Black was arrested in Florida this morning. I want you to go to Miami and post bail for him. I'll have someone meet you at the airport and explain how to do it. There is a flight leaving in forty minutes from El Dorado Airport. Okay?"

Lili could not believe it. It had to be a trap. "Martin? Arrested? In America?"

"Yes! Will you go?"

Impossible! she thought. How could his own people arrest him? El Patrón would suspect him, no matter what Martin did now, unless he truly was under arrest. But that could not be; it simply could not be!

"I'll go, but why was he arrested?"

"Something about taxes. There is no time to waist. I'll have the ticket waiting for you at the counter. I owe you one, Lili. Good luck."

"Wait! What do I do when I get him out?"

"When you arrive in Miami you will be given all the directions by my people, okay?"

"Okay. Good-bye."

No sooner had Rafa hung up when the telephone rang again.

"¿Diga?" Rafa said.

"¡A sus órdenes, Don Rafa!" At your command, said Lucio.

"Lucio, the house might be under surveillance. I want you to move the weight immediately. Do not take it out the front door. You know what to do. Remember the plan, okay?"

"Of course, Don Rafa. I'll get right on it."

"Good man. Call me when you've moved the weight."

Rafa hung up and breathed in deeply. He was not out of the woods yet. He was still responsible for the fifty million dollars stashed in the house. Until the coke had changed possession, it would be his responsibility. If the DEA seized the coke, he would have to pay. He would be killed.

There was no anger in Rafa. He had expected something like this for a long time. El Patrón had told him to expect it like that. The big things always could be taken care of, because they could be foreseen. It was the little things that mattered because they were unexpected and always took one by surprise.

Suddenly Rafa looked up at the sky, realizing at once that he might not see another day. If the coke were seized and Martin was taken for good, and Lili were to be arrested, he would pay. He would not see the sun rise and feel the cool Medellín breeze gently caress his face again.

Now all Rafa remembered were El Patrón's words echoing in his ears. We don't get to lose often, at least not in America, but especially not here in Medellín. But it happens.

Was this the test El Patrón had mentioned in Bogotá? Rafa wondered. How would it come? Would he be asleep in his bed? Would the woman he was sleeping with suddenly stab him? Would he become a muerte de prueba for some sicario-to-be? ¡Madre de Dios! But it had been a good time while it lasted! It sure beat planting coffee for forty centavos a day. Now, whether he lived or died, his family would never know another poor day in their lives and that was worth the price of his life. You don't lose all of them, but sometimes you do. Things happen.

# CHAPTER 23

It was incomprehensible to Don Harkin. His head whirled as if he had blundered into a whirlpool of contradicting thoughts, or, as if he were slowly emerging from one nightmare into another, except this wasn't a nightmare; it was real and someone had turned the reality into a nightmare.

Don put the hand over the sticker the IRS had stuck on Windraider, as if that would reveal the secret to the whole story. Then he heard a noise below in the aft cabin and he felt elated. No, elated was the wrong word, he thought: elated meant joyful and that word didn't fit the situation, because what he felt was anger and despair. If the sticker were a joke it certainly wasn't an amusing one, but if...

Another thought came to him. What went wrong? How could the IRS have picked Martin to be a target and why? Why hadn't the DEA computers picked up on the IRS trace? He began to think his idea through, but the noise from below came again. It was a tinny noise, so he unholstered his pistol and stepped down into Windraider's lower decks.

Suddenly a cat ran passed him and up the steps until it disappeared, scaring him enough to make him jump out of the way.

Then he recognized the handiwork of recklessness. He thought he could feel Martin's rage fill the cabin, expand like hot air in a balloon. Dear God, what had happened?

He ran up the steps as fast as his bulk would allow him and disembarked. He waved at Lisa, motioning her to pull up the car by the side of the dock.

Lisa saw something was wrong the moment she saw Don running. She had never seen Don run in her life and the sight unsettled her. She started the car and moved it forward to meet him as he stepped off the dock.

Don opened the door and got in. He was hyperventilating.

"What's wrong?" she asked.

"Just get me to a telephone. Fast!"

Lisa slammed the car into gear and drove to the nearest restaurant, where Don got out and, beyond belief, was running again! She followed him into the restaurant and watched him ask the manager for the use of a telephone.

The manager was about to ask what for when Don showed him his badge. The manager immediately pointed towards his office. Don nodded and hurriedly walked down the hallway.

Finally, Don was able to call Alfred to tell him that his Titanic had metaphorically struck an iceberg and was beginning to sink.

"What happened down there, Don?" Lisa asked timidly. "Is Martin dead?"

Don didn't hear her, because Alfred came on the line at that moment. "It's me. Martin Black's yacht was seized by the IRS and it looks like they told the local boys to have a go with it. They smashed the boat to bits. Yes, I'm sure. They put stickers on her so that a blind man could feel the braille. What do we do? No, no, no! Bust the coke now! We can always find out why the IRS went after Martin and where the hell they took him. Our first priority is to let Martin know its just a big fuck-up... Of course, I'm fucking upset! This is going to mean lives if we don't get to the bottom of it and fast!... I'm on my way to Lauderhill, right now!"

Don hung up and nodded for Lisa to follow. He opened the door and walked out of the office, with a wave thanking the manager, who was only too happy to see them go. The DEA was bad for business; it wasn't the image the restaurant was seeking in this drug-crazed State.

Lisa said nothing. She felt as if the wind had been kicked out of her and, consequently, turned two shades of lighter gray. She was scared and didn't know why. She wanted to stop feeling scared, defeat it, but the fear wormed its way into the pit of her stomach and began to grow. She couldn't say exactly what scared her, but, deep down, on an instinctive level she could sense something dark and grotesque.

When Don and Lisa arrived at CHUCHO'S TRUCK REPAIR in the early evening, the place was mobbed with DEA agents wearing dark blue coats. From a hundred feet away a man could read the DEA logo on the backs of the blue coats. Don forgot why it was necessary, but he was sure they were there for some reason other than vanity. He parked the car beside a Metro-Dade squad car and walked into CHUCHO'S. He and Lisa were asked to show I.D's, until they heard Alfred's assistant's voice say, "It's okay. Let them through."

Alfred's assistant was a small, thin man, with balding hair, and took to wearing bow-ties. His real name was Anni Chipoor, a name which he hated, so he called himself A.C., but everyone called him Chip. When he spotted Don and Lisa he lifted his hand to his lips and nodded for them to follow him into an office. It was a typical garage-like office with glass walls where a supervisor could observe the work-in-progress from his desk. Calendars with photographs of bikini clad women holding car parts dotted the walls. The smell of grease and oil permeated the air along with a recent smell of cigarette smoke.

"On time?" Don asked without preamble, but he could read the answer to his question on Chip's face.

Chip shook his head. "Gone. All of it."

"How?" Lisa asked. "We had it on round-the-clock surveillance."

"Tunnel. The dogs sniffed it out. It's over there behind the far wall, beside the pickup truck. It leads to the apartment building next door. The experts say they hauled it out in three cars, subcompact ones. Don't ask me how they knew, but they did. It really doesn't matter."

"And Martin?"

"He's gone, too. Vanished. No longer among those present." Alfred's assistant paused, and then lowered his face. "We screwed him over good on this one."

"Where was he?"

"The Broward County Jail. A woman by the name of Allison Gorman posted a quarter million dollars in bail and walked out with him. The curious thing is that Allison sounds a lot like Liliana Santander, by the way the officers on duty described her."

"Has Martin called?"

Chip sat down on what had been the supervisor's chair, despite the grime on it. "No, he hasn't called."

"How, sir?" Lisa asked. "How did it happen?"

"They used little carts to move it faster..."

"No, that's not what I mean. How did the IRS target Martin."

Chip lifted his hands in disgust. "It," he began to say, but then became quiet. It was as if he didn't know where to begin and didn't care anymore. The man seemed unequal to the task. Events had spiraled out of his control.

"It, sir?" Lisa prompted.

"Who knows. The truth is we might never know. The cartel might have persuaded some IRS agents to dig up some dirt and...it doesn't matter. There's not much we can do, 'cause if we ask the IRS why they're going after Martin, word'll get back to the cartel that Martin's with us. Think about it; the idea of the IRS going after Martin Black out of all the possible tax cheats in the country is ludicrous. The seizure, Alfred's determined through highly reliable sources, was legitimate. It seems Martin made some sort of snafu with his taxes in 1989. It's all above board, the spectre of the seizure appears to be within the law, etc., etc...Christ! who are we kidding? The IRS was-fucking-tipped-off! Maybe it was one of us, or, maybe it was the cartel itself. We'd be wasting time trying to figure it out."

"So we let him run alone?"

"We've got no choice." Chip shook his head in abject resignation. "We've lost, Martin."

"You think he's dead?" Lisa asked nervously.

"That or he's gone over."

"You mean crossed over and become a drug runner for real? Impossible!"

"It happens."

# CHAPTER 24

At the beginning, in the first hours of his incarceration, Martin's first vivid impression was the stench. The smell of urine and dried sweat intoxicated the air.

Now, in his seventh hour, he hardly noticed it. And then he wondered if he were simply becoming careless by not keeping alert, because, sooner or later, the attack would come. It would have to come. Imprisoned people didn't take kindly to being locked up with a former law enforcement officer, despite the fact he had never made a single arrest in his life.

Martin was surprised by how some of his cellmates slept so soundlessly when the jail itself was so noisy. The slamming of steel bars shutting on some prisoner and said prisoner cussing loudly, because his imprisonment was without question, 'unfair.' Every cellmate, Martin had come to learn, was innocent, and he was no exception.

He watched the minute hand sweep up towards six in the afternoon and he began to wonder if he had not made an error in judgment by calling Rafa. Maybe he should have called Alfred, he told himself, but then the operation would have been blown and Lili would be dead.

"What you in for?" a prisoner asked Martin. He was the biker sort; the kind with long scraggly beards and tattoos imprinted on every available square inch of fair skin.

"You talking to me?" Martin asked, looking around him to see if the man had made a mistake.

"Yeah."

"Armed robbery," Martin replied.

The biker man seemed to shake his head. "Did you get rid of the piece?"

"Huh?"

"The piece? The weapon? Did you get rid of it before they arrested you."

Martin had no idea what that had to do with anything. "Yeah."

"That's good," the man said. "The piece adds five years onto your sentence automatically, but you're still looking at twenty -- hard..." Then, "Jeeeesus!" the man added, interrupting himself.

Martin turned around to see what he was looking at.

Lili stood in front of the steel bars while the officer pressed the automatic control that would open the cage. She walked down the corridor with the officer and stared at Martin, while all the prisoners began to hoot and yelp like a bunch of wild coyotes.

She's beautiful! Martin thought as he looked into her eyes and saw the desperation in them. It sobered him up quickly. He understood at once that she was risking her life and this was not what she had intended at all. He, after all, was supposed to be the one bailing her out.

"Is that him, miss?" The prison guard asked Lili.

Lili nodded.

"Number seven!" the officer shouted and Martin's cell opened. "You!" The officer pointed at Martin. "Let's go. Your bail's been posted."

Martin walked out of the Broward County Jail with Lili holding onto his arm. He could feel her trembling as they walked towards the rented Chrysler. He didn't know what to say, so he remained quiet.

Then Lili stopped in mid-stride halfway to the car. She moved her arm away from his and stepped back. "Martin, what are you trying to do?" Then she grabbed him by the arms. "Tell me! This is my life and my family's lives you're fooling around with, goddamn you!"

Martin lowered his head and, in shame, said, "I'm sorry, but I don't know what's going on."

Lili looked at him, her eyes narrowing in disbelief, but she remained silent and angry. She didn't believe him; how could she? The people she had asked for help had arrested their own man, thrown him into prison and now the cartel was bailing him out? How could the American authorities not know about it? Didn't they talk to each other?

"I swear," Martin said, feeling the unspoken charge, "I don't know what's going on."

"We have to go. There's some sort of boat waiting to take us to some island. The man who gave me the money for your bail gave me some directions. He said you would know how to get there."

"Where are they?"

"In the car," Lili said and handed him the car keys.

The directions were straight-forward. He was to be at pier thirty-six in the Miami Marina and look for a cigarette boat with the name of Death Child painted on her stern. Martin put the car in gear and drove away from the Broward County Jail.

Death Child was a white, V-bottomed, twin 500-horsepower cigarette which easily could cut across a smooth ocean surface at over ninety-miles per hour and with some change left over for extra measure. It was an eye-catching boat that literally said speed.

Lili and Martin climbed aboard Death Child and became alarmed, because her bow seemed to be pointing skyward as if she were a missile or worse; she was taking on water at the stern. The boat's pilot, however, saw their alarm and laughed. "First time on a cigarette?" he asked them.

Lili and Martin nodded.

"When its dead in the water she looks like she's sinking, but she isn't. The engines pull the stern down, so the bow comes up like a pointy missile. She'll level off once we get her over open water, though." The pilot then let out another laugh. "If you're scared now, just wait 'till you hear her start up; she'll sound like she's ready to fall apart."

The pilot was unlike any seaman Martin had ever known. His hands were delicate, unlike a sailor whose brittle hands had to bring in a sail during a full gale. The man's face was smooth as a baby's instead of the worn leather looks most seaman develop after spending time under a glaring sun, or a wild and wet day in the Atlantic. This pilot was the new breed of seaman, the kind Martin detested, the electronic kind, the type who couldn't find their way out of their cabins in a fog bank.

"Why don't you go below and settle in. There's some coffee in a thermos and some life jackets."

"Life jackets?"

The pilot turned from the wheel and said, "It's my boat. Do it my way or its the highway. If I get stopped by a Coast Guard vessel I don't want them impounding my boat for not wearing a life vest. Of course, that's if they can catch me," he added with a gigantic laugh.

Lili and Martin looked at each other and went below, wondering what insanity awaited them in the open sea. Down below they found the thermos and Styrofoam cups. They poured each other a cup and looked around the cabin. It was rather small. It had an FM radio and a bed. There were also some well-thumbed paperbacks on the floor, but the place reeked of alcohol.

Martin raised his cup of coffee in toast and then drank it. "That hits the spot," he declared.

Lili, on the other hand, took a sip and said nothing. She had seen Martin's face cloud over with worry and then seen him force the worry out of his features, for her sake. She loved him, but she began to believe he was not letting her in on everything. It was just as well, because she knew, sooner or later, they would be found out -- she was sure of it.

"Come on up!" the pilot shouted from the top deck. Lili and Martin finished their coffees and did as the pilot told them. The pilot was behind the steering wheel that controlled the boat's rudder, his eyes scanning around the deck for any anomalies. Then he began turning switches and knobs and the instrument panel lit up, casting a greenish glow on his face. Then he turned to look at them and said, "Sit in those chairs and strap yourselves in. If you feel the need to get up, ask me first and I'll let you know if you can."

"Why?" Lili asked.

"The wind's a monster at the speed we'll be sailing. If we hit a wave you'll be in the water. And even if your mate sees you fly off, it'll take me some time to turn this baby around."

The pilot turned to a crewman who Martin and Lili hadn't seen before.. "You! Untie her and push us off from her mooring. Use that pole beside you if you have to."

The crewman unclipped the pole and moved towards the bow, then untied the ropes holding Death Child to the pier. Martin was amazed by the fact the crewman's added weight hadn't lowered the bow by more than an inch. Finally, when the crewman hauled the ropes aboard and stowed them away, he pushed the boat away from the pier.

Death Child slipped away easily from her mooring.

The pilot looked at his gauges and then made sure Lili and Martin were strapped in. "We'll be using only one engine to get us out of the marina, but even then it should tell you something about its power, all right?"

Lili and Martin nodded.

"Where are we going?" Martin asked.

"Bimini. There you'll transfer to a plane and head straight for Medellín."

The pilot turned the key in the ignition and the engine came to life with an explosive roar, causing the water behind the stern to bubble as if it were boiling. The boat vibrated for a moment and then settled, but the sound remained deafening. The pilot turned on her running lights, moved the throttle forward and Death Child eased into the channel. Then, with his left hand, he moved the throttle into neutral and then slightly forward as he kept his right hand on the wheel. Death Child began to move and the pilot became busy twisting knobs and gauges as he kept a steady lookout for other craft in the area.

Finally Death Child cleared the channel and the last of the safety buoys, then the pilot engaged the second engine and again the cigarette shook for a moment, then settled.

Martin watched the pilot move the throttle forward and then felt the blades engage and cavitate. The stern sunk deeper for a moment and then shook slightly as the propellers grabbed and began to move the boat ahead. He watched the pilot hit the trim tabs and the cigarette shot forward as if out of a slingshot.

Suddenly, they had gone from a near-standing-still position to fifty miles an hour in a matter of seconds. Death Child was a bullet being rifled across the sea.

Martin looked up at the night sky and watched a full moon rising. Everywhere across the heavens he saw stars sparkle like diamonds on a black velvet cloth, the sea black and suspicious, and smooth like an obsidian surface. He turned to Lily who had become pale. He reached for her hand and squeezed it reassuringly, but he knew she was finished with pretending, with the games, and that now she only had room for the truth. And in that moment of insight he knew she was stronger than he was, because he didn't know how to face the problem; he only knew how to die for a cause, and the thought made him remember what a poet had written long ago.

*I have a rendezvous with Death*
*At some disputed barricade,*
*When spring comes back with rustling shade*
*And apple blossoms fill the air.*

# CHAPTER 25

The pain was extra-special. It was as if she were skinned alive and salt had been added to the wound. It wasn't fair, she thought, she had kept control of the habit. She had never asked for it in the first place. He had had no right to take it away!

Well, she would ignore the matter. He had not called her, perhaps because he had forgotten about the package. Maybe he was busy and was unable to call her. His job demanded that he fly all over Colombia and it wasn't easy for him to contact her all the time, but there would be hell to pay when she told him he had not sent her the gift. First, she would pretend it hadn't bothered her, but she would tell him that the slight was just another signpost on the road of his waning affection. Yes, she would tell him as much, but when he began to apologize for his lack of courtesy she would cave in immediately. That was, of course, if he had the stuff on him.

She sat by the telephone, waiting, imagining how she would lead the conversation -- taunting him and making him beg for forgiveness, but four days had passed and the pain was blistering. Why hadn't he called? Was he dead?

Suddenly she was overwhelmed by fear. What if he were dead? What if he had become one of the disappeared? Like so many of his colleagues. It could be weeks, months before they could confirm his whereabouts, alive or dead -- and then what would she do? How would she get her stuff? She needed her stuff! The pain! The pain! It was too much! She needed her coke.

Why hadn't he called? Was it because she had ignored his request? No, impossible! He had asked for worse in the past. Could he be angry for not having sent him what he wanted. Was it? No! She had sent him something, just last week. It was nothing major, nothing compromising, just something to titillate and whet the appetite.

The telephone rang and she answered it. She cursed herself mentally for being so eager, because he would know she had been waiting for his call. She steadied her voice, but the voice trembled badly under the shakes of withdrawal.

"Yes?" she said with a trembling sound in her voice.

"Hello, love," he said. "I'm sorry I haven't called you, but I was out of town and where they sent me they didn't have a telephone. Well, actually they did, but I could hardly be expected to make a call on such an insecure line, could I? No, of course not. It was one of those public telephones in a bar where everyone can hear you talking; of course, that's one of the reasons why they put them there." He laughed as if he had no cares in the world.

"I might have to go out of town for a few days, love," he continued gravely, as always, changing the subject spontaneously. "It's business. Anyway, that's why I called, so you wouldn't worry. I have to go now..."

"No!" she screamed.

"Shut up!" The DAS captain said. "You sound like a desperate woman. Why haven't you given me what I have asked for? Huh? I have never asked you for anything, and yet, I give you everything. Can't you once do what I ask?" The voice was cold, hard and held a threatening note to it.

She knew him now to be a man pressed by others, because she had figured out who his real bosses were, so why hadn't she figured it out before?

"Lisa," the DAS Captain continued, "if you want your gift in the next few minutes you better tell me everything on Martin Black."

"That's way past the deal we agreed on!"

"Fuck the deal! Get it or you're finished!"

She listened in disbelief. "Is that a threat?"

"Call it what you want, I don't care." The man paused, then he added, "If you don't send it, they'll wash you out with yesterday's laundry."

"Who are they? You, I suppose? Don't make me laugh," Lisa said with some bravado; she wasn't frightened.

She knew who would wash her out; perhaps she had known all along, but she definitely knew when the IRS had seized Martin's boat. She had suspected it before then, but she didn't want to believe it at the time. She had sunk so low that everything she thought and did and had done was now tainted with deceit and betrayal.

The man laughed and said, "Don't be silly, you know who!"

"No, I don't know."

"You have my number..."

Lisa began to cry silently, wondering how she had let it happen. She thought of running, packing up and leaving to Brazil, Bora Bora, wherever, somewhere else rather than where she was. No one could force her to do anything if they couldn't find her.

"...Are you listening to me, Lisa?"

"Uh-huh."

"Who is he?"

It didn't matter any more, she thought; even Alfred had said the case was beyond salvage.

"You're asking me to betray my country."

"Tell me... You do want another gift by tomorrow, don't you? Or do you want to dry up like a prune? You're already shaking, aren't you? It'll get worse. You will feel cold, colder than being naked in the middle of a winter storm. You will feel as if someone had cut you up with a knife...the pain will be unbearable."

Lisa thought about all the arrests she had made on people like herself. The drug addicts who committed crimes in order to support their habits. She remembered how she had considered them disgusting and weak, because they had no control over their lives and how she had become one of them. It had been so easy, so good and yet so monstrous. How had she devolved to such a thing? No! She had gone far enough. She had to end it, but, first, she would have to make it right, or try to, at least.

"I thought you loved me?" she asked him.

"Love," the DAS Captain replied sarcastically, "is a two-way street. Now tell me what Martin Black's job was?"

"Good-bye." Lisa said and hung up. She wiped the tears from her eyes and stood up from her bed. She would go to Alfred directly, because she would never be able to look into Don Harkin's face again. It was over. Everything was over.

Suddenly her apartment door crashed open and three men stormed in with their weapons drawn. They were Federal Agents and she knew they had come for her. The government knew.

Lisa noticed that the two men were nervous, as agents usually are when arresting one of their own. The thought of one of their own betraying them reminded them of their own vulnerability. If it could happen to one of their colleagues, they thought, it could happen to them.

Lisa read their thoughts and realized she would rather be dead than have to face another policeman. And prison! The hundreds of inmates she had jailed would only begin to count their blessings and start thinking of ways to take their revenge on her.

Lisa reached for her gun.

Everything exploded at once. Starpoints began to dance in her eyes, as if she had been hit by a wooden croquet mallet. Except that no one died from such a thing, and she, she knew, was going to die.

She was seized by a blind all-encompassing panic. Where was she? She tried to look around, but her head would not move and whatever peripheral vision she ever had possessed was gone. Had she been shot? She wasn't sure, because she didn't hear any shots -- and she remembered her father telling her once that, if one heard the shot, it meant one probably would survive. He said that he had learned that in the war.

Lisa felt the fabric of her sofa behind her neck, but where was the rest of her body? She felt nothing, no clothes, no wounded limbs, nothing! It was almost as if she were floating on air. Would it be like this always in death? Would she go to heaven or hell? Was she really dying?

Her vision became tunnel-like and for a moment she thought she saw Chip and Don coming towards her, but she kept falling into a vortex faster than they could reach her. Everything was becoming darker now...darker than the blackest night she had ever known.

    Finally the light at the end of the tunnel became microscopic and she trembled in fear. She no longer could feel her own head. She was floating into darkness. She did not want to die, she thought, just before it went completely black.

## CHAPTER 26

The efficiency of the cartel must have astounded Martin. In Bimini he and Lili were led to a seaplane that was nothing more than a converted Cessna with pontoons instead of wheels, which flew them to Great Inagua Island. At Inagua, the Bonanza A36 Martin had flown into Florida the night before was waiting for them.

A man then handed Martin a sheaf of papers that had the landing coordinates for the Guajira Peninsula and then another set for Bogotá, Colombia.

"What's wrong, Martin?" Lili asked Martin, noticing his puzzlement.

"Rafa wants me to fly to Bogotá."

Lili smiled. "That's good."

"Yes, I suppose," Martin said, unconvinced.

"Okay," Martin said to the man and then asked, "Why Bogotá?"

The man shrugged. "I don't know, señor. I am just a mule."

"A what?"

"He means he's just a coke-carrier," Lili said, her spirits rising for the first time in hours. She believed that if they were being sent to Bogotá they would not be killed, because the cartel didn't like to hold public executions in the capital. Too much publicity.

Martin noticed the change in Lili, so he didn't tell her that the situation felt odd, because if he were Rafa he would want to hear everything first-hand and then make his own judgment.

"Thank you," Martin said to the mule-man.

"Wait, señor!" the mule man said as he hurried to the trunk of his car and retrieved a small plastic box.

Martin opened the box and saw twelve separate double-sided, high density, micro-floppy computer disks. Each of the disks had a name or a code on it that he recognized immediately. Instinctively, Martin knew they were important, because they had the codes that stood for cartel members; CONTRAS, Hi-Fi, RR... Martin remembered the codes: CONTRAS stood for the Contreras family's cocaine. Hi-Fi was El Patrón's code for his load, and RR, which belonged to Rafa, meant Rolls Royce.

"¿Señor?" the man asked Martin. "Are you all right?"

Martin nodded and grabbed Lili's hand. "Let's go," he said and together they climbed aboard the Bonanza.

"Martin, what's in the box?" Lili asked.

"I don't know exactly, but I think it's why we're flying to Bogotá instead of Medellín." He touched her cheek tenderly and added, "I think it could be our insurance."

The taxi's floorboards were old and rotted out, so much so, that Martin and Lili could see the potholes in the pavement a few inches below their feet. Outside the city-skyline was sharp, crisp, and framed against a gun-metal gray sky that threatened to do just about anything. They were on their way to the Tequendama Hotel, according to Rafa's instructions. Somehow he knew he would have to make copies of the disks before he gave them back to Rafa. First, however, he would check into the Tequendama and then go out and find a place where the disks could be copied.

Once Martin settled on the plan he glanced around the inside of the taxi. He noticed the folded newspaper on the top of the dashboard and asked the driver if he could read it. The driver looked into his rear-view mirror and shrugged, hoping Martin wouldn't take it.

Martin did and settled back into the seat. He only wanted to read the headlines. The lead article was of the current negotiations between the Colombian Government and the M-19 guerrillas. He turned the paper over so he could read under the fold and the caption rocked him.

FABIÁN PACHA KILLED IN ARMY RAID

BOGOTA. -- Last night, in what military officials described as a daring nationwide raid on Colombia's top

drug barons, the army shot dead Fabián Pacha, a.k.a., "The Mexican." However, in Medellín, Juan Calderón, a.k.a., El Patrón, managed to elude capture.
Sources in the military high command...

Then he read further down the column.

Man sought in connection with Calderón's escape

Authorities in the department of Medellín are also seeking an American by the name of Martin Black. He is believed to have warned Juan Calderón and then spirited him to safety. All ports and airports have been advised and a thorough search is now being conducted in Bogotá.
However, when authorities were asked why they were searching the capital they had no comment, except to say that a $10,000 reward leading to his arrest had been posted by leading industrialists.

Martin sat straight up. There was no time to waste.
"Stop!" Martin shouted at the driver, waking Lili from her sleep.
The driver looked into his rear-view mirror in confusion. "¿Qué?"
"Stop! We want to get out!"
"The Tequendama Hotel is not for another six blocks."
Lili was wide awake now. "What's wrong, Martin?" she asked.
Martin ignored her. "I said stop, now!" Martin bellowed at the driver.
The driver shook his head and reached under his seat. Martin saw the black blur coming up from under the seat and he punched the driver in the back of the head. The driver bent forward and smashed his forehead on the steering wheel, knocking himself out.
"Martin!" Lili screamed as the taxi careened out of control.
Car horns blared and people scrambled from the sidewalks as the taxi side-swiped a lampost causing the right win-

dow to shatter. Then the front end of the car made an awful grinding metal noise as it ran over a fire hydrant. But the taxi kept moving and the constant lurching threw Martin off balance as he was unable to gain control of the steering wheel. He crouched as a bullfrog and pushed himself over the front seat, hitting his head against the dashboard and nearly knocking himself unconscious. Finally, in dizziness, he managed to put his hand on the steering wheel and steady the car.

The car came to a halt in front of a book store while people ran for their lives. Martin and Lili got out of the taxi just as steam began to erupt from under the car's hood. The taxi, smashed and hissing with steam noises, threatened to explode, but Martin and Lili were already running away from it and blending in with the frightened bogotanos.

They were all right, Martin thought, as he ran, holding onto Lili's hand, before anyone could take a serious look at them. But even in the madness Martin was able to notice that Lili was hurt and was bleeding from the side of her face. He could do nothing about that right now; their first priority was to get away, to hide.

Lili had felt the warm syrupy liquid run down her face and knew it was blood. She didn't care, because she was alive. She felt it congealing like wax as it cooled with the Bogotá air. She, too, had seen the taxi-driver raise a pistol, had seen Martin's sudden explosion of violence and now she could feel Martin's hand grip her like a vice as he led her through a maze of city streets, away from the main ones that could spell their doom. Her right hand hurt, but she didn't want Martin to let her go, because, without him, she was nothing; she might as well be dead.

Finally when he slowed the pace and she realized he was lost, she spoke. "Where do you want to go?"

"I don't know," he said, turning to face her and he grimaced at seeing the blood on her face. Quickly he retrieved a handkerchief from his pocket and wiped the drying blood from her face.

"Does it hurt?" he asked her.

"A little," she replied softly.

"I need to think, Lili, someplace quiet. I also need a telephone. Do you know where?"

"Yes."

He kissed her.

"Martin," she mumbled. "My brother..."

Martin lowered his head. "I can't do anything for him. I would if I could, but I can't save him. Nobody can. His family...they're at the cartel's mercy."

"What about us?"

"Maybe we can save ourselves, but first we need some place to rest and think."

Martin awoke later that night, clear-headed for the first time in weeks and knowing what to do. He twisted slowly in bed, disentangling himself from Lili's limbs that were intertwined with his. He felt a rush of desire come over him, but he suppressed it. Then, slowly, he raised himself from the bed and began to look around the apartment.

It was a comfortable apartment on a fifth floor which overlooked carrera 11 in the northern section of Bogotá. It was in the neighborhood known as Chico, an exclusive one, and he vaguely recalled Lili telling him that the woman who owned it was the daughter of some important cabinet minister in the Colombian government. Lili also had mentioned that her friend was away on her honeymoon and had asked Lili to water the plants in the apartment while she was gone.

The apartment was well-furnished with art deco pieces and ultra-modern design furniture. However, the lighting was subdued, so that the sharp edges of the furniture seemed somehow less threatening.

Martin looked at the luminous dial on his wristwatch and was surprised to see it was only eight-thirty in the evening. He had slept through the afternoon, he thought, which was good. Then he peered out the window and watched the heavy evening traffic.

Bogotá amazed him. It was a large cosmopolitan city with tree-lined avenues and well-lit streets. Lili had explained to him that there had been a construction boom in the past two decades, but which now seemed to be slowing down. She also had told him the nation's economy had been invigorated by the drug money.

"My brother is one of the people who figured out how to deposit the money in a bank and make it look legal," Lili had said. "To my brother it didn't matter where the money came from or what paper the cartel had in its possession to back its supposed legality; all bankers knew it was drug money. The nation's economy exploded after that.

"Ernesto went to El Patrón once and said that he could no longer work because the banks didn't want anything to do with him. The bankers had informed him that they couldn't prove he was depositing drug money, but they knew it, despite the lack of evidence and wanted him out. El Patrón simply laughed."

"How then did Ernesto continue to deposit money?" Martin had asked Lili.

"El Patrón ordered Ernesto to set a private meeting with each bank president and while they were in the meeting he was to pullout a gun and threaten them. Well, Ernesto said he couldn't do it because the bankers were his longtime friends. El Patrón didn't care, because he ordered Ernesto to do it."

It was madness, Martin thought. Colombia was a country under siege by a handful of drug lords. Martin then quickly shook his head free from the grim thoughts and headed for the shower, because he wanted to clean himself, physically as well as mentally.

Martin showered and shaved, using an unused lady's razor, but, before entering the shower he put his clothes into the wash-machine. Once he emerged from the shower he headed back into the laundry room and put the damp clothes into the dryer, then he walked around the apartment in a towel while his clothes dried. For the first time in days he felt clean and light, his mind sharp and alert. He had one more thing to do before waking Lili up and that was to write a letter.

Martin searched the apartment for pen and paper until he found them in the small night-table. It was a woman's stationary, rose-colored with little flowers on the corners, nicely packaged in a box with a clear plastic top. He found a pen and then walked into the dining room and sat down at the table. He looked at the blank piece of paper and tried out the pen. He made little circles and then a number of straight lines until he was ready to start writing. He retrieved a clean paper from the box, took a deep breath and began to write.

    Dear Dusty.
    You warned me all along that something like this would happen. Well, you were right. I guess it's because of our present situation, because we are sentenced to die by the cartel, that I thought it would do no harm to get the story straight before everyone starts covering their backsides.
    It's turned into a godamm mess, Dusty, and it seems to be all our fault...

Martin must have written for at least an hour, because in the letter he explained how he thought they might get themselves out of Colombia. He wrote about how he had fallen in love with Lili and how his life had seemed to take on a new perspective. But what seemed remarkable to those who would later read the letter, even months after the events had transpired, was the fact that Martin had never written a single word of resentment towards the DEA who had sent him on such a fool's errand.

Martin returned to the bedroom and woke up Lili. "Lili," he said, shaking her lightly by the shoulder.

"What time is it?" she asked, rubbing the sleep out of her eyes.

"Ten o'clock. Night."

"Why did you let me sleep so late?"

"Because I'm not sure when we'll be able to sleep next. We'll be moving soon. Do you want to take a shower before we go?" She nodded. "Then do it, I'll go see what your friend has in the fridge..."

"Fridge?" Lili's English was excellent, but every now and then Martin would use an English expression that would make her question him, as if he were in the habit of inventing words.

"It's short for refrigerator. Frigidaire, ring any bells?"

She smiled and Martin felt a warm feeling spread from his solar plexus all the way to his head. He leaned over and kissed her tenderly on the lips, but she didn't settle for just a kiss, because she put her arms around his neck and brought him on top of her and then removed his towel.

Later, when he had assuaged her, he walked into the kitchen and began to make sandwiches for the trip they would make. Sometimes he would hear Lili hum a tune in the shower and his thoughts would scatter like dust, but, on the whole, he felt confident of their escape. He had a plan and they would escape; he was certain of it.

They had studied the map, prepared and rehearsed the excuses they would make, just in case they were stopped by the police. They had settled on the roads, because they were the least likely to have military patrols and were not known for guerrilla ambushes. She would do the talking and the driving. Everything had been planned in the small hours of the morning -- logically, precisely and matter-of-factly; nothing was left to chance, or, at least, what was not known was minimized, and it was all done in a friend's kitchen who neither knew of their plans nor would ever want to know.

They settled on leaving just before dawn, because Martin had remembered something Rafa had told him: the best time to drive through Colombia was in the first hours of light, because the military would be having breakfast and the guerrilla would be retreating with the night.

They drove out of Bogotá an hour before dawn -- but not before Martin dropped off his small package containing his letter and computer disks into the building's mailbox -- northeast towards Tunja, Duitama and Soata. The green plains of Bogotá soon turned into lush rolling hills and finally into mountains.

At midday, Martin and Lili argued about stopping because he felt they were pressing their luck, but Lili reminded him that if the military was going to post a spot-check on the road to Bucaramanga, it would be in the afternoon, sometime after lunch. Martin relented and agreed with her assessment.

Their luck turned sour in the small town of Piedecuesta. Two soldiers had set up a spot-check and were examining papers. The traffic had backed up and Martin wished he had brought a gun with him, but he knew that if the military searched the car and found the weapon he would be taken out and shot. The worst type of criminal in Colombia was not the drug lord, but the arms' trafficker, that is if one believed the military. It was something Rafa had taught him, he thought with irony, because he was now using Rafa's own knowledge to make his escape.

"Check how much money is in my pocketbook," Lili said as she moved forward in line, inching closer to the soldiers. Their vehicle was a jeep, an Isuzu Trooper, navy blue with a gray stripe, with extra-dark windows and less than six thousand miles on the odometer.

"What?" Martin asked.

"I think we might be able to circumvent this little trap."

Martin looked at her and then rummaged through her pocketbook. He was amazed that she had so much money with her. "Where did you get all this money?" he asked her.

"Rafa," she said. "He gave it to me for incidental expenses on my way to bail you out."

"Jesus! There's got to be ten thousand dollars here."

"Good. Count out five hundred dollars and give it to me. Then hand me the car papers that are in the glove-box."

Martin did as he was told.

"When I get out, love, get behind the wheel. If the soldiers motion for you to pull out of line and come up, do so. I'll wait for you up there."

"Lili, you're not..." Martin began to speak, but she was already getting out of the car and moving towards the two soldiers.

The soldiers eyed her suspiciously, but they must have thought she was no threat because they returned to harassing the motorists in front of them. She approached the furthest soldier of the two, because he controlled the gate.

The soldier was a corporal in the Colombian Army, serving out his two-year draft enlistment. He was a young teenager with pock-marked skin and dark brown eyes.

"Perdón, mi capitán." I'm sorry, my captain, said Lili knowingly using a rank several grades higher than what he displayed.

"Señorita, a sus órdenes." At your orders, the soldier said impishly.

Lili then took over. "I have a problem. My colleague and I have a conference to attend to in...Barranca-Bermeja," she said, instead of telling him that they were going to Bucaramanga. "We were wondering if there was a way of jumping the line."

The soldier shook his head in proud resolve. "No, that is not possible, señorita."

"Oh, captain, please accept my apologies if I have questioned your integrity. No, no, no. That was not at all what I meant. I was saying that we would merely pay double what today's...rightful toll to Barranca-Bermeja is."

The soldier looked at her with a steady gaze. "You realize, señorita, that this is highly irregular and that my compañero and I could be in breach of military orders? I could also arrest you for trying to bribe an officer of the army."

"Yes, of course. Please accept my apologies. I would not want you to do anything that would be misconstrued in such light. In fact, I shall go back to my car and wait my proper turn. By the way, what is your name, captain?"

"Why?"

"Because when I return to Bogotá, I would very much like to tell my father, the Minister of the Armed Forces, how well you have done your job." Lili then gave him a radiant smile and saw the man pale visibly.

The corporal gulped. "Perhaps, if you showed me some papers I...we could make an exception."

Lili handed him the papers to the car that belonged to her friend. The corporal read the name and almost stopped breathing.

"Oh, how silly of me," Lili declared. "I've left my license in the car, shall I go back and get it? Oh, but then that would mean unpacking the entire trunk and..."

"No, that will be quite all right. Stay here."

The corporal moved towards his mate and they talked for a few minutes. The two of them became agitated and then smiled at each other. Then they seemed to settle their argument and finally the corporal returned.

"You understand, Señorita, that this is highly irregular. However, my compañero and I will allow it this one time, but you will have to pay a triple toll and the regular toll is twenty dollars."

"Of course, of course," Lili said hurriedly. Then she grabbed the soldier's hand and shook it, pressing a hundred dollar bill into it.

The corporal pretended not to have felt the money pressed against the palm of his hand. Instead, he waved the Isuzu Trooper jeep forward with official decorum while the other drivers looked on, aghast.

Martin watched the soldier wave him forward and he pulled out of the line and stopped a few feet away from Lili. The corporal was already lifting the gate and waving them through.

Martin and Lili traveled northward towards the city of Bucaramanga, the capital of Santander Province. Their mood was quiet and reserved, knowing they had just made a minor escape.

"How did you know the soldiers could be bribed?" Martin asked, the curiosity getting the better of him. He also slowed the speed of the jeep as they entered heavier city traffic.

"I read it in the papers," Lili said, responding to Martin's question.

"What?"

"Two weeks ago there was an article in the paper about the sudden rise of spot-checks around the country. The military stated that it was a new way of stepping up pressure on the guerrilla, but there was a lot of evidence that it was nothing more than a few enterprising soldiers setting up illegal tolls and calling them spot-checks. In fact, the controversy began when a comedian made a skit of it on a comedy show." Lili let out a chuckle. "The comedian referred to them as the unmarked tolls."

Martin laughed. "How do Colombians tolerate it?"

"If you grow up with such things you become used to them; they become part of life. We even have a saying for it,

'Así es como es.' That's how it is. Bribing soldiers or police officers is a matter of negotiating tact and most Colombians would know how to do it, and wouldn't think it wrong at all. It's just the way it is."

"Why doesn't anyone complain to the ministry of whatever and get them to stop? Why doesn't anyone protest, or do something?"

Lili let out a chuckle. "You know, we have a Constitution and a Bill of Rights here in Colombia which is exactly like yours in America? We even have free speech!"

"Yes, which further states my point."

"Ah, but in Colombia when a person stands on a street curb and denounces the government it is called free speech, because he is thought of as crazy. However, if half dozen people stop to listen to that person, that person is then believed to be a subversive and is, therefore, arrested."

"You're joking?"

"No. Despite Colombia's long-standing democratic government it's still very weak. We are literally one tank away from a coup d'état. People like my brother have made the place worse, because now graft and corruption rule the hour."

"You see that restaurant?"

"Yes, the Restaurante Bolívar?"

"Uh-huh. We can have dinner there and wait until dark. Then we can continue on."

"Are you sure?"

"Yes, the guerrilla make their ambushes after midnight, and by then we'll be out of their range."

Martin brought the jeep to a stop in front of the restaurant. "What range are you talking about?"

"It's the outer limit of the guerrilla's perimeter. They like the Barranca-Bermeja area because of its oil refineries. Cúcuta is about as far as they could get if their intention was to harass the refineries on a daily basis."

"How do you know all this?"

"It's common knowledge; even the military knows it."

"So why doesn't anybody do anything?"

"Because it's a thick and dangerous rain forest. I think the proper word would be...impenetrable. Any more questions before we have dinner?" Lili asked him with a wink in her eye.

# CHAPTER 27

"What does Cúcuta mean?" Martin asked Lili as she drove the Isuzu Trooper north, past Pamplona, feeling the cool air temperature as they reached the summit of the Occidental Cordillera and then slowly began to descend into Cúcuta.

"It was the name of an Indian Chief who lived here during the time of the conquistadors," she answered. "Cúcuta was discovered by the German conquistador Nicolás de Federmann. Somewhere along this cordillera in 1539, three great conquistadors came upon each other, by chance. Sebastián de Belalcazar, Gonzalo Jiménez de Quesada and Nicolás de Federmann. Federmann and Quesada had been feared lost in the wilderness...what's wrong?"

"I love you," Martin said. Then, with a smile, he added, "Please, continue."

"I love you, too," she replied easily and they both laughed. "Anyway, it must have been something to be here on that day when they came upon each other by chance. Cúcuta is also historically important because Simón Bolívar passed through here in his campaign against the Spanish in 1813. It was in Cúcuta where he made the famous speech to his soldiers."

"What speech."

"Bolívar was a very great thinker. You've probably heard some of his words and never recognized them as his. For example; Those who have served the cause of the revolution have plowed the sea. However, you might be more interested to know that Cúcuta is a haven for black market items."

"What do you mean?" Martin asked, suddenly excited by the prospect of acquiring a weapon.

"Contraband."

"Can I get a gun?"

Lili glanced at him. "I suppose," she said, hiding her nervousness. She had never liked the use of guns.

"Then we'll stop in Cúcuta."

"Martin?"

"Yes?"

"I want to call Ernesto."

Silence.

"I can't help him, Lili. You can't either."

"I know, but I would like to say good-bye. Please, Martin?"

Martin wanted to tell her that he was probably dead, but he didn't. Instead, he said, "All right, but on a few conditions. You don't say where we are and you take less than thirty seconds on the telephone."

"Thirty seconds?"

"Thirty," Martin said sternly. "That way they won't be able to trace the call."

Lili nodded.

Lili's call went through rapidly. She called from a telephone booth in Cúcuta. The night-sky was blocked by passing clouds and the wind brought with it the aromatic smell of the rain forest. On the third ring the telephone was answered and a voice broke into Lili's thoughts.

"Ernesto?" she asked timidly.

"No," said a gruff voice that Lili didn't recognize.

"Who is this?"

"Fabio. Who's calling?"

Lili glanced at Martin, wanting his permission to say her name. Martin shook his head.

"Esperanza. Is Helena home?"

"One moment."

Lili heard voices on the other end.

"¿Aló?" Helena said. "Who is this?"

"It's me, Lili. Where's Ernesto."

"Run, Lili!" Helena shouted just before she was cut off. Had she heard Helena say 'run,' or just imagined it? Finally, she collapsed into Martin's arms and began to weep.

230

Martin didn't have to ask what was wrong, because he could hazard a guess. Ernesto had died violently by the same violence he had helped to perpetuate. Martin walked Lili to the jeep and held her in his arms. There was nothing more Martin could do for Ernesto. His job, in that respect, was technically over, but now he could do his all to save Lili -- even if it killed him. After a few minutes passed, Martin said to Lili, "I'm sorry for your loss." And then he held her for twenty minutes.

Finally they went in search of a gun in the black market. He had wanted to call Alfred and let him know that he and Lili were on their way, but that was too risky. Someone at DEA already had betrayed him and he wasn't about to trust them again. They were on their own. Nobody could help them. In Colombia, except for a few men and women, all the authorities were corrupt. And America was not much better, because an inter-agency rivalry had exposed and sold him out. They were doomed.

## CHAPTER 28

The sky was no longer black velvet, but a charcoal tinged with streaks of purple. Dawn was breaking as Martin kept the jeep's throttle pressed to the floor. He was close now, maybe five or six miles at most he thought, because he could already smell the sea in the air.

They were going to make it, Martin told himself. It could be done. The gas gauge in the jeep was reading empty, but that didn't concern him as much as the dawn. His escape depended on the cover of darkness.

Then as if in a dream he saw the entrance to the airfield and slowed the jeep down to make a right turn. The paved road led to an unpaved one and clouds of dust began to billow from under the jeep's tires. Martin drove for a hundred meters and then brought the jeep to a stop beside a small, sandy ravine. He looked around for a place to hide the jeep, but La Guajira Peninsula was a region with small sandy dunes and small desert like bushes. There was simply no place to hide a jeep, so they left it by the side of the road.

"Where is it?" Lili asked.

"Not far," Martin replied. "Four hundred meters, but we have to skirt around the entrance. They have guards on duty, at least they did the last time I was here."

They skirted around low bushes -- just like Texas brush, Martin thought. They spotted the gatehouse and got down on their hands and knees. Then they worked their way around the gatehouse, but Martin was worried about time. The color of the sky was changing fast. Then he turned his face the other way and spotted the planes. He smiled, he couldn't help himself.

Lili, noticing the grin on Martin's face, asked in a whispered voice, "What is it?"

Martin crouched and raised Lili to her feet. "There," he said, and pointing with his right hand he showed her where a Bonanza A-36 parked beside a Piper Cheyenne. It was Juan Calderón's air-field near the town of Ríohacha.

"My God! We're really going to fly out of here, Martin." Lili said.

"Yes, we're really going to fly out..." Martin began to say, but his voice fell away in surprise as they walked towards the plane.

"What's wrong?"

"She's loaded with coke!" Martin whispered urgently. "We'll have to unload some of it. We can dump the rest of it in the air. By the way, how much do you weigh?"

"What?"

"How much do you weigh? I need to know how many kilos I have to unload."

Lili cocked her head and said, "I don't know, Martin. It's been years since I've weighed myself."

Martin held her at arms length and viewed her body. She was five feet nine, at least, which would probably put her in the one hundred and twenty pound range. So to be extra safe he would unload one hundred and sixty pounds.

"How many kilos to a pound professor?" Martin asked her with a smile.

Lili closed her eyes and whispered, "Libra al kilo, multiplique la libra por cero punto cuatro cinco." Then in English she said, "About seventy-two kilos."

"Let's go," Martin said and they ran towards the Bonanza.

He opened the rear hatch and pulling out duffel bags filled with coke.

Then they froze at the sound of Rafa's voice. "Buenos días, Compadre," Rafa said holding a MAC-10 in his hand and shaking his head with pity. He had a cigar in his mouth and spoke through clenched teeth. "You almost made it, but...you didn't. Where are my disks?"

Martin and Lili said nothing.

Rafa took two steps forward and raised his left hand. Two of El Patrón's pistolocos stood up from a small gully by the side of the air-strip. They had been hiding in the drainage ditch.

"Raise your hands!" Rafa ordered. "Walk away from the plane! Move!...Hurry! Get on your knees."

As if they were dreaming, Martin and Lili, their eyes still on the MAC-10, did as they were told. They had lost and they were going to die, but Rafa would make them before he killed them. They watched Rafa circle him as the two pistolocos stopped beside him.

Martin watched the small guard break away from his partner and come around, until he stood so close he could hear his breathing. Martin then heard the rustle of fabric and knew the blow was coming...

The blow came to the base of the neck, rifling pain to every nerve ending in his body as he slumped forward.

Suddenly Lili turned and shouted, "Stop it!" and then lunged herself at Rafa.

"Shut up," Rafa said and kicked her on the jaw.

Lili fell backwards in a daze, but managed to get back on her knees. She had to find time for Martin to recover. It was their only chance, she owed him that.

"Please, Rafa," she said. "I can give you the disks, but don't hurt him. I will do anything you want, but..."

Rafa hit her again with his boot opening a gash under her left eye. Then, suddenly, unexplicably he was doubling over, wondering what was happening to him. Then as he put his hand out to cushion the fall he saw Martin firing a pistol at him and the two pistolocos retaliating.

Martin felt the ice-cold stab of pain just above the hip as he emptied his weapon on the pistolocos. Then everything was quiet and Martin fell to his knees and Lili rushed to his side.

"Lili, help me up."

"Where are you hit?"

"The stomach," Martin said squinting in pain, feeling as if he were going to black out. "We have to get out of here. Help me into to the plane, we don't have much time. The guards at the gatehouse should be coming this way soon."

They walked back to the Bonanza.

"Help me up onto the wing," Martin ordered.

235

Lili gave him a boost-up and watched him sway on the wing and then lose his footing. He fell flat against the fuselage, like a flour sack thrown over a horse. Martin grunted in pain, but managed to recover. She watched him open the hatch above the pilots seat.

"Get in," he said as a car engine turned over in the distance and roared to life.

Lili climbed aboard and then watched Martin struggle painfully into the cockpit. She closed the hatch for him. Martin then closed his eyes and breathed deeply, his lungs seemed to be out of breath and his wound felt as if it were on fire. Then he checked under the seat for the ignition key. When he found it he started the engine.

The whining crescendo of the engine built rapidly, the muffled pop with the whistling hoot followed soon after as the fuel caught fire and the propeller spun-up. Martin waited for the propeller to pass the vibration stage, a few seconds that seemed eternal. Finally, the power stabilized and he moved the throttle forward and the plane began to roll. Then as he put in flaps, he caught a glimpse of bright car lights.

"Martin!" Lili said in warning, as she spotted the headlights of a jeep approaching from the right. "They're shooting at us!"

"Do you see a wind sock?!" Martin asked, angered that he hadn't taken a reading on the direction of the wind.

"What?"

"A windsock, something that tells where the wind is blowing."

Lili searched, but shook her head as she did. "No, but Martin..."

"Shit!" Martin shoved the throttles to the stops. The Bonanza lurched forward and they began to gain speed slowly.

God! We're too heavy! Martin thought in wild panic. I should have thrown more of the coke out!

The Bonanza reached air-speed and Martin pulled back on the control column. She bit into the air like a slow and graceful sea gull, skimming the land at first in level flight and then rising effortlessly into the sky. The Bonanza rose over the

Guajira Peninsula as the first light of dawn scratched across the Eastern sky.

He leveled off at four thousand feet and set the automatic pilot on. Then he glanced through the pilot's flight book and punched in the code for Puerto Rico on the Loran. Now all he had to do was call Puerto Rico Air Control and ask them to call Alfred Stevens. The rest would take care of itself. His wound was bad, but he would get to Puerto Rico on time to see a doctor. He would have an ambulance ready and waiting to stabilize his pressure. Then all he had to do was begin a new life with Lili.

Martin reached over with his hand and caressed her face. "It's going to be all right, honey. Nothing can stop us now. Nothing!"

# EPILOGUE

The Congressional Investigating Committee met under the eyes of the press. It was a public display from the powers-that-be to say, that, the Santander Case would never happen again. Because it was here, as the gentleman from the State of Georgia pointed out, "...where the manure stopped rollin' down hill and justice would be suhv'd. Heea' the blind hand o' justice will fall on the guilty."

The law was blind, indeed, but it could still sniff out the rats and ferret them out for prosecution. There was to be no delay, because explanations were needed and blame was to be apportioned. Those who had business with the Santander Case were to draw near and be heard, or at least until the hullabaloo fell to a whisper and the crowds had, metaphorically speaking, watched some heads roll down the steps of the capitol.

But the Congressional Investigating Committee after a few days of sitting and listening to the supposed eye-witness testimony, delivered a short speech with a lot of tough talk and then sent the investigation to the sub-committee level where a more thorough job could be done. Then the sub-committee, not wanting to be left holding the bag, appointed a Special Task Force, otherwise known as the STF, to find what had caused the disaster, but, by then, the astute Congressmen had discovered more urgent business elsewhere and distanced themselves from the STF with an almost blinding speed.

People were called in to testify. Congressional subpoena's were sent out and very serious note was taken. Oh, yes! The janitors who cleaned the offices at DEA were the first to be called in, but the questions, for fairness' sake, were the same for everyone. What had he or she seen? What had they heard and with whom? And who was holding the smoking gun and when was it fired. Then came the secretaries, and all sorts of threats were made to them, but they knew on whose side their bread was buttered on and they remained as silent as the grave.

Finally, they called in Alfred to testify and he gave it to them straight. Yes, he was in charge, he told them. Yes, the President had been informed during each phase of the operation, which was immediately followed by a series of questions that stunned Alfred: How come he did not inform the sister agencies, primarily the Customs or the Coast Guard, etc., etc., and, moreover, why hadn't the Colombian President been informed?

"Because it was too risky for our man," Alfred replied.

The crowd and the press roared in laughter.

"...The Chair recognizes the gentleman from the State of North Dakota."

"Thank you, Mister Chairman," said the Congressman from North Dakota. "Mister Stevens, can you tell us in a simple sentence what was the objective of the Santander Case?"

Alfred's face relaxed and he replied, "Our mission was to displace Mister Camacho from Colombia in exchange for testimony against the Medellín Cartel."

"Mister Stevens, I suppose that when you say the cartel you mean it to be Juan Calderón and not the other two hundred drug traffickers that presently make up the cartel, correct?"

"That is correct."

"Why would this government want to do that?"

"In order for us to successfully put Juan Calderón on trial in this country, we need an eye-witness to the crimes committed."

"I see. So, basically, what you're saying is that we trade off a lesser evil for a greater good."

"Yes, that's it exactly."

"Ernesto Camacho was a lesser evil, was he?"

"Yes."

"Let me see here..." The Congressman shuffled some papers in front of him. "Ah, here it is! In your own report it states that Mister Camacho was a top man in the cartel, Mister Stevens, so how could he be a lesser evil."

"Well he was not, in the sense that you mean it, but in a court of law his testimony could convict anyone in the cartel. Mister Camacho would have been a reliable witness."

"Because of his integrity and sense of decency, eh?"

"Yes, sir."

The Congressman scratched his chin. "Mister Stevens, was Mister Camacho involved in the murder of over one hundred passengers because he exploded an aircraft in midair?"

The crowd whispered in the room. Stevens realized the trap, but there was nothing he could do about it now. "It's unconfirmed whether he was involved, sir."

"Un...con...firmed," the Congressman said, dragging out the syllables. "Well then, perhaps you can tell us what happened to the Camacho family?"

Alfred removed his handkerchief from his coat pocket and wiped his brow. "They were killed, Mister Congressman."

"All of them?"

"Yes, sir. Mister Camacho's body parts were dropped off in front of the F-2 Police office in Bogotá."

"And what about the family?"

"Camacho's wife and children were killed. Their throats were cut and then dumped in a small ditch beside the main street in Medellín."

And that's how it went for Alfred. He replied to every question in the plural form we rather than in the singular I, in the sense that we did this and we did that.

Don Harkin was the next person to testify before the Sub-Committee. He was well-dressed for the event and answered the questions that were put to him calmly. In fact, it seemed for a while that Don might escape from the committee's investigation unscathed, until the lady from Oregon began to ask questions.

"Mister Harkin, you've stated in your report that Lucio Bonilla was Mister Rafael Sanchez' right hand man, is that correct?"

"Yes, ma'am."

"Did you know this prior to the Santander Case?"

"Yes, ma'am."

"Therefore, you must have known Mister Sanchez, as well."

"That is correct; we had been tailing...rather, the Miami DEA office had been tailing Mister Sanchez for several months."

"Why didn't you arrest him? Was he not a wanted man?"

"Yes, he was a wanted man, but we figured that if we tailed him we could catch his Miami network."

"Prior to the Santander Case, why was he a wanted man?"

"He was believed to be the trigger man in the killing of two Miami Police officers."

The crowd whispered in loud tones.

"Ladies and gentlemen, please remain silent or the chamber will be emptied," the committee chairman announced as he banged his gavel.

The distinguished lady from Oregon continued. "Where is Mister Sanchez today?"

"He's dead. The F-2 police in Colombia found him on Juan Calderón's private runway in the Guajira Peninsula."

The Congresswoman from Oregon narrowed her eyes. "Help me, Mister Harkin; why is that familiar to me?"

"It is the runway from which Martin Black and Liliana Santander escaped."

"Oh, yes. Can we assume then that Martin Black or Liliana Santander caused Mister Sanchez death?"

"We've confirmed it, ma'am. One of Mister Sanchez' bodyguards was arrested two weeks ago and he offered testimony in exchange for a lesser sentence."

"I see." The Congresswoman paused and drummed her pen on the table. "Mister Harkin could you please inform the committee of what has been gained from the Santander Case?"

"Gained?" Don replied in surprise. "I don't exactly know what you mean, ma'am?"

"What did we gain from this operation? Is the cartel in jail either here or in Colombia? Has drug trafficking been reduced since this operation took place? And let me remind you that you are under oath, Mister Harkin."

"Uh, well...nothing was gained..."

Donald Harkin's inability to answer the question was later viewed as loyalty rather than ineptitude, but he survived and cleared off to make room for the next witness, who, because of his remoteness to the case, would be blamed for the whole affair.

"Captain Ray Sullivan," said the sub-committee chairman, "would you please describe to this committee who you are and what your connection to the case is?"

"Uh, yes. My name is Captain Ray Sullivan of the United States Customs Service. On the morning of December 16, 1991 I was on duty at Homestead Air Force Base..."

"Captain, Perhaps, if you clarify what it is that you do we might understand the events that transpired that late morning."

"I am the captain of a Blackhawk Helicopter. My job is to intercept any aircraft that is suspected of drug-trafficking and force them to land for a visual inspection."

"And if they refuse?" the Congressman from Massachusetts asked.

"We give them a warning shot."

"If they still refuse?"

"We force them down."

"How?"

"We shoot them down."

The Congressman from Massachusetts nodded. "I see, captain. Please continue."

The captain removed a small note pad with notes written on it. "On the morning of December 16, 1992 at 10:43 hours my crew and I scrambled to intercept an aircraft that was suspected to be a doper."

"Why was it suspected?"

"It was flying under false colors."

"Will you explain what that means, captain?"

"It had a bogus registration number on its fuselage. The aircraft was not flying with legitimate numbers, also, Miami International had been unable to make contact through normal channels and it was flying in an irregular traffic route. At 11:05 hours we intercepted the suspected aircraft, it was a Bonanza A36, the same aircraft which had slipped through us a few nights before."

"I am assuming you made a positive identification of the aircraft?

"Yes, sir."

"What did you do next?"

"I attempted contact over the radio and then flew beside the aircraft and made my intentions to force the pilot down if she did not land."

"You say she, why?"

"Uh, well, the person behind the captain's seat was a man, sir, I think."

"Think?"

"Sir, the man seemed to be out cold."

"Is this committee supposed to infer that the aircraft in question was on automatic pilot?"

"No, sir. There was a woman aboard and she seemed to be flying the aircraft. I had my co-pilot signal her to land, but she continued to fly for another fifteen minutes. Then I fired a few warning shots. She did not respond."

"Then what?" The Congressman from Massachusetts asked, the committee chamber hanging on every word.

"I fired a round into the aircraft's rudder. The aircraft descended after that, but I thought it was making a run for it because it power-dived."

"You mean, it was trying to evade you?"

"Yes, sir. So, I fired another round into the engine and disabled the propeller."

"Tell me captain, while firing at the aircraft did you ever have any doubt that maybe the aircraft could've had a legitimate reason for doing what it was doing"

"None, sir. I saw the cocaine duffel bags in the aircraft."

"And you knew they were full of cocaine just because they were duffel bags?"

"Uh, eh, I didn't mean it that way."

"I'm sure, but please continue."

The captain looked down at his notes with a strange look in his eye. He knew something was transpiring, but he couldn't put a finger to it. "I, uh, then noticed the aircraft flying erratically as it continued to descend, so I backed off..."

"Was there an air field nearby, captain?" The congressman from North Dakota cut in.

"Yes, sir. Homestead was two miles in front of the doper."

"Do you think the aircraft in question saw it."

"Absolutely, it, well, attempted to land on it, sir."

"Captain, I am sure you now know the circumstances involved; therefore, let me ask you this: knowing that Mister Black had been shot in the stomach by Rafael Sanchez on the Guajira Peninsula and was slowly bleeding to death, would you have shot the aircraft?"

"I didn't know..."

"If you knew the person flying was a woman who had no experience in flying aircraft, would you have been so quick to shoot?"

"Sir..."

"Haven't you ever heard of pilots who have heart attacks in mid-air and of passengers with no experience in flying who are forced to fly the aircraft because of circumstances beyond their control?"

"Yes, sir."

"Then couldn't this aircraft be one of those?"

"The duffel..."

"Ah! The duffel bags gave them away, did they not?"

"Yes, sir."

The Congressman from North Dakota rubbed the skin between his eyebrows. "Captain, are you aware that over a million of our servicemen have those green duffel bags? Should I assume then that you would shoot down an airliner because you saw a green duffel bag in one of the windows?"

The captain remained quiet, because everything he said was being twisted to fit circumstances he had no control over. He only realized too late that he was the scapegoat and there was nothing he could do about it.

"Please, captain, don't think that we are putting the blame on your shoulders. No, no, no! That is not the intention of this committee, because we know how you brave boys put your lives on the line every day. No, please don't take this questioning to be a witch hunt of some sort." The Congressman from North Dakota then turned to the House stenographer and added, "We will note in the record that Captain Sullivan has had an exemplary career in the service of his country."

The stenographer then nodded to indicate that he had done as he was ordered.

The Congresswoman from Oregon however, continued the inquisition. "Captain, when you mentioned you disabled the aircraft's propeller what happened after that?"

"The aircraft glided towards the Homestead runway, but as it was about to touch down..."

"Yes?"

"A gust of wind flipped it over and it crashed... It became a huge fireball after that. There were no survivors."

When the Special Task Force finally closed their doors, the speculation about the testimony began in earnest. The talk was not really about who exactly was to blame, but rather who would survive the STF. Washingtonian insiders began betting at cocktail parties and luncheons on who was in and who was out, and who would be transferred to such and such place if anyone managed to survive the long knives. But, as days drew into weeks and weeks into months, the interest in the Santander Case began to wane, and everyone, except for Alfred, returned to their old jobs.

Alfred was quietly re-shuffled and given the post as head of the Department of the Interior, where the President decided Alfred couldn't mess up as badly as he had at the DEA. But, as the newspaper would carry in a much later edition, Alfred had been selling millions of acres of wild preserve to the big industrial giants and the EPA and the environmentalists were squaring up for a fight. Don, on the other hand, had been promoted to DEA Administrator. Lisa Mejia was buried without honors and left to rot in some grave outside of Miami. She left no surviving relatives and she was quickly forgotten. El Patrón expanded into the Baltics and Middle East markets and was still at large, despite the fact that he could be found in the local Ríonegro bar every Tuesday and Thursday nights.

It all looked bad, especially in view that Calderón was still out there making millions, because some good had emerged from the case. Eleven days after Martin and Lili crashed on the runway, Dusty received, by Parcel Post, the computer disks and the letter which Martin had mailed to him before leaving Bogotá. The disks led the DEA to the confiscation of a billion dollars, which must have hurt Calderón where it counted most, his wallet. The downside of the disks was not publicized, because the evidence was being used to jumpstart another case, which Dusty was told was the biggest thing to hit the DEA ever! Dusty, though, was already feeling sorry for whoever was involved in that case. Martin's letter, however, did turn out to be his last will and testament. He left Dusty Windraider because he thought he needed a career change.

And as for good ol' Dusty? He was commended by the highest notables in the land, north and south of the Caribbean Water. Yet, he typed his resignation on his old IBM S electric and turned it in. Then he packed his belongings into a cardboard box and drove south to the end of the road in the American dream. Key West. He was hoping against hope to find something there, aboard Windraider, because there was nowhere else for him to go. But he was not feeling sorry for himself; on the contrary, he was happy for the first time in his life. He had a small legal practice there and it kept his bills paid. He was living alone, but still hoping that would change some day. The locals were nice to him, perhaps, because they recognized a quality in him they saw in themselves: burnout, dropout, or whatever, but they took him under their wing anyway.

Dusty would think about his ex-wife every now and then, because she was one of the crosses he had to bear. He walked out on her and never said why. He let his attorney inform her of his intentions. She kept everything, which was fine by him. Her remembrance was a painful one for a different number of reasons, but it was a pain he would not trade and would gladly bear until his dying days. She was a part of him and to forget her would be the ultimate act of cowardice on his part. Sometimes he thought of picking up a telephone and calling her to ask how she was getting along, but the urge didn't last long; it was all water under the bridge.

Yet, despite his new life, Dusty never forgot what had made his new life possible, especially when the orange sun dipped in a blaze of gold and red, and the breeze rustled the sails aboard Windraider, and the Northern Star twinkled in the cool dusk light, he would lift his head up to the heavens and dream of Lili and Martin and what might have been.

Otros títulos publicados por
**Ediciones Nuevo Espacio**

Benedicto Sabayachi y la mujer stradivarius
Hernán Garrido-Lecca
Como olas del mar que hubo
Luis Felipe Castillo
Cuentos de tierra, agua... y algunos muertos
Corcuera, Gorches, Rivera Mansi, Silanes
Exilio en Bowary
Israel Centeno
La lengua de Buka
Carlos Mellizo
La última conversación
Aaron Chevalier
Los mosquitos de orixá Changó
Carlos Guillermo Wilson
Melina, conversaciones con el ser que serás
Priscilla Gac-Artigas
Prepucio carmesí
Pedro Granados
Rapsodia
Gisela Kozak Rovero
Ropero de un lacónico
Luis Tomás Martínez
Simposio de Tlacuilos
Carlos López Dzur
Viaje a los Olivos
Gerardo Cham
Visiones y Agonías
Héctor Rosales